The Ladies of

Harrington House

Spirits of Charleston

JUDY HORNBECK

Without these two people this book would never
have been completed.
Thank you both for your faith in my writing.
Amy Wright - Chief Editor
Walter Hornbeck - Chief Encourager

TABLE OF CONTENTS

CHAPTER ONE

Maggie

The letter came in the mail, late that day, the return address was from Charleston, South Carolina! Too excited to open it she ran upstairs to find her Grand-mamma.

"Granny, oh my goodness, will you open it, I'm too nervous, do you think I got it? I can't believe this is happening so fast."

"Calm down child, let me see."

Handing her the letter Maggie closed her eyes and said a silent prayer to Lakshmi, the Hindu Goddess of Abundance. In turn she heard her Granny mumble something in Creole. She listened to the envelope being torn open and Granny gasped. Opening her eyes she saw a big beautiful grim on Granny's face.

"You did it child, your first nursing job!!"

Magdalena thought back to the interview, so different than any other one she had, the virus changed everything in their lives. She sat in front of the laptop computer on her Grannys old antique desk gazing out the window, as she waited for the recruiter to appear on the screen. Teli-view worked just like you were sitting across from the other person except you weren't. The computer allowed her to apply for and interview for a job over 700 miles away. The process was relatively painless, it took 45 minutes start to finish, having sent her resume into them weeks prior. She had her heart set on working at The Medical University in Charleston, never having been there her friends couldn't understand why she wanted to move so far away. After all New Orleans was her home, all her friends and family were here. They didn't understand, her spirit guides knew where she needed to be and she always trusted them. After all it was her Spirit that guided her to nursing school.

Waiting for her mother to get home was emotional agony, she was so excited about her acceptance letter that she thought she would burst with happiness. She paced up and down the living room, gazing out the second floor window every few minutes. Watching the tourists weave their way around the street vendors. Wondering where all those people were headed, were they as happy as she was at this very moment. She allowed herself to imagine what it was like in Charleston right now, were the skies just as blue with billowing white clouds as they were here?

Her mom had been more like a friend growing up, and in turn Granny had been more like a mom. They both had been so supportive of her decision from the very beginning. Granny always connected with the Creole spirits and evidently they approved. This is going to be one heck of a journey you guys are taking me on, she thought, not knowing a soul in South Carolina, it was a giant leap of faith!

Her life was far from exciting but it kept her happy and busy. Growing up in a suburb then in the city of New Orleans she was always aware of the dark side of town. The voodoo shops, the seers and the Mambo priestess always intrigued her. Granny warned her not to dabble in such things without protection. But as a teenager years ago she did, for a while it was fun. Her and her friends would drive out to St Louis Cemetery and find Marie Laveau's crypt to leave offerings. Looking back, that seemed like years ago now.

Another overtime shift and my car will be paid off, she thought happily. She loved her red Rav 4, it got her everywhere she needed to go, and hauled all her belongings with her. She worked part time as a delivery driver for a medical supply company. It had been a long three years of working extra shifts and going to college to accomplish this. She was proud of herself.

From finishing college early to paying off her car a year sooner. Once she set a goal she was driven. Her mother once told her it was a curse to set goals.

"It's the devils way of tripping you up, fail once and you will fail again, let the fates lead you." She would always say.

Having been raised in a Creole community with her mother and Granny she knew this came from their beliefs. Growing up she thought everyone had a spirit altar in their living room, crystals and chakra amulets, Ankh necklaces and sage oils. Her Granny wore bright colors and always had a head scarf on. But it didn't cover her still jet black hair, falling over her shoulders to the middle of her back. Her feet were always barefooted, she loved the feeling of the earth. She claimed it kept her grounded. Some of the neighborhood kids called her the old gypsy woman and teased Maggie about her giving them the evil eye. When she was younger she wasn't sure what exactly that was, but it didn't sound good.

Magdalene was her birth name but her family called her Maggie. She was a small child for her age, but once she reached puberty she blossomed. She was as tall as her mom now and they could almost pass as twins. They both had long jet black hair, same as Granny's with green eyes that sparkled when there was a secret to be told. The only difference was that her mom, Geraldine, tended to dress like Grand-mamma in bright colors with long flowing skirts. Maggie dressed a bit more conservatively with the exception of her jewelry, An ankh necklace with her crystal quartz always hung around her neck, both wrists were adorned with bracelets of all kinds, most of them from decades gone by.

Their house had originally stood in the ninth ward, but after Hurricane Katrina they had to move, their home was literally washed off its foundation. Friends of Granny's took them in after the storm until they could find a place of their own. The Goddesses helped guide them to a wonderful family, who had decided to move out of New Orleans after the storm. They owned a two bedroom condo near Jackson Square that they were willing to rent. After agreeing on their terms the ladies moved in. Thankfully it was semi furnished so they only had to buy a few things. Living in the Quarter made their lifestyle easier. There were so many different cultures that no one looked at you strangely. Which was good for Maggie, not wanting to be accused of giving the evil eye, whatever that was.

CHAPTER TWO

Leona

"Mom, I can't look at another apartment, just to be disappointed," said Maggie.

"It's the last one today honey, I have a good feeling. Come on, what can you lose. I'll treat you to an early dinner," she said with an encouraging smile.

It had been a long couple of weeks, getting her acceptance letter, deciding on a start date and flying to Charleston to find an apartment. Her Mom came with her for moral support but mostly because she loved just being with her best friend.

The afternoon sun was starting to go down just below the tree tops as they parked the rental car, at the visitor center. They decided to walk to the next apartment. It was actually located a few blocks from the Medical Center on the Peninsula.The breeze off the bay felt good in the early summer heat. Shadows from the buildings provided more coolness as they walked down King Street.They passed windows filled with old antique furniture, then windows filled with old and new jewelry. Scattered among them were cafes with outdoor seating.The store windows told the story of old Charleston, antiques of days gone by and the families that no longer lived there. She had no idea that the city held so much history, she would love exploring it in her time off. As they stepped off the curb to cross the street a bicycle bell caught their attention. A handsome man wearing a helmet whizzed by them waving a hello.

"Whoa, I guess we need to look for all kinds of traffic here," Maggie giggled as they continued crossing the street.

Once they reached Beaufain Street they turned right and walked down to Rutledge. They rounded the corner to the left onto Rutledge Avenue and Maggie was stunned. The beautiful old Victorian mansion stood majestically, just as it had in her dream many times! The coral pink color shone on three stories. A cascade of steps on either side led up to the front door. Four white pillars held up two stories of porches. She noticed how the ceilings were painted blue to appear as only the sky was above.

"Oh, Momma, it's her! The house I've seen in my dreams since I was little."

Standing there staring at it took her breath away. Her Granny had always told her to believe in her dreams. She said they were just different timelines, we have the choice of where our timeline ends up. She knew this was where she wanted to be!

"Maggie,it's beautiful and look at the window upstairs!"

As they both gazed up to the window, Maggie gasped. A 'For Rent' sign said to apply at the front door. They looked at each other wide eyed and both started laughing, knowing that the Spirits had brought them here.

Traditionally, in Charlestonian times gone by, the women were meant to go up one side of the steps while the gentleman used the opposite steps. Maggie and her Mom gave each other a smile and chose a different side, meeting at the front door laughing. The huge double wooden doors stood like centuries guarding their master, a lions head knocker was on the right. To the left was a beautiful wrought iron piece reading 'Harrington House.' Nodding to each other Maggie grabbed the large Lions head and banged on the door.

The door opened revealing an older woman. Her shocking white hair was braided and fell over her shoulder reaching halfway down the front of her chest.The bright colored shift she wore reached the floor. Her smile was warm and inviting with a hint of mischievousness.

"Come in, please, I've been expecting you."

She walked ahead of them into a large Victorian decorated drawing room of reds and gold. The furniture looked as though it was from another era, but in excellent condition. Crystal chandeliers hung from the ceiling with sunlight reflecting off the diamond shaped glass making a rainbow of colors appear on the wall of velvet brocade paper.

"Excuse me. I'm sorry, maybe you are mistaken. We just saw your sign and were wondering about your apartment for rent," Maggie blurted out.

The old woman assured them she made no mistake, she was expecting them. She had only just put the sign in the window that morning knowing that they would see it.

Maggie and her Mom looked at each other with eyebrows raised. They were used to the spirits giving them hints in their lives but never had they been pushed!!

"My spirits said they would send me someone to help, and here you are," she said, with the infectious but mischievous smile.

Leona introduced herself and motioned them to sit as she rang an old bell. A young woman dressed in faded jeans and a sweatshirt appeared through a door, it had been built into the wall of the room. She asked her to bring tea and biscuits

7

for the guests. The girl nodded and disappeared once again through the door almost magically.

"Please don't go to any trouble for us. I am Maggie Beaumont and this is my momma Geraldine. We are from New Orleans and I am looking for an apartment. We saw the sign."

"Yes, you are most welcome to see the apartment. But first, I get so few visitors, indulge an old lady, tea and some conversation?"

Over tea and biscuits Leona told them a bit of herself. She was a widow who had inherited the house through her husband's family. They had lived in Charleston for generations and made their money first in rice, when they owned a plantation on the Ashley River. It had been a large and profitable business with the unfortunate use of slaves. After the war of northern aggression the rice plantation could no longer support itself. The family invested in the turpentine business further up the coast near Georgetown. She paused, took a breath and drank some tea. She didn't seem to be in a rush, rather the opposite, she was sizing them up, watching their reactions.

Maggie and Geraldine looked at each other as if to say, why is she telling us all this? We don't even know her. But in a strange way they did.

Leona saw the look between mother and daughter and was pleased. She continued,"Someone in my husband's family, we believe it was his great great granddaddy, Jonathan. He decided to build this house after the war. It was originally supposed to be a summer home, but actually became the family home in 1875. Many were born here and many died here as well. They enjoyed an era of wealth with great balls and family gatherings. There were rumors of famous people that had visited the house at one time or another. My mother in law had passed down many stories of the house's history," Leona told the story of the house. She had a far away look in her eyes, almost as she was reliving the story.

She continued on, "My husband Herbert Harrington, was a prominent physician. He passed away after a bout of pneumonia, he was only 60 years old. I was 14 years younger than him when we married. He worked tirelessly to save his patients. Through flu epidemics and diseases he was always there for them, but no one could save him," her face revealed her sadness. "I had lived alone since my son got married over five years ago. He married late in life never finding the right woman, then one day he up and told me it was time he married and brought an heir into our family. He married within a year of that decision. Sometimes I wonder if it was really love or just a need to have a son to carry on our lineage. When he left, he had made arrangements for a young woman to come look after me everyday for a few hours. Her name was Marie and she is very shy. I am getting on in age, it's time I have someone else live in this big house with me, as company mostly," she said, looking at Maggie hopefully.

Maggie and Geraldine were drawn more and more into the story. They both felt a knowing.

Leona went on to explain that the upstairs had been converted to an apartment for her son and daughter in law to live in. But sadly they were killed in a car wreck on Highway 17, just the other side of the bridge in Mt Pleasant. It was late one night they were returning from dinner. The rain caused it, they said. Her sadness returned. The apartment was never lived in, they were just finishing the renovations when the accident happened.

As they finished their tea and biscuits, Marie once again appeared magically and took away the empty tray. Leona seemed to come out of her trance, memories went back to their hiding places.

"Now, ladies, would you like to follow me? We can see if the apartment is right for you." She led the women up the wide mahogany staircase, complete with stairs that creak as you stepped on them. For Maggie, it was as if she was in her dream. Never seeing it from the inside, it was like opening a beautiful gift.

The apartment was large with four rooms overlooking Colonial Lake. Each room was beautifully decorated as if the owner had just stepped out. Walking into the bedroom made her smile. Done in pale greens and yellow the canopy bed stood in the center with small pink pillows carefully placed near the headboard. A writing desk facing the window overlooking the lake looked so inviting that Maggie sat down. She could see herself here, it felt like home. Geraldine walked into the room smiling. Her daughter belonged here.

"Mom, it's furnished. I won't have to buy a thing. And everything is so beautiful, almost too nice for a simple girl like me."

"It was meant for you, I feel it in my bones. The fates have spoken as Granny would say," she said, hugging her daughter.

Leona sat patiently on the cream colored settee in the living room, ankles crossed as a proper southern lady would. Every few minutes she would rearrange the bright red throw pillow under her elbow, a nervous reaction she thought to herself. She knew Maggie was the one, but she must let her make the decision on her own. After all it was the same spirits that brought her here as a young bride, that also brought Maggie to her today.

CHAPTER THREE

New Friends, New Job

Maggie locked her apartment door and headed down the beautiful mahogany stairs, loving every creak of the steps. Still not believing this was home. There were some mornings that she was half tempted to slide down the banister like a child, but refrained. The thought of it made her smile. She found Leona in her usual spot this early in the morning, the enclosed courtyard garden. The walls of cinder blocks were six feet high and draped with Carolina Jasmine. It was particularly potent this morning due to the thick humidity, typical summer day in the Carolinas. Leona's tall frame was kneeling over her flowers, weeding them gently while she whispered to them like they were her children.

"Good morning, Leona. I'm off to work. Can I bring anything home for you?"

In the six months since she moved in her answer was always the same, no, have a pleasant day. Smiling, she would return to her gardening. Today was no different.

The walk to the Medical University was about five blocks and Maggie loved it. The street was lined with intertwining branches covered in moss from centuries old magnolia trees, forming a canopy of sorts. When they were in bloom the smell was intoxicating.

As she walked along a horse and carriage carrying a group of tourists caught her eye. The driver tipped his hat and smiled,"Good morning, Missy."

She waved and smiled back. She imagined the people who had walked these streets years before. How elegant they were in their horses and carriages. Women walking along with parasols blocking the sun from their delicate faces. How different the time was back then.

On occasion she would see the gentleman that almost rode over her and mom their first day in Charleston. He passed her today and waved. It felt so good to have local people recognize her as one of them. There were so many bike riders you really had to be careful you didn't get run over.

Work at the Rutledge Tower was different everyday. There were always new experiences and sometimes sad outcomes. Her Granny had told her nursing was a calling. Not everyone had the compassion needed to minister to the sick and more often than not, the dying. But Maggie loved it. She looked forward to each day knowing that maybe she could make a difference.

The first few months had been rough, learning her way around, meeting new co-workers and dealing with their personalities. The worst part was the computerized charting for patients. She had been trained using paper charts in school. Now each hospital had its own computer charting program to learn. Like everything else in her life she set her goal, I will accomplish this crap and be proficient within one month. She hated taking the time away from her patients to learn this, but in the end she met her goal.

Maggie and Allison had become fast friends her first month working at The Tower as they called it. They met during Maggie's orientation to the step down unit. Allison was assigned to be her mentor. They quickly bonded while taking care of a few of their long term dialysis patients. The girls seemed to have the same sense of deep compassion for the older patients. One day during their shift there was a commotion in the hallway,

"What the heck is going on Carol?" Maggie asked the charge nurse, "everyone's all excited."

"There was an accident. A celebrity of sorts was admitted to the ICU two floors above us," answered Carol as she headed back to her desk.

Christian Belle, was one of Charleston's famous historical mystery writers. He had been riding his bike down King Street and a car came out of one of the alley streets. The driver claims he never saw the bicyclist. Unfortunately he was in a coma and placed on a ventilator. So no one would be asking for his autograph any time soon. Having read a few of his books the girls day dreamed about where he got his inspiration from. Maybe after he was off the ventilator he would be transferred to their unit and they would get to meet him.

Their schedules worked out so they had the same days on which gave them days off together to hang out. Allison was from Savannah originally, her family moved to Charleston a few years back for her fathers business.

"Our shop in Savannah was bought out by a chain. They made my parents an offer they couldn't refuse. They had always wanted to retire in Charleston one day so they decided why not open another shop here," Allison had told her.

They owned an antique shop on King Street and lived in an apartment above the shop. Allison still lived with her parents, more out of convenience for work, the shop being so close. She was deeply religious which led to friendly banters about spirits. Tall and thin she could have been Miss Savannah in a beauty contest growing up. Her blond hair had curls in curls causing it to spring to life on humid days, which is why she wore a ponytail most of the time.

Maggie's first introduction to Charleston had been a horse and carriage ride that Allison insisted they take.

"It will give you a baseline history and flavor for what Charleston was all about."

She happened to know a driver named Tim who was especially animated with his storytelling and thought Maggie would get a kick out of hearing his version of history.

Tim carefully guided the horses down the cobblestone streets lined with magnolias. She listened intently as he told stories of the old city. They piqued her interest to know more.

Tim explained, "As we ride past these homes I will tell you how you will know if they were built before the quake of 86, and I don't mean 1986." The driver said mysteriously.

"In 1886 Charleston had a great earthquake. It was August 31, at 9:50 on a hot and humid night. It struck with no warning, a great rumble filled the earth as people ran out of their homes into the streets. As far as they can tell it was about a magnitude 7. Around 60 people lost their lives that night. Some of those that died were killed from the facade falling off the walls of the building." As he went on with his story, Maggie felt chills run down her spine.

"Weeks after the quake people realized how unstable some of the houses were. Engineers came up with a plan. If you look up to the second story of these homes you will see a black disc like shape about ten inches wide."

Everyone looked, Allison pointed and Maggie nodded.

"What they did was drive a bolt through and attach it to the timber frame to stabilize the exterior wall. Some homes actually have a more decorative piece that was added over the top of the plate to make it look fancy."

Maggie was hooked, she loved the history of Charleston and this driver had taken her on an imaginary trip she would always remember. She knew she would seek out Tim again for more of his storytelling.

Once a month the girls would plan a day of exploring. They would pick a spot to go, then they'd have an early dinner before returning back to their favorite neighbor bar, The Hood for a drink or two.

The bar was a small hole in the wall so to speak, the mahogany wood gave it a dark and mysterious aura, especially in the winter early evenings. It was rumored to have been there for over 150 years and some nights it smelled like it. Maggie often wondered what spirits were hiding in its air space. Allison turned out to be somewhat of a tour guild herself. Since living here longer she knew the historical spots to highlight.

One of their favorite things to do on a day off, when not exploring,was just to wander through the streets South of Broad, better known as SOB, it was where the elite lived, old money. Their mission was to find the oldest homes. Each of the houses would have an oval copper or metal plaque identifying the year it was built. They would walk up one street and down another, gawking at the beauty of the homes and the gardens that often sat behind large courtyards. At times, when they made sure no one was looking they would peek around the walls to get a better look. Now that they took the carriage ride they could also identify how well they withstood the great quake by their bolts on the second floor. The homes stood like majestic guardians, standing at the entrance of the bay. Their walk usually ended up along the Battery, watching the waves splash along the wall. There was always a breeze off the water that renewed their spirit.

Some days they would just sit on the steps of the Gazebo that was in the middle of the park and watch people as they went about their day. But Maggie's favorite was Rainbow Row along East Bay Street, a group of homes, some attached and painted all different colors. The Caribbean flavor of colors were chosen during a renovation of the area in the 1930's to reflect the heat and keep the homes cool. She imagined what it was like long before the renovations when it was a wharf and slum, the people that would have walked these cobblestone streets and worked the boats that landed in the port city. These walks always led to great stories they would make up about families that lived long ago.

CHAPTER FOUR

Tales of Old Ladies

It was Sunday. Leona always planned a special meal for dinner if Maggie wasn't working. Their relationship had grown warm and Maggie looked forward to spending time with the old woman, listening to her stories.

"My dear, if you don't mind I have invited a friend to dine with us this afternoon."

"I don't mind at all, is it someone I know?" Maggie asked.

"No, an old friend from the Charleston Society Club I belong to. We do, or we did do charity functions, now we're both too old."

"That sounds like fun. Maybe she can give me more pointers on places to explore," she said smiling.

Dora arrived right on time, she disliked tardiness. It was as if the wind blew in a breath of fresh air, her whole being drank you in. She was short and had flaming red dyed hair which drew your eyes to the top of her head. Leona had been friends with her since she moved here as a new bride. It was Dora who introduced her to society in the city.

"After all, my dear, you are a prominent physician's wife, you must join our group." Dora convinced her the very first time they met. Their friendship and spirit hunting grew over the years.

Dora made a bee line right for Maggie. Taking hold of her shoulders with both hands, looking straight into her eyes she said, "Yes, you are right my dear Leona, she is the one." Then she hugged her.

As Maggie hugged her back she looked over Doras shoulder at Leona with pleading eyes as if saying, what the heck.

"Yes, I felt it the minute she stepped into the house, her mother has it also."

"Excuse me ladies, I'm right here. What is it that I have?" Maggie said anxiously.

"Why my dear, you have the sight, of course," Dora said, smiling.

The women went on to tell Maggie of 'the sight', a special person who was in tune with the spirit world, one who could see through the veil of death. They both agreed that Charleston had called her here, she had work to do.

"Ladies, I have always been in touch with my spirit. It's a family gift. But not in the way you explain it. My spirit gives my clues or realizations. I've never conjured up the dead!"

"Maybe not yet, but you have the gift. It just needs to be cultivated, like my garden," Leona smiled.

For Maggie this came out of the blue. She knew the spirits from growing up in New Orleans. But conjuring up the dead was bad juju. She really didn't want any part of dark magic. Over dinner the conversation got lighter. The ladies explained that they had no interest in anything sinister, just with helping spirits that were stuck to pass over. They had been doing this for years, ever since Herbert came to Leona after passing away. The old ladies looked at each other, nodded and Dora explained.

One evening about a month or so after Herbert passed, Leona had a dream. A dream so real she felt that it really happened. During the dream, Herbert woke her, sat down beside her on the bed and told her of important papers that needed to be found. He was very insistent, but at this point she woke up. This dream occurred two more times before Leona finally told Dora out of fear.

Dora had the sight. She didn't share it with many people as it would scare them off or think of her as a witch. She also knew Leona had the same ability. She saw it in her at their first meeting and that's why they became fast friends. At this point Leona couldn't contain herself. She jumped into the conversation to explain what came next.

"Dora taught me that my fear was waking me up during the dream. We worked on a meditation that would clear the fear before bedtime. Sure enough the next time Herbert came to me he revealed a little more."

Once again in her dream, he woke her up, sat on the bed, told her of the paper that needed to be found. They were her financial freedom!! Then she woke up.

"Well," she said, "I got a tad further into the dream but it still scared me, that's what woke me up."

Now Leona and Dora were more determined to find out about these papers. As Leona had depended solely on Herbert for her livelihood and her savings were dwindling. It took another month or so of meditation and learning her spirit skills, as they called it, before another dream came.

One evening as Leona prepared for bed there was a calming presence in the room. As she was falling asleep she felt a gentle touch on her cheek. Then she dreamt, she knew there was no fear. This time Herbert didn't have to wake her, she was waiting for him. He sat down beside her, gently stroked her cheek as he did many times in life.

He told her without words, ***"My love, I left you too soon. There is a safe in the basement, in it is your security."*** Leona immediately woke up!!

"He was gone. I felt it. His spirit had one more thing to do before passing over. He made sure I was going to be ok. I cried but I also knew that his love for me kept him here until I understood."

Sure enough the following day the two women ventured to the basement, rummaged through what seemed to be centuries of family heirlooms before finding a small safe. It was black about one foot square with beautiful gold leaf designs on it. A large dial with numbers was in the middle of the door. They looked at it and smiled, for they knew that if Herbert directed them to the safe that the Spirits would give them the combination!

They made a game if it. Of course they could have taken it to the local locksmith, but what was the fun in that. They meditated, lit candles, gave offerings during the full moon, but no combination came.

Leona's son,who had now grown,had been a soulful child, the kind that could entertain himself for hours with imaginary friends when he was younger. What they didn't realize was that he had the sight also.

At lunch one afternoon he said, "Mama, I was reading in the front room this morning and got distracted by the horses out the front window. When I turned to leave the window I saw some carvings on the backside of the fireplace mantle. I never noticed them before, what is it?"

"Lord, son, this house is so old, who knows. I'll look at it later." And it was forgotten.

About a week later, Dora had come for lunch. While chatting about their dilemma with the safe, her son again said something about the engravings.

"Mama, those carvings were numbers I saw. Remember, I told you last week," he said excitedly looking at the women, back and forth, "maybe that's the combination!"

"Long story short, they were the numbers to the combination. It was the year the house was built! The papers inside were investments that turned out to make me a very wealthy woman. Even in death Herbert looked out after my son and me," Leona said with a sad half smile.

The afternoon sun was starting to drop below the tree line, their luncheon had been quite an eye opener for Maggie. She needed time to think, to absorb what had just happened. After thanking the ladies, she excused herself to allow them their time to visit with each other.

Dora was a character, she knew all the old families and their secrets. She claimed to be the secret keeper in polite Charleston society, but of course she wasn't. Most of her conversations started off like, "I don't want to gossip but...." Leona adored her, they would put their heads together whispering and laughing like school girls. It warmed Maggie's heart to see these old ladies reminiscing with joy, not regrets.

CHAPTER FIVE

Sorrows

Maggie met Allison at their usual place for coffee before work. It was a corner deli that could only fit a few people at a time but brewed the best high test in the area. They each got a cup to go with a cinnamon bun, Maggie's downfall. While they walked to The Tower discussing where to go on their monthly exploring trip, a man accidentally bumped into Allison who appeared very flustered.

"Oh, I'm so sorry, please did I spill your coffee?" he stammered.

"I'm fine, really, didn't spill a drop. Are you ok?" she smiled.

"Yes, yes, it's just my mom, not good news. I'm on my way now, they told me to hurry," he said, jogging off in the direction of The Tower.

The girls agreed, this wasn't a good way to start the day off.

Maggie's assignment for the day was relatively light so she decided to visit one of her favorite long term patients on her break. Most of the staff had become attached to her and some called her Grandma, she had kidney disease and required dialysis three times a week. She reminded Maggie of her

Granny, caring but firm, able to tell a story while delivering a message made only for you. She had a following of sorts. People would come regularly to sit with her. They reminded Maggie of the Gypsies in New Orleans, dressed in brightly colored clothes with lots of jewelry. Sylvia loved gum drops so Maggie stopped by the gift shop to pick up a bag.

As Maggie approached Sylvia's room she heard crying. Quietly she opened the door. His back was to her, he sat holding Sylvia's hand whispering to her in between sobs.. Maggie slowly backed out and went to find the nurse taking care of Sylvia today.

"Carol, what's happened to Sylvia? There's a man in there crying, is she gone?" she said, almost crying herself.

"It's not good Maggie. She really took a turn for the worse early this morning. That's her son with her. I have to go change her dressings at her dialysis port site. Would you like to help me?"

Maggie helped Carol gather her dressings and meds and they headed down the hall.

Apparently Sylvia's son was from out of town and just drove in this morning. He hadn't seen his Mom in awhile. It was the typical excuse she heard all the time. I'm too busy now, my job is crazy, the kids are in school. Didn't grown children understand how much their elderly parents needed them. But to his credit he was here now, hopefully she knew he was at her bedside.

Carol knocked on the door and walked in, he was standing at the window, looking out, deep in thought, not moving.

"Excuse me sir, we need to do a dressing change and give your mom some meds, would you like to stay or step out?" Carol asked.

He turned around and both he and Maggie gasped at the same time.

"You….." he stammered.

"Yes, it's me. Can I buy you a cup of coffee while Carol takes care of your mom?"

He nodded as Maggie pointed him out the door, leaving Carol with a startled look on her face.

They found a table in the hospital cafeteria. After making their coffee, Boyd introduced himself and told her how utterly ironic this was after bumping into them this morning.

He hadn't seen his mom in six months, due to a travel schedule at work. "If I would have known she was this sick, I would have been here a long time ago. She told me she was fine, just here for dialysis. That it was easier to stay in the hospital then to go back and forth," he said, looking helpless.

"She probably didn't want to burden you, that's what moms do," she replied, deep in her own thoughts.

They talked for the next twenty minutes about family. He told her of his mom's strange lifestyle and how he was raised. She was a believer in the spirits, they led her on every decision she made. Some people thought her a little weird. Now Maggie knew why she was so drawn to her.

As they were headed back to the room Carol came to find them, Sylvia was awake and requesting to see her son. She told Maggie in a whisper things weren't good.

Boyd practically jogged down the hall to her room. The girls gave them some privacy. Carol explained that while they were gone, Sylvia had requested and signed a DNR document. Do Not Resuscitate, this meant she was to die in peace, no heroics.

Boyd came to find Maggie and Carol, Sylvia had requested it. They gathered around her bed and held her hands. She smiled at them, her radiance in death gave you chills.

"Thank you for all your care," she said, looking at the girls "Boyd, you know what you have to do son, let my spirit go. Don't hold me here, I want to soar," she said weakly.

As Sylvia lay dying a ray of beautiful sunlight came through the window. It was as if to welcome her home. Boyd quickly opened the window, the girls looked at each other.

"Your spirit can soar now, Mom, go, your path is clear," he said with tears rolling down his cheeks. Looking at the girls he said, "It's her belief, the open window helps her spirit depart from this physical building."

The past week had been a tough one emotionally for Maggie. She lost two patients, one being beloved and the other way too young from cancer. From time to time she got assigned one of her favorite patients. He was an older gentleman named Mr McGinnis, who was in a coma and required total care while on a ventilator. As she took care of his needs, Maggie would talk to him. She knew he could probably hear her, maybe not totally understand, but her voice could be a comfort. She would tell him of her days off and of settling into her new home while tending his needs during her shift. He became a silent father confessor, she could tell him anything without recrimination. There were days that she couldn't stand the thought of another sick person, it drained her. But then she remembered and Granny's words came to her.

"We are all here for a reason, you are a healer my child. Some days will be joyful, some days will bring sorrow. But you must remember that each person you minister to, has their own reason for being here, their own Karma. You must be careful not to take on their juju. Love them, heal them if possible but always let them lead the way."

When Maggie had bad days she found herself in the garden alongside Leona, it gave her peace feeling the earth in her hands, helped her stay grounded. The old woman never said a word these days, it was as though she felt Maggie's sorrow. They would work side by side pulling weeds, replanting and pruning until it got too warm. Marie would appear with a tray of sweet tea, signaling it was time to sit on the veranda and enjoy the breeze. These mornings seemed to rejuvenate Maggie, they gave her hope that life goes on.

CHAPTER SIX

Tea Time

As the days grew into months, Maggie realized that it had been a year since she moved in with Leona. A year of growing in her profession and growing new friendships. Her mother visited almost every other month or so, sometimes bringing Granny with her. Leona and Granny had hit it off right from the beginning, kindred spirits of sorts.

During one of their visits Leona decided to introduce the ladies to high tea. In Charleston this tradition had been around for years. It was first practiced at home, the parlor to be exact. Ladies of society, in fine dress and beautiful hats would sit and chat while drinking tea and enjoying tiny cucumber sandwiches. Later around the early 1950's, the first Tea Room was founded as a fundraising event. It was held in the old St Andrews Church that hadn't been used for over 50 years. It became so popular that over the years smaller tea rooms were opened. There was no need to be a part of high society now. Anyone could enjoy a cup of tea in elegance. In fact, some tea rooms actually encouraged it. They had wide brimmed colorful hats and boas hanging on the walls to choose from as you enjoyed your tea. Leona explained that her and Dora would do this high tea the old fashioned way every few months.

"It will be great fun. I'll ring Dora and make reservations, she can meet us there," she said excitedly.

The ladies got all gussied up like school girls. Leona dug in her old trunks for a few outdated gowns from times gone by. They each picked one that called to them, even finding some old hats in the attic that hadn't been worn in years. Leona and Granny actually found matching dresses of dark red brocade with silk overlays. Their wide brimmed hats cocked to one side gave them an air of mystery. They almost looked like sisters if it weren't for the hair color. Geraldine had gone more conservative for her taste. It was muted yellow with white lace around the bodice falling straight to the floor. Her hat sat neatly on her head with a white netting falling over her eyes. Maggie chose an emerald green ball gown to match her eyes. It was sleeveless with a low cut bodice, almost scandalous for the time it was designed for. On her head sat a wide brimmed black hat with emerald green ostrich feathers. They were such a sight, coming down the mahogany staircase Marie thought she had gone back in time.

"Why, ladies, you all look positively lovely, and where are you off to in such finery?"

"Oh, Marie, thank you, we are going for high tea."

"Leonia, you really need to do this right. Let me add a bit of magic to your day," Marie said, opening the front doors with a twinkle in her eye.

There stood a horse and carriage! The ladies were all laughing and talking at the same time. Leonia hugged and thanked Marie for her grand idea. The driver assisted all the ladies into the carriage and headed to King Street where Twenty Six Divine was opened for tea. For Leona it was great fun showing off her city to the others. They agreed that one day she must visit New Orleans.

CHAPTER SEVEN

Herbert

Maggie had always listened to her Spirit. It brought her to Charleston, it brought her to Leona but it was always done so in subtle ways. Today's intervention was not so subtle! She was trying to remember his exact words, it was important. She took out her pen and started writing it down on a copy of her work schedule that was folded in her pocket. She must tell Leona!

It was a typical day, she met Allison for coffee, they walked to work, nothing unusual. Maggie clocked in on her floor and got her assignment for the day, nothing unusual. She went back over in her mind the day's events, what could have brought this on? Again, nothing unusual, just another day. Thank goodness this didn't happen until her shift was over, she wouldn't be able to contain herself.

She speed walked down Rutledge to get home, if the side walks weren't so caddy wonked she would have ran, but fear of tripping did not allow that. Finally, she felt that she would burst when the house appeared. Running up to the front door it magically opened!! What the heck, she thought, but then again it made sense.

"Leona, Leona, where are you?" she yelled, very unladylike

"Why, dear, I'm right here. I saw you coming up the steps and opened the door for you," she said, with her one eyebrow raised

Maggie doubled over trying to catch her breath and laughing at the same time. Of course she opened the door, you silly girl, you thought he did it? Leona guided her to the settee and asked Marie to bring Maggie a glass of sweet tea. After calming down and Leona watching her patiently she explained, "It was a typical day, really, I didn't do anything to bring this on," she said, looking at Leona like she had done something wrong.

"It's ok Maggie, whatever this is, we will take care of it, calm down and tell me."

As Maggie was clocking out for the day she decided to stop by the gift shop for some flowers. That was the only unusual thing that had happened up until that point. It was like a Spirit thought, bring home daisies. So she bought a bouquet of daisies and as she was headed out a different door then usual she saw him!

It was a rather large picture of Dr Herbert Harrington, dressed in his physician white lab coat, stethoscope around his neck and a big beautiful smile. She had never seen this picture before as her usual entrance was behind her. He stopped her cold in her tracks.

As she stood there she heard him, ***"Bring her the daisies. Tell her to remember the night on the river in Savannah."***

As she finished telling Leona, she looked up to see her crying and smiling at the same time.

"I'm sorry, I've made you sad, I shouldn't have said anything, maybe it's just my overactive imagination."

Leona stopped her, got up and hugged her. She went on to tell Maggie of her meeting Herbert for the first time. It was many many years ago. She had been walking along the river early one evening when she decided to sit awhile. She found a bank filled with daisies. Lost in her own thought she heard a man ask her for directions. Looking up the sun was to his back and he appeared like a God with a halo around his head she thought. She started to get up from sitting when he offered his hand, as she took it the warmth of his touch went through her.

"It was on this date that we met all those years ago. Thank you Maggie."

"But how?"

"Don't question Spirit. You have the ability, just let it flow. We will help teach you, there is still much to learn," she ended with a prayer of protection from the dark.

CHAPTER EIGHT

The Angel Tree

When Maggie told Allison of her encounter with Herbert, Allison insisted they use the front door of The Tower all the time now. She also insisted on a strange ritual whenever entering or exiting past the picture. She crossed herself, as if in church. Allison had been brought up Catholic and had some strong beliefs. Her crossing herself made her feel as though she was helping Herbert in some strange way. Maggie on the other hand knew. Herbert was fine, living in another dimension, another timeline of sorts. He didn't need any mumbo jumbo but if that made Allison feel better, whatever.

The girls decided to drive over to Johns Island later that week, it was time for some sightseeing. The island was between the Ashley and Stono Rivers, with loads of marshland between and magnolia lined streets. They were on their way to see the Angel Oak when they spotted Sweet Belgium. It was a pastry shop with small hand held waffles. You could add all kinds of toppings, like a donut.

Agreeing that coffee and sweet waffles would taste wonderful they stopped for a quick treat and weren't disappointed. In fact they bought extra for the ride home.

"Oh my goodness, these are awesome! I could eat two more," Allison said, then did, laughing at herself.

The Angel Oak was off the beaten path. If you weren't looking for it, you missed it. There was an old dirt road off Main Road just past Rt 700. The dirt road winds in about ½ mile or so into the woods. Then there, on your right you see it, standing majestically, her 500 years old moss covered limbs stretching like arms to embrace you. Some of the branches have reached the ground and then grown back up as if to reach the sun. She stands over 60 feet tall and is about 160 feet wide. The girls were awestruck, agreeing that it was wonderful of this family to save her. A small gift shop with a porch and swing add to her charm. No fee is charged to see her but a donation is encouraged. Turning onto the dirt parking area they noticed hardly anyone was there,

"Wow, I thought there would be more people here," Allison said.

"I like it like this, more quiet time to enjoy the Angel tree," replied Maggie.

Maggie stood mesmerized by the tree. The blue skies and white clouds made a beautiful backdrop for its majestic limbs. She was immediately drawn to touch it. The breeze had suddenly stopped and there was a presence. An Indian woman and child stood crying and holding hands, she thought for a moment they were real. But then a cardinal flew right through them and she noticed nothing but grasslands behind them. She closed her eyes and muttered a prayer of protection from the dark, allowing only light into her surroundings. When she opened them they were still there, completely unaware of her.

As time stood still she watched them. She knew what they were saying to each other without hearing the words. It was a ritual for her dead husband, the tree was just a sapling then. The mother compared the tree to the son. One day he would grow mighty like this oak would, standing tall to protect the ones he loved just as his father had.

"Maggie, are you ok?" She felt Allison's hand on her shoulder.

The image was gone, the woman and child forever now in her memory.

"Oh, yes, I'm fine, sorry. Just thinking how much my Granny would love this tree."

There was no way she was telling Allison the truth this time, she'd spend the rest of the afternoon crossing herself! They spent the next few hours enjoying the grounds, reading plaques, buying a few postcards of the tree and taking pictures. They had been blessed with a beautiful day. Maggie couldn't wait to tell Leona and Dora about her experience. She could see them now, almost salivating for her story, she loved these silly old ladies.

The jasmine in the garden was overpowering, Leona and Dora agreed. The two old ladies had their sweet tea on the veranda and waited. It was as if they knew she was coming home to tell them something of her adventure. Allison dropped off Maggie in the rear alley to the house. The kitchen entrance was the best to clean your shoes off first before going in, hers were full of dirt. She spotted the ladies and headed their way after removing her shoes. The old mahogany wood floors felt cool on her feet even though it was warm outside, almost like the house knew.

It took restraint on the old ladies part. They waited patiently for Maggie to settle in, take a breath and pour herself some tea. She knew they were anxious and played for just a little more time, giggling to herself.

"So, ladies, what have you been up to?" she said, laughing.

"You little minx, tell us!! We felt it, your sight, what happened?" Dora whispered as if others were listening.

She told them of the Indian woman and child, her heartbreak of losing her husband and the ritual of the tree. They discussed the sapling and knew the story had to be about 500 years ago, that area was inhabited by the Stono Indians then. They questioned her about her protection prayer, she assured them she was careful not to allow any darkness. With the woman not being aware of her being there they felt that she was just a part of the tree now, her history was embedded in the tree. What a beautiful story it was, she wished she could share it. But knew people weren't ready for this, only those that were awakened would understand.

CHAPTER NINE

Home

It had been over a year and half since Maggie left New Orleans, she was feeling a little homesick. Her mom hadn't made the trip in over four months and she was missing them both. She planned a trip with Leona, and they decided to surprise Granny.

"Oh what fun this will be, I haven't surprised anyone in years," Leona said as she was packing her suitcase.

"Hopefully Mom can keep a secret from that old crone. She has the sight, one wrong answer or look and she'll know Moms up to something."

Geraldine met them at the airport on the hottest day of the summer, the humidity was so thick you could cut it. Granny and Geraldine still lived in the two bedroom condo in the Quarter. It was a short 15 mile drive from Louis Armstrong Airport to their place.

Leona was like a teenager with a secret, barely able to sit still. As they drove past the ruined homes still waiting for repair or demolition, it was hard to believe it had happened back in 2005.

"Oh Maggie, it's overwhelming." Leona could feel the sadness from the dead, she sensed the anguish. She knew there were many souls stuck here.

When they arrived at Granny's she was in the kitchen cooking up a huge pot of jambalaya. Stirring to the right, always to the right, making her intentions known. She smiled to herself knowing they had been on their way, imagine them trying to get one over on this old cron.

After many yells of "surprise " and hugs all around the ladies went to the dining room. The table had been prepared with candles and glasses of wine.

They stood together with glasses in hand, raised, as Granny said,"Laissez les bons temps rouler" as they toasted each other by clinking their glasses together laughing.

Leona, not quite fluent in French looked at Maggie questionly with that one eyebrow turned up.

Smiling Maggie said, "Let the good times roll!"

Granny brought out a huge cauldron filled with her special jambalaya and a loaf of crusty French bread. She dished out healthy portions into individual bowls then broke off a piece of bread for herself. She passed the bread to Maggie who tore off her piece. She passed it to Leona who did the same, then on to Geraldine. There was no need for hot sauce but if you needed more heat Granny had her own special blend made of local hot peppers. Geraldine was the only one who gave the bottle a few shakes into her bowl.

Dinner was a great success. The ladies ate their fill and sat at the table talking for hours. Granny brought out her famous chicory coffee, of course they added a bit of Frangelico liqueur. Cookies and bite size pastries rounded out the evening. As the evening wore on Maggie and Geraldine gradually made their way to bed to leave Granny and Leona by themselves.

Talk eventually led to the many lost souls wandering in their air space as Leona called it. Granny confirmed she felt it also. In fact, she had already helped a few crossover. It could only be done if the soul was ready. Some souls thought they were ready but when it came time to go, they couldn't. These were the souls Granny regretted not helping.

"I was drawn to a few of the homes we drove by on the way here. They called to me," Leona said sadly.

"While you're here we can drive over, maybe we can help a few. We'll have to sage the houses before we can do anything."

After agreeing to find some time for lost souls they went to bed. The music from down the street was intoxicating. Leona had never heard anything like it, the horn was almost mournful. No wonder there are so many lost souls here, she thought as she fell asleep.

The next morning Leona found Maggie in the kitchen. Geraldine was still in the shower and Granny was out doing her morning errands in town. After inquiring how Leona's night was, Maggie poured her a cup of chicory coffee.

"I've never had this before last night, why use chicory?" she asked.

"You'll have to ask Granny but from what I gather it's low in caffeine and has other medicinal purposes. For me, I grew up on it so it's my kind of coffee."

The back door opened and in walked Granny carrying a big brown bag with scattered oil stains on it. Maggie knew what she had.

"Oh Granny, Beignets, from Cafe Du Monde?"

"Yes my dear, powdered sugar and all," she said beaming.

Leona had never had a beignet. she dove right in, as did Maggie. Geraldine found them all sitting around the table with powdered sugar all over their faces laughing.

"Y'all have better saved one for me," she said, as her hand grabbed one from the bag. "Mom, you could have at least put them on a plate," she said, as she stuffed half of it in her mouth moaning in pleasure.

Their leisurely morning turned into a crazy afternoon. Maggie and Granny decided to take Leona on a walk about the French Quarter, to feel the flavor. There were many similarities to Charleston; the history, the ability to walk the city with ease and the numerous souls taking up air space! By the time they dressed and were out the door the city was bustling. The bike taxis and carriages were in full swing, the tourists loved them. Their walk took them down Decatur Street where they sat for a while in Jackson Square. Leonia was in awe of the fact that from the park you looked up to see the river,

"Oh my, I feel like I'm in a bowl, how can this be?"

After Maggie explained about the layout of the city Leona totally understood how it could flood so badly. From the park they walked up the steps to the river. The barges and tourist river boats were gently gliding up and down the river, never coming anywhere near each other. They sat for a while there also, Maggie knew her Granny had to pace herself.

CHAPTER TEN

Old Soul

While sitting on a bench, the sun at their backs, Maggie felt a draw. St Louis Cathedral stood across Jackson Square, it sat like a beam of light in a dark space. She had been here many times before but never experienced this feeling. It was as if the same feeling hit the others,

"I think we need to visit The Cathedral,' Granny said, as they all got up at the same time, almost knowing she was going to say that.

They walked back down the steps, through the park, commenting on the statue of Andrew Jackson for a moment. Then they stood in front of the cathedral. There were street vendors and people playing instruments all over Chartres Street, the blend of sounds were surreal.

The blended music from the street performers sounded like voices to Maggie. At first she thought it was her imagination, but then she saw Granny and Leona tilt their heads as if to listen.

"Help her, please, she's drowning. Please hurry!"

It was as if they all heard the same thing at once. What the heck, thought Maggie! Leona knew, she felt it driving in, she knew where they had to go. Without a single word the older women turned and started walking toward the taxi stand. Maggie followed, knowing not to say a word.

They arrived in a neighborhood that had been shuttered for years since Hurricane Katrina. The homes were falling apart, trees had actually grown through porches. When the ladies asked the driver to stop and wait for them, he looked at them as if they were crazy. But when they offered to double his fee he agreed. The sadness was overwhelmingly for Maggie.

"There are so many here," Leona whispered.

"I feel it also, but one calls to us," Granny said solemnly.

Maggie looked at them both, not wanting to break the spell, they walked down a few houses when they both stopped.

"Here," Leona said and Granny nodded.

The house stood about 20 feet off the street. There was dirt where grass used to be and tall weeds grew through the holes in the porch floor. It was painted white at one time, but now the paint was peeling so bad it was mostly bare wood. It bore the scars from time gone by. By the looks of the roof, half the shingles were gone and a hole could be seen over the porch. The porch railing had fallen into the dirt and a few floor boards were sticking up as if to say, come near me and I'll trip you. They approached the front door with caution.

As they touched the door they heard again, *"Help her please, she's drowning, please hurry!"*

Maggie joined the women and touched the door. It was as if they were laying hands on the house. As they stood on the porch touching the door, time stood still. They felt the coldness of the water, the darkness of the night and the panic of the house. The house who loved the old woman who lived there. In a flash the spell was over, the sun was shining and the taxi driver was beeping his horn. The women walked together as if in a trance back to the taxi.

Granny gave him her address and made a strange request,"Step on it son and there's an extra ten for you!"

By the time the taxi pulled up to Granny's back in the Quarter Maggie was wondering if she had imagined the whole thing, then again she remembered the Angel Tree incident, she couldn't wait to talk to the ladies.

"What the heck just happened," Maggie blurted out as they opened Granny's apartment door Leona and Granny exchanged knowing glances and went on to explain. The plea they heard for help was not from a person, it was from the house.

"But it's a house, not a person, how can this be?" asked Maggie.

Evidently the old woman had lived in that house since it was built. Her very soul was in the house, they were one. The house is mourning still. It doesn't know what happened to her. They went on to explain that all objects have cellular memories. This house became attached to the woman, she must have loved it very much.

"We have to free the house from its sorrow," Leona said.

"I think I know how," Granny replied.

The next day, after much planning the previous night, the ladies headed for the courthouse down on Chartres Street. It was still early and the street performers weren't out yet. Maggie felt a sense of relief, she didn't want to hear that plea for help again this early in the morning. She would much rather be across the square at Cafe du Monde having chicory coffee and a beignet. It was only a short couple of blocks and they arrived just as the attorneys and other workers got there.

Their plan was to find out who owned that house and what happened to them. It sounded too easy, it wasn't. Since Katrina many people were displaced, records were lost and properties were just abandoned. The lady at the courthouse informed them that since that property had been condemned by the city the records were moved to a county office that handled federal funds from the disaster. Not to be swayed the ladies persevered, it made them want to know even more.

The next few days they visited the Orleans Parish Assessor's Office with no luck. But a kindly older man pointed them to the Orleans Parish Land Records Office where they finally got lucky. It seemed that the house was owned by one family by the name of Landry. They had been evacuated during the storm to Houston and as far as any records were concerned they never returned. The letters sent out to find them by the city had all been returned. So the house was condemned and became property of the Parish. Leona asked the clerk if anyone had died in that house. The clerk looked at her very strangely and said only the Sheriff's Department would have those records. With their new information in hand the ladies decided to call it a day and head back home.

"Well, we have a name at least, it's a start," said Granny

They agreed that it would take more digging. Maggie opened her laptop and started searching, thinking she might find a lead. It was then that she realized that Leona loved a good Spirit driven mystery, or maybe she just attracted them. The older women searched through some old phone books they found with no luck. There were many Landry's but none with that address. Maggie decided to do a search of Houston for the name and came up with two possibilities. It turned out that one family had lived there for many years and the other just moved there recently, it was a dead end. After some leftover jambalaya and a fresh loaf of bread the ladies decided tomorrow was another day, maybe they would have more luck. Saying their good nights each one turned in early.

Maggie woke up with a start. She felt her first, a presence. She knew enough not to panic. I'll just lay here and see where this is going, she thought. The entity was female. A calm loving aura surrounded a now appearing very old black woman. Her back was bent as if she had done a lifetime of hard work. She had shocking white hair that was pulled back in a neat bun. Her clothes were worn but neat and she had bare feet. Maggie knew this was the woman who lived in the house!

There were no words spoken aloud, but they still communicated, as though they were reading each other's mind. Her name was Mahalia, she was born in 1916, to a family of sharecroppers in Alabama. At 15 she moved to New Orleans where she worked as a hotel maid until she met her husband. It was after the Great Depression that the city allowed squatters to build tin roofed and cardboard houses on the outskirts of the town. That was the land that the house stood on now. Like others around they gathered whatever materials they could to make shelter. Soon many destitute families came and they became a small neighborhood looking out for one another.

As new money from the north moved south, in the late 30's, Mahalia went to work for a wealthy family as a maid again. She loved the family and the family's children loved her. As those children grew they saw the horrible conditions she lived in. In 1965 one of the children had become a big wheel in the oil business off the Louisiana coast. He started a fund to convert these makeshift homes into real wood

47

structures. Mahalia had her first real home, built right where her cardboard one was.

During her lifetime she had two children. One died in childbirth, when she was very young. She wouldn't say anything more about that. The second was a daughter, born in 1950. When she was 34 years old and, she thought, too old to have a child. She named her Lillia Bell. She lived with Mahalia until she passed away giving birth to an unwanted child in 1967. Mahalia and her husband raised the child, naming her Bell after her momma. Bell was born with an unusual birthmark on her chest, almost like a faded tattoo was the outline of a heart. Mahalia's husband died in 1980. Her granddaughter, Bell went to work one morning in 1985 and never came home. Mahalia never saw her again.

Maggie woke up, shaking her head not sure what happened. Did she dream this, was it real. Physically shaken she made her way to Granny's room. Not finding her there she went down to the kitchen. There sitting at the table was Granny, Leona and a beautiful black woman. She wore a dress of bright colors with a headpiece to match Her hands had long slender fingers with nails that were painted bright red. The strange part was she was barefooted. They were all drinking coffee in silence. Not sure how to react she looked to Granny. Smiling Granny told her to get a cup of coffee and sit. The woman came here asking for Maggie, she wouldn't say anything until she met her. They all looked at the woman now, she smiled as if to say "your not going to believe this…."

Grace started her story. She had to find Her, she wasn't sure who Her was, but she had to find Her. In recent months she had dreamt of water, darkness and an old house. Sometimes in different settings but never making sense. Then last week her spirits told her she must go to New Orleans. Grace had been living in Gulfport, Mississippi ever since the accident. The accident happened over 30 years ago. She woke up in a hospital, two broken legs, broken arm, concussion and no memory.

Her nurses named her Grace because it was by the Grace of God that she was alive.The name stuck. She never regained her memory and there was no trace of any missing person that they could connect her to. She took the last name of Charity, to honor the hospital that kept her alive for nine months, The Sisters of Charity Hospital.

During the past few years different flash backs would occur, an old couple, kitchen table, a small front porch. But she never knew where they were from. Over the years she just accepted that there was no family because there was never a missing person report to match her. She never married or had children. There was always a piece missing that she couldn't find, at least until now.

She arrived in New Orleans two days ago, not knowing why. But then sitting in Jackson Square she heard it.

"Oh my God, don't tell me, oh my God!!!!" Maggie blurted out astonished.

Leona and Granny were also talking at the same time. Grace looked at them all.

"Help her, please, she's drowning. Please hurry," she whispered, as if she was afraid of their reaction.

A group Yes was heard….Granny tried to get everyone calmed down enough to listen to the rest of her story.

Grace sat in the square and heard it. She knew the message was for her, but how. Trusting in her Spirits she waited. The next day she came back to the square but never heard anything. She did however see a woman with an unusual aura surrounding her. The Spirits told her to be patient, she was Her. Later that afternoon she saw Maggie and followed her here. She waited until this morning to attempt to see her.

"I don't know exactly why I need to see you," she said looking at Maggie, "But it's important and I trust my Spirits."

"I think I do," Maggie said, taking a deep breath, she told Mahalias story.

It was a long morning. Through many tears and hugs the women bonded, a bond that would last a lifetime. When Grace revealed her birthmark there was no doubt she was Bell, no doubt that Mahalia was her Grandmother. She had a family history to be told. They had one more thing to do. They piled into a taxi and drove over to the house, the house that had called to them all. As the woman put their hands on the house it spoke to them through unspoken words.

"She waited for you, Bell, never left, never gave up. Even when the flood waters came she waited, just in case you would come home. I tried to save her but I couldn't, she died here with me. We loved each other, you couldn't save her. Please save me."

Not only did Bell save her Grandma's house, but she saved four more in the neighborhood. A new era began. Over the years Grace had worked and saved. She had the funds to start rehabilitating old homes and it turned out to be very lucrative for her. You can see a sign on Grace's new offices, Mahalia's Place, if you drive down that old street on the outskirts of town.

CHAPTER ELEVEN

Back in Charleston

As Maggie and Leona headed home they talked about their adventure at Granny's. If this was any indication of what was to come, living with these old crone's Maggie was in for one heck of a ride. Leona congratulated her on the expansion of her abilities, reminding her of the many Souls occupying our air space yet to be helped. Maggie just smiled and rolled her eyes. Leona could tell Maggie needed a break from the spirits for a while. She let her rest as the airplane headed back home.

Home, Leona thought, it had been such a comforting thought. She had spent the better part of her life in that house. Her memories were imprinted into its walls just as the others were. She wished those memories could be shared with family, but sadly she had none left. Hopefully Maggie's abilities would help her connect the dots of her life.

The plane touched down at Charleston Airport. It was overcast and rainy, one of those days you just want to curl up with a good book. They hailed a taxi and headed home, it was good to see the familiar surroundings. When they arrived home Marie had left them a pot of warm soup and sandwiches, knowing they would be hungry after the trip. After devouring the food Leona went off for a nap while Maggie unpacked and put things in order for work the next day. She was looking forward to things getting back to normal for a while.

Morning came too early for Maggie. She felt more tired than normal, maybe the trip caught up to me she thought while in the shower. She dressed and headed down the stairs to check on Leona before going to work. Although it was a beautiful morning, she wasn't in the courtyard garden. Maggie checked the kitchen and no Leona. Maybe she's just tired like me and sleeping in. She headed out the door and down the street. Her head was in a fog, trying to shake it off she bumped into Allison.

"You're late, is everything ok?"

"Yes, I just couldn't find Leona , I think she just slept in. Coffee, I need coffee bad!"

They got their coffee and cinnamon bun and headed to The Tower. Allison asked her about her visit to New Orleans. There was no way Maggie could tell her that they solved a mystery of a house's soul. Allison would definitely freak out.

"We had a wonderful visit. Leona and Granny are great friends. They did the tourist thing while my Mom and I hung out," she said nonchalantly. "I feel like I have jet lag cause I can't seem to wake up, I'll need lots of coffee today."

"My dad thought you might want to bring Leona by the store sometime this week. He got a couple of vintage pieces that he said she might like."

Maggie thought about it a minute, Leona, old furniture, spirits….

"I'll ask her but I think her house is already full of antiques," she said, as they got to The Tower. Just as they got to the door the bicycle gentleman rode by waving. Maggie waved back smiling. Allison went through the door, stopped at Herbert's picture and crossed herself. Maggie half expected her to genuflect as she walked by smiling at him, knowing his spirit was long gone.

CHAPTER TWELVE

Antiques

Leona felt it, something was amiss. She had felt it since they got home, first the lethargy now this. She called Dora who also felt it. After checking Grandmother Moon's phases, they knew it wasn't that. Maggie found the two of them with their heads together kneeling in the courtyard garden, hands deep in the earth pulling weeds. But they weren't giggling as usual.

"Good morning ladies. Good to see you again, Dora."

Dora just nodded, Leona barely looked up. Maggie got the feeling she was intruding.

"Well I'm off to meet Allison at her parent's store, then some wandering around town. See you later."

She turned and walked out as they muttered something like have a nice day. That whole situation was strange, thought Maggie. Those two are up to something,

"You could have acted more normal, Dora, at least said good morning or something," Leona said exasperated.

"I could barely look at her, it's her. She attracts them and we feel it. Lordy what's next!"

The two women made a feeble attempt to stand when Marie came through the rear gate. She assisted them both to the rocking chairs on the back veranda. She proceeded to chastise them for not having a walking stick close by to lean on. Then she was gone, disappearing into the rear door of the kitchen.

"I'll bring you old crones some sweet tea and a walking stick," she said, calling over her shoulder giggling, which was very unlike Marie.

The two old ladies looked at each other, what just happened? Things were definitely out of whack, Marie, who never says a word, now was calling them old crones.

The walk to the B & B Antique Shop was pleasant. But Maggie's mind was elsewhere, not really paying attention to her surroundings. It was a good thing she had walked these sidewalks before and knew all the uplifted spots or else she would have tripped at least three times already. The sound of horses hooves clapping against the black top of the street brought her back to the present. Gosh, I was so deep in thought I don't even remember walking here.

The antique store was located within a group of attached buildings three stories high on King Street. Each storefront was something different, a jewelry shop, a hairdresser, a cafe. The businesses were on the street level and apartments were on the upper levels. Some shop owners tended to live above their businesses, as did Allison's family. As Maggie approached the store she realized that Allison hadn't met her half way. Strange, she always did.

"Good morning," she called out as she walked through the door and the bell rang out.

"In here, Maggie, we're in the back," She heard Allison's father call.

She threaded her way through all the old furniture and statues to the back room where she found Brooks and Blair Parsons, Allison's parents. They were sitting at an old desk looking through a ledger of some sort, it looked very old.

"Allison had to run an errand for us at the bank, she'll be back shortly. Please sit," her father said, pointing to the chair next to the table.

As Maggie sat down Blair couldn't contain herself. She blurted out a long line of conversation excitedly that ran together not making any sense.

"Allison told us you can help, it's really strange, why is it just now happening? I never expected this, the town's old but, my goodness......"

Brooks attempted to calm his wife down, "Please, dear, let me speak to Maggie. Why don't you bring us some tea."

Mrs. Parsons, Blair gave her husband such a look. Maggie had to turn away so as to not smile at the interaction.

"I will, dear! But I better not miss anything!" she said, as she stomped out of the room.

Allison came through the back door, calling out that she was back. She found them sitting around the desk sipping tea, waiting on her. Having no idea what had happened earlier she thought it so strange that they seemed calm. She had left her mother in an absolute tether.

"Well, this is cozy, waiting on me are you?"

They all nodded and then the flood gates opened once more. Maggie watched as they all spoke at one time. She gathered that there was a reason they wanted to speak to her, something about a ledger and Mr. Calhoun. Putting her two fingers into her lips she whistled loudly. The conversation stopped immediately!

"That's better, now can one person explain what the heck is going on?"

Mr. Parsons looked at his family, they gave him a nod and he told Maggie the story.

They had owned the antique shop for three years now, never having a problem. But it seemed that they might have a ghost living with them now. For the last month or so every morning they came down to work, this old ledger would be opened to this page. It was an accounting of a Mr. Calhoun, he said pointing and looking at Maggie for answers.

"Ok, first of all, they are not ghosts. They are spirits, lost souls who haven't crossed over yet, usually for good reason. Secondly, could there be a breeze that just blows the pages open?" she said, knowing damn well there wasn't.

"As it turned out," Brooks continued, "We put the ledger on that shelf, every morning," he pointed once again, "then the next day it's back on the desk!!"

"At first we thought Allison was messing with us. We didn't say a word to her thinking she would finally fess up, but she didn't. When we asked her about it she freaked out."

Maggie looked over at Allison who was nodding her head.

"It was then that Allison told us you can speak to the dead!!"

"Whoa, slow down. I don't speak to the dead, that's dark, no, no. For some reason I can help spirits who haven't crossed over, nothing sinister, please," she said, now looking at Allison. "I thought you didn't believe in this, Ally, crossing yourself and all that religious stuff." It was her turn to ramble on.

Mr Parsons could see this was getting out of hand. He clapped his hands and called for a time out. They all stopped and you could see them collectively take a deep breath. Maggie needed more information, in an organized conversation, perhaps with the spirit itself. She stood up, stretched and walked over to the ledger. Without saying a word she put both hands on the book. She felt it, the old cracked brown leather was worn bare in spots. It's twelve by twelve size was big for its time. There were traces of gold lettering on the cover, she couldn't make out what it said. The binding of the book looked as though it could come apart if not treated tenderly. She waited, waited to hear or feel something. Nothing, she got nothing, just an old book, not revealing anything.

"I'm sorry, there's nothing here for me to see. If there is a spirit it's not for me to discover or even help," she said helplessly.

But Maggie was already thinking of someone else who possibly could, the old crones. They were up to something, they felt this!

"Mr Parsons, you mentioned to Allison that Leona might be interested in some new furniture you bought at auction. Why?" Maggie asked.

"Actually I don't know, she just popped into my mind when I saw the table," he said, raising one eyebrow. "Does that mean something? Does she talk to ghosts, I mean spirits also?"

Maggie and Allison slowly walked back to the coral house on Rutledge, keeping their thoughts to themselves until, as usual, Allison couldn't keep quiet. She admitted that she believed in Maggie's abilities. She knew there was more to life and death. She just needed time to understand it all, maybe Maggie could teach her to understand. She didn't want to talk to them, oh heck no, she just wanted to be a part of something that also helped people heal. They helped heal the sick at work. This helped heal souls who were stuck. As Maggie listened she was stunned, and excited, it was so much more fun to have others to share these adventures with.

She hugged Allison and said, "Are you sure you're ready for this? I'm not the only one who speaks to spirits."

Allison hugged her back and said, "Bring it on, sister!" they laughed the rest of the way home.

Leona and Dora were eating lunch in the kitchen, that's where the girls found them. Strange, Maggie thought, Leona never eats in the kitchen. When she asked Leona why she was eating in the kitchen, especially with company she just replied that Marie had said it was best. Accepting that was a little weird as Maggie had only heard Marie say "yes" the whole time she's been here. She thought the girl was a tad simple.

Maggie was trying to figure out how to begin the conversation when Dora asked, "So, when are you going to tell us about the ledger?"

The girls looked at each other and Maggie winked, as if to say, see I told you so! Allison started, she explained about them finding the ledger every morning opened to the same page. Then Maggie told her experience with touching the ledger and feeling nothing.

But there was one more piece of this puzzle Maggie said, "Mr Parsons wanted you to see a table, Leona, He wasn't sure why, your name just popped into his head when he acquired it."

Dora not one to waste words or time stated, it was settled, they would call a taxi and all head back to the antique shop!

The bell on the front door rang out as the group entered the antique shop. Leonia felt it immediately, the smell of lavender overwhelmed her. She asked the others if they could smell it, it was lovely. But they only smelled the musty old building. The group stood back and let her explore, she had a look of serenity on her face. Leona wandered in between pieces of furniture, touching some, smiling and moving on.

"There are many souls in the air here," she declared, "most are happy to stay at this time."

Allison had quietly gone in the back and gotten her parents who watched in awe as Leona picked her way through the shop. Leona suddenly stopped, her face grew angry, she turned and screamed, then fainted!

They all ran to her, Maggie getting there first felt her pulse, Allison making sure there were no cuts or bleeding, doing what nurses do without thinking. She slowly opened her eyes to see them all looking down on her. What the heck was she doing on the floor! Mr. Parsons gently helped her up to the closest sofa and put her feet up.

"Leona, what happened?" begged Maggie with tears in her eyes.

"I'm not sure, it's a blur. Please, a glass of water." She needed time.

Allison ran for a glass of water. The others were quiet as to not interrupt Leona's thinking. Waiting patiently for answers. It was Dora who suggested that maybe Leona needed to go home, this was all too much for one day. Maggie agreed.

She felt so guilty for bringing her here, what had she done, it was all her fault. It was weird but every other person in that room was thinking the same thing, they all felt guilty.

The taxi brought Maggie, Dora and Leona home. The Parsons stayed back at the shop not wanting to intrude any longer. Leona's color and demeanor seemed better now that she was there, in her own surroundings. They settled her into her comfy bed, brought her tea and left her to sleep for a while, which she was more than willing to do. Suddenly she was exhausted.

While she slept Marie made tea for Dora and Maggie who looked like they lost their best friend, both feeling guilty. It was Marie who once again chastised them.

"She's not dead you know. She loves what she does, it's for a reason! It's not your fault, it's just time, time for things to be known. Things she can only uncover," she said, as she disappeared behind the door.

The women looked at each other and suddenly laughed, things couldn't get more wacky. Now that they realized Marie also had the sight, things were getting a bit complicated. They both decided to call it a day, with so many things happening. They needed to let them marinate as Granny would say. After Dora called for her cab they decided to meet again, tomorrow mid morning. That would give everyone time for proper rest, if the spirits would allow it.

CHAPTER THIRTEEN

Old Memories

Leona slept and dreamt. But was it a dream, maybe another timeline, another lifetime, it seemed so real. The courtyard garden was so beautiful. Sitting here on the veranda watching the gardener tend it was agonizing. She wanted to be doing it, it was her garden! If I just try I know I can do it! Looking down Leona saw that she was sitting in a wheelchair, yes, I remember now. I can't walk, the accident, the horse, oh God no…..she felt the gut wrenching anger and self pity. Then she saw him, how dare he come here! His face full of guilt, good, he needs to feel it. It's his fault! Her anger grew more and more. Then Leona became him. He fell to his knees in front of her, crying, begging her for forgiveness. She laughed, a laugh that woke up Leona. She had broken out in a sweat and found herself crying, what the hell was that.

Maggie woke up suddenly. She needed to get to Leona, she needed her. She threw on her robe and ran down to her room as she heard sobbing. Knocking softly she entered to see Leona kneeling at her bedside.

"Leona, here let me help you." She gathered her up in her arms and helped her to sit on the side of the bed. "Are you ok?"

Suddenly she felt old. Was it the dream or did her body just realize that too much time had gone by. Looking at Maggie for answers she told her of the dream, or of the other timeline. As she spoke they settled themselves into the bed, Maggie listening as Leona explained. Then something strange happened.

The sun shining through the window woke Maggie up. She was there in Leona's bed with her, she didn't remember falling asleep. Leona stirred, opened her eyes and looked stunned. She didn't remember falling asleep either. Both agreed that after Leona's explanation of her dream that they both slept without dreams. In fact they both woke up feeling well rested, but confused.

Dora arrived promptly mid morning, polite society wouldn't visit any earlier. She blew in with a basket of goodies, some to eat but others for different uses.

"Good morning ladies, I expect you had an eventful night my dear," she said looking at Leona "I think we need to bring Marie in this morning, the child has much to offer," she said, unpacking her basket.

Following Doras suggestion, Maggie went off to find Marie, leaving Leona to explain the previous night's occurrences.

As all the women gathered around the kitchen table the story unfolded. They all felt something last night, it affected them all in different ways. After Leona had told her story, yet again, Maggie told her part, then they listened to Dora.

She had been woken up by a horse, neighing loudly under her window. Strange, she thought, there were no stables close by. As she gazed out the window she saw a girl riding bareback laughing, but not a happy laugh, more like a sadistic laugh. Not knowing if it was a dream or real she felt very tired. The next thing she knew was the phone ringing, waking her up, it was Marie. It was her turn to explain her connection.

"The evening was normal. I went to bed as usual after my bedtime routine, thankfully so. My dream took me to you, Leona, I saw what you saw and more. But I saw it as an observer, I felt none of the emotions you experienced. We have here a very angry and unforgiving spirit. She has been in the courtyard for many years, I think over a hundred as far as I can tell."

They all looked at her with awe, who was she? How did she know these things?

Marie continued, "Leona, she reaches out to you as a kindred spirit of sorts. She was brought here as a bride also, from a well to do family that spoiled her. Her husband denied her nothing, she played on his feelings, never really loving him. Theirs was a marriage of convenience for fostering the wealth of both families," she stopped and took a breath.

No one moved, it was as if they were all in a trance listening afraid to break the spell.

"The story goes on," Marie said, "her name is Abigail Calhoun."

Leonia and Maggie gasped, "the ledger."

"There are many connections here," Marie continued, "The spirits try to get our attention in whatever way they can," she explained. "Abigail wanted a horse, a certain horse, it was high bred and wild like her. Knowing her husband would not deny her she bought it. At that time there was a stable behind the courtyard where she kept him. Her husband hired a man to take care of the garden and the horse. Never having ridden a horse before she needed to be taught, the new man was tasked with teaching her. Long story short….they fell in love."

"Her husband, who had grown to love her, found out they were having an affair and fired the man. Abigail was enraged, she ran to the stables to find the man but he was gone. She jumped on her horse bareback and galloped off at breakneck speed to find him. Unfortunately for Abigail, she fell off and broke her back, landing her in a wheelchair never walking again. Her husband stayed by her side throughout the following year always coming before her begging forgiveness for buying the horse, for without that indulgence this never would have happened. She never forgave him, she died a bitter woman a year later of pneumonia. It is he that seeks forgiveness, his soul that feels the guilt, he needs to cross over."

The women were exhausted just listening to the story. Now the questions would start.

Maggie asked the first one, "Marie, who the heck are you?"

Before she could answer a borage of other questions followed. Is Abigail stuck here? Why the ledger? What's in the courtyard? We have to find this family, it must be part of my husband's side, was Leonias last question.

By this time the ladies needed time to absorb the details. They decided it was time for a light lunch. They all pitched in, pulling things out of the cabinets and refrigerator until they had a small feast in front of them. While they ate Marie emptied Doras basket of the remaining items onto the counter and began arranging them. Maggie knew them, items sent from the Goddesses: incense, oils and sage, the same that Granny had on her altar.

When they finished eating Marie asked Maggie to sage the room of any negative energy. She took the sage bundle, lit the top and waited for the flame to die off and the smoke to rise. As she walked the room, gently waving her arm into each corner, she spoke a prayer of protection, as Granny had taught her. Returning the sage bundle to Marie she sat down with the others. Marie lit the incense with the end of the sage and said a prayer of her own, then applied some oils to her forehead. She asked permission of each woman to apply a small dab of oil to their forehead. They all agreed and watched once again in awe.

Marie could now finish what they had started. Abigail needed to be exorcised from the courtyard where she has been stuck for decades. Her anger has kept her here, she will not cross over as her spirit is evil. Once her spirit is gone it will free up her husband's spirit to cross over. He was loving and loyal, it's her that holds him here.

Marie continued her work, kneeling with purpose, speaking in another language and suddenly a loud clap of thunder was heard. Then a ray of sunshine came through the kitchen window, so bright it was as if a spotlight was on them. As quick as it came, it was gone.

"It is done," Marie stated as she rose. Standing, she opened the window and smiled. Maggie understood that one, but there was still the question of who she was.

CHAPTER FOURTEEN

A Sons Love

Marie knew this story from her grandmother who had told her over and over while she was young. Her grandmother's guilt over keeping the young couple apart was the driving force behind Marie knowing the whole truth, a real love story:

Ronald had been a good son, after all he was the one who found the combination to the safe. He was a tall boy now, towering over Leonia and very handsome. His hair was the color of yellow, just like his fathers. Once Herbert died, something in Ronnie died also, he went from being a studious child to being a tad mischievous. In his teen years he would sneak out at night, thinking no one knew, but of course Leonia always did. He had loved his father and wanted to carry on his work as a physician. But when he saw that regular medicine couldn't cure his pneumonia, Ronnie lost faith. He began to seek out other methods of healing. If only he would have confided in his mother, she could have guided him. He didn't know she had the sight. But then again Leona was just new at her abilities also.

Ronnie was sitting on the Battery Wall one afternoon, staring at the water lapping at his feet daydreaming, when a young girl sat down beside him. She wore a brightly colored skirt that touched the ground and her ears had large gold hoops dangling from them. He first noticed the color of her feet. They were bare and a beautiful light chocolate color that matched her face. Her nappy hair had long dreadlocks down her back tied together with a ribbon. It all seemed very natural. They sat without a word between them for about thirty minutes, then she left. He wondered if he would see her again. As he wondered, he knew he would.

He made a point of sitting on the wall everyday for a week and she never came. It was while he was running an errand for his mother the following week that he saw her, sitting on the wall. He went over and sat down. He dangled his legs over the side and stared out into the water.

Again, no words were exchanged. She got up and left after a few minutes. These meetings went on every few weeks for the next two months.

Fatu lived up a few blocks on Gadsden Street with her Nana. Her parents died when she was young, she never really knew them. Her Nana was a slave descendant from the rice plantations across the river. Her people settled on this side of the river after the war. They were considered a Gullah community. Many of their people came up from Louisiana, the Creole people, and blended their beliefs over the decades. Fatu didn't trust easily, she had lost too much. Her own community treated her like an outcast, being a half breed and blaming her for her parents death.

She didn't have any friends and liked it that way. But this boy was different, she felt it. Sitting alongside him, she could almost have a conversation with no words. Her Nana called it Ecknowledge, Gullah for knowing. She decided that she could trust him. And today I will speak, she thought, hoping he would be there. He didn't disappoint her. As she walked along the battery, her long brightly colored skirt flowing in the breeze he saw her and waved. He had never done that before. This was a sign from the spirits, she thought, he was ready.

She sat down next to him, threw her legs over the side and let the waves splash at her feet. She noticed that today he was also barefooted, she looked at him and smiled. His heart melted, it was a smile of pure unspoken trust. He had never seen something so beautiful. He reached down and gently touched her hand. She responded by turning her palm over to hold his fingers first, then his hand. They sat for a few minutes, staring out into the waves.

"I am called Fatu, I live a few blocks up there," she said, pointing.

Ronnie thought her voice sounded musical, it had an odd twang to it.

"I live just over there," he pointed, "My name is Ronald but Mamma calls me Ronnie."

She thought it was a lovely name, Ronald, very strong and manly.

"I will call you Ronald," she declared, got up and walked away.

Their courtship continued this way for a few weeks. They would sit barefooted on the wall holding hands, exchanging one sentence conversations, then she would be gone.

Then one day as they were sitting staring out into the water a man came up to them. He was very rude declaring that what they were doing was disgusting. They needed to take their behavior elsewhere. He walked away in a huff. The couple looked at each other as if what was that all about? They really had no idea why someone would find them disgusting. Their innocence added to their relationship of trust.

One afternoon Ronald decided to ask Fatu if they could walk the Battery instead of sit. They enjoyed a beautiful sunny day, free of humidity. As they walked they spoke more. He learned of her family life and she learned of his. When they got to the end of the sidewalk to say their goodbyes Fatu stood on her tiptoes, kissed him on the cheek and ran. Ronalds heart soared, he felt things he had never felt before.

Eventually Fatu and Ronald became lovers. They found places that no one knew about in Charleston to meet. They pledged themselves to each other. Ronald had asked her to marry him many times but she refused, her Nana had forbidden it. She must only marry one of her own kind. This was the downfall of her mother. She married a Buckrah, a white man, became pregnant with Fatu and died in childbirth. Her father was so distraught that he took his own life a year later. The couple thought about running away but Ronald knew his mother depended on him. He couldn't leave her alone. Their relationship went on until Fatu's Nana found them. Enraged that it had gone this far she sent Fatu to relatives in New Orleans.

Ronnie was heartbroken. He tried to find her but the Creole community in New Orleans closed ranks around her, she simply disappeared. He finally gave up on finding her but never gave up loving her. Years went by. He became obsessed with his business and became very wealthy, all the time never marrying. As his mother grew older he realized that they needed a grandchild to leave the legacy of his father to. The house needed to stay in the family, it had been in their family since 1875.

Leona introduced him to many socialites to date, none made him feel like Fatu. He decided just to pick one as he would never find another love like hers. Patrice was the daughter of a wealthy builder in the Charleston area. She was nice, not snobby like the rest. She understood Ronnie when he explained about Fatu. He didn't want to start a marriage with secrets. She would give him time and, hopefully, he would love her. They married later that year. Ronnie was happy, he was learning to love Patrice. Learning that there were different kinds of love, theirs was deeper, a respectful love.

The years went by and Ronnie could see his mom needing more help in that huge house on Rutledge. Patrice agreed and they started renovations on the second floor for them to move in with Leona. Ronnie and Patrice never had any children, it was a big disappointment to Leona. She needed to know what would happen to her house once Ronald was gone. Maybe they would adopt, who knows.

Ronald's secretary knocked on his office door and opened it slightly,"Sorry sir, but there's a young lady out here insisting to see you. What shall I do?"

"Who is it, Lizzie. What does she want?" he said, feeling very out of sorts.

With that the young woman burst through the door. Her multi colored long skirt reached the floor, her hair was long and straight and pulled up in a ponytail. Her light brown skin shone in the light streaming through the window. Ronnie was stunned!

"Fatu?" he whispered, not believing what he was seeing.

"No, FATHER! I am called Marie." She let that sink in…..

They sat together, holding hands, just like he did with Fatu. This was his daughter. He said it over and over in his mind. Then Marie explained. Her grandmother found out Fatu was pregnant three months after she was banished from Charleston. Her heart was broken, she tried to leave but they wouldn't allow it.

"She died giving birth to me, just as her mother had. I don't want to repeat history," she said sadly.

Ronald knew what he had to do. Marie would come live with them. She would be the grandchild his mother wanted, one that would keep their legacy going. There was only one hitch, Marie refused. She would take no charity, she was her mother's daughter. She would earn her place in his life. She would earn her grandmother's and new mother's love on her terms. She had heard so many stories of Charleston society and their ways. She couldn't just show up, disrupting their lives.

Marie agreed to her father's idea. She would be a hired helper to Leona. She would help a few hours every day Monday thru Friday, hoping that a relationship would form. He bought an apartment for her to live in until she felt comfortable enough to tell Leona and Patrice. Their arrangement went well, that was until that rainy night in Mt Pleasant. After that Marie just let things settle. She grew to love Leona and she knew that Leonia loved her. The spirits told her to wait, it wasn't time yet. Another young girl would come, then it will be time!

They all looked at Maggie.There wasn't a dry eye in the room, no one moved. They didn't want to break the spell. Leona couldn't wait another minute, she jumped out of her chair and went to Marie. They stood together looking into each other's eyes.

"Oh child, all this time. You have your fathers eyes, I see it now, yes," Leona hugged her tightly, not wanting to let go.

Marie was crying and hugging Leona back. The others were wiping away their tears and laughing,

"What a grand surprise! Just like his father, taking care of Leona even after death," Dora exclaimed.

CHAPTER FIFTEEN

There's all kinds of storms

The following week was filled with many changes. Marie moved into the house on Rutledge but insisted on still helping Leona. Leona agreed only after she won the argument about hiring a cleaning lady. Maggie and Marie started taking turns cooking, which Maggie found very relaxing. Leona also insisted on a cook for the weekends, that was time off for everyone! They made quite a family, the three of them.

Living on the south east coast during hurricane season kept you on your toes. Between living in New Orleans and Charleston, Maggie's had her fill of direct hits and close calls. If there was anything Katrina taught her it was to be prepared, sometimes to the point of obsession.

"Maggie, I need you and Marie to update the storm cellar inventory. We have been so caught up with spirits that I didn't think about it until I saw The Weather Channel this morning. There's a storm brewing and I don't want to be caught off guard," Leona said, as she was sitting with her feet up on her tapestry covered footstool, knitting her purple and green aphgan.

"The weather has been so nice, I completely forgot about them also. Sure, we'll get to that this afternoon when Marie gets home from school."

Marie's dream had always been design, specifically architecture. Her renderings of Rainbow Row were phenomenal. When Leona found her one day drawing a fictional office building surrounded with gardens she questioned her.

"Marie, that's beautiful, is your hobby drawing? you're very talented!"

"Actually Nana, I like designing them."

That was all it took. The following semester, Marie was enrolled in a satellite program with the Savannah College of Art and Design in Charleston.

Between Maggie's schedule working three days a week and Marie's classes Tuesday thru Friday they tended to lose track of the calendar and each other. Leona's reminder was a good thing. Plus it gave Maggie and Marie time together to catch up. The calendar said September but it felt like July, hot and muggy with no let up in sight. The waters off the coast had gotten warmer, not good during hurricane season. Although the temperature outside was in the 90's the storm cellar under the house was a cool 68 degrees.

"Watch your step, the cobblestones are uneven in a few spots. Lord, it feels so good down here," said Maggie.

"I never knew this was here. How awesome would this be as a storm shelter!"

Maggie could see the wheels turning in Marie's brain.

"Don't get ahead of yourself girl. Remember, flood waters fill cellars! That's why we bring the perishables up a few days before a storm. The canned goods can survive the water."

They worked together, making lists, counting and rearranging foods according to dates. Moving things around led to a few empty spaces on one of the upper shelves. Marie thought it would be better to put items high up, just in case of water. Maggie agreed and got a step ladder. They started taking jars from the lowest shelf and stacking them on the highest one. As Maggie placed the first jar on the top shelf she noticed something odd. She pushed aside the jar and looked closer,

"Marie, do we have a flashlight down here anywhere?"

Looking around she found one and handed it to Maggie.

"What is it, some kind of dead rodent or something?"

It was something all right, an old bundle was stuffed far back into the stoned wall. Just as Maggie reached for the bundle they heard a scream. It only took a split second and the girls were up the stairs. They found Leona in the drawing room, her back to them, kneeling on the floor. Maggie panicked.

"Oh, my God, Leona, are you ok?" she said gently touching her shoulder

As they came around to face her they realized there was a broken picture frame and glass on the floor in front of her.

"I'm fine, but the strangest thing happened. That picture has been sitting on the sideboard for years, it's the only picture I have of my great granddaddy. It had fallen over, face down. I went to straighten it out and the minute I picked it up it felt so hot that I dropped it and it shattered."

The girls assisted Leona to the chair. Maggie made sure she had no cuts from the glass while Marie got the broom and cleaned it up. As she was sweeping up the glass she noticed there were actually two pictures on the floor. Picking them up she saw they were the same person, only the hidden picture looked like he was dressed as a sea captain.

"Leona, there are two pictures here. Was your great grandfather a sea captain?" she asked, holding the pictures out for Leonia to see.

"Yes, he was. Oh my goodness, I never knew that was there," she reached out to look at it and quickly withdrew her hand. "Marie, how can you hold that, it's hot!"

Both girls looked at Leonia like she had lost her mind. Maggie even questioned if she'd hit her head when the frame broke. As they all stood there staring at each other, not knowing what to say, the emergency weather radio started beeping.

The storm had been upgraded to a category one hurricane. It was well off the coast out in the ocean. The path was unsure, depending on the wind currents. The best cone of prediction was the east coast of Florida in three days. Leona knew better, that storm was headed for Charleston!

"It's time to prepare girls, we have a storm coming. It will not be pretty."

Leona gave orders. Maggie and Marie followed, even though the local TV still reported it was headed for Florida. Extra drinking water and batteries were purchased, perishables were brought up from the basement. During all the excitement Maggie had forgotten about the bundle on the top shelf. Leona insisted their local handyman test the generators on the second floor veranda and close the hurricane shutters on the top two floors. The first floor would be the last so they had some light. Neighbors followed her lead, they trusted her intuition.

Similar readiness was happening at The Tower. Anytime a storm was off the east coast the hospitals were on alert. Ever since Hugo in 89, they take storms seriously. Their manager assured them it was only precautionary, we hadn't seen a hurricane in years. Maggie worried about the ventilator patients, especially her favorite, Mr McGinnis. The back up generators were being tested the day Maggie was taking care of him. She knew there would be a split second pause once the power went off before the generator kicked in. She wanted to reassure him it was okay so she stayed and told him of Fatu and Ronald. Maggie thought as she was talking to him, he must think we are one crazy family. Leona still insisted it was coming their way. She told all her friends, even encouraged those living alone to evacuate inland. Charleston had flooded during Hugo and she was afraid they would see that again.

The sky was dark and the rains had started, bands of light rain then heavy on and off. Maggie knew the rains came well before the winds. She remembered Katrina and it made her shiver in fear for a moment. Why did these storms always happen at night, Maggie thought. They were scarier when you couldn't see what was happening. They sat watching The Weather Channel, all three huddled around the TV. It was happening! The storm was now a Category Three and turning north toward the mid Atlantic states, predicted to miss Florida and now Charleston was in the cone of prediction.

"Leona, how did you know. What made you so sure it was coming?" Marie asked.

"The spirits warned me, the picture. I knew my great granddaddy was a sea captain but had never seen that picture. It was him warning me!"

They had finished their preparations and now just waited. Flashlights and candles were on the tables ready for when the electricity goes out. They played cards while the TV kept them updated in the background. As the storm got closer, sleep was out of the question. The sound of heavy rains and howling winds kept them awake as the bands got closer. Every now and then you could hear a tree branch hit the shutters. As the storm got closer something very strange happened yet again. Great granddaddy's picture fell over!

"Yes, yes, I understand. Thank you, thank you Granddaddy!" Leona said almost trancelike. "The storm will not hit us directly, it will turn at the last minute. This is the worst of it!!"

Just as Leona was saying that, an update came across the TV station. There was a small possibility that the storm could turn north. They looked at each other and laughed. It was a laugh of shear relief, knowing they had an inside source. Never ones to question the spirits they all put their faith in great granddaddy and decided to go to bed. Even though the wind still howled and the rain blew they knew the worst was over.

Charleston had dodged another bullet, it was spared the worst of the storm. The streets were scattered with tree limbs and some power lines were down but nothing that couldn't be fixed in a day or two. There had been a low tide so no flooding occurred with the exception of minor low lying areas from the rain. The girls helped open the shutters to let the sun in. Today they welcomed the heat and thanked the spirits for their guidance.

CHAPTER SIXTEEN

Leona

Leona appeared deep in thought as Maggie walked in the drawing room. She sat with her tiny feet propped up on her tapestry covered footstool, knitting needles and yarn in her hands, but lost in thought. Not wanting to disturb her Maggie started to back out of the room when Leona stopped her.

"Come in, child. I was just on another plane so to speak," she said smiling.

Maggie could always tell when Leonia was reminiscing in her mind, she had a far away look. These must be very precious memories. Maggie wondered why she never shared them. In fact, Maggie thought, I really knew very little about Leona.

"I'll be seventy next week," she said unemotionally, "I still have so many questions. There's a piece of me missing," she said, as if talking to no one.

Maggie knew how old she was. In fact even knew her birthday was coming up but didn't let on. She didn't act her age. In fact, most days she was as spry as a cat. It was unusual to see her so melancholy. She questioned if there was something she could do for her. She was going to suggest that they invite Dora over to celebrate, but she didn't look like she was in a celebratory mood. Maggie knelt down beside Leona and took her hand.

"What can I do for you?" Looking into her eyes she could feel her despair.

"I have so many unanswered questions the older I get. I am no closer to the answers. I'm sorry, Maggie, this was not meant for you to see," she said sadly.

Leona seemed to shake it off as fast as it came. Her mood changed and she continued her knitting smiling. Maggie thought, how can she do that, just turn a switch on her emotions. Hopefully, one day she would trust her enough to confide in her. It was hard to keep a secret from someone like Leona, who had the sight, but the women did a good job of it, keeping her busy with meaningless things. Maggie had arranged for Geraldine and Granny to make the trip up to Charleston to help celebrate Leona's birthday. Dora was picking them up at the airport and they would spend the night at her house. A few days before the women were coming in, Marie decided how to sidetrack Leona so they could prepare the house for the party.

"Nana, our class is having a showing of our term projects. Remember that picture I drew that you loved of the office building and gardens?"

"Why, yes, that's why I insisted you go to college."

"Well, I did a 3D rendering of it and got an A! The showing is tomorrow afternoon, will you come?" Marie begged.

"I would be honored to go, in fact we should all go!" Leona exclaimed.

Maggie quickly made an excuse that she had a staff meeting to attend and acted very disappointed.

The day had come. Leona suggested that they all meet for dinner after the showing since they couldn't all go, they would celebrate afterwards. Maggie panicked, turning to Marie she signaled with her eyes to make an excuse. Marie had other plans.

"That would be wonderful! In fact let's ask Dora to join us for dinner."

What the heck was she thinking! Maggie knew that wasn't going to happen, but evidently Marie had something up her sleeve. Waiting to see what happened next she just listened.

"Oh that's a grand idea. I know Dora has her regular hairdresser appointment that afternoon but she should be free for dinner, I'll phone her," she said as she reached for the phone.

With no time to warn Dora, Maggie held her breath and listened. Leona explained her plans to Dora, but Dora was quick thank goodness.

"Really, oh my, that's terrible, is there something I can do?" Leona said into the receiver

"Well, keep me updated, I'll talk to you soon, bye."

Leona turned and explained to the girls that Dora's niece, who just moved here got in a fender bender. She was ok but hurt her arm. She needed help with the children till her husband, who was away on a business trip could get home. So Dora was forgoing her hair appointment and going straight to her niece's house once they hung up. Marie and Maggie looked at each other and were barely able to keep a straight face. Wow, could Dora spin a tale!

Leona and Marie headed out the front door as Dora, Granny and Geraldine came in the back alley door. With laughter and their arms filled with bags of goodies they started organizing the decorating.

"How the heck is Marie going to get out of going to dinner?" Dora asked.

Maggie laughed, "That was really quick thinking on your part getting out of dinner. Although I was panicking on the inside, I can tell you that!"

She explained to the others the plan Marie came up with. When they were done with the show, Marie would secretly text Maggie. Then Maggie would call her and say there was a problem with a water leak in the kitchen. They knew Leona would want to hurry home with that news.

"Remind me never to try and get away with anything around you gals," said Geraldine, laughing as she was putting up Leona's favorite colors, purple and green streamers from the chandeliers.

Allison and her parents arrived carrying a beautiful sheet cake decorated in purple and green saying 'Happy Birthday Leona' and a handful of the same colored balloons. Presents were piled up one end of the dining room table while the other had the catered food and cake. A few more ladies from the Charleston Society Club arrived and the group was complete. The ladies from the Society brought the making of a very secret southern punch, complete with punch bowl and glasses.

"My mama used to make this years ago during the 'Season'. She passed down the recipe. They called it Peach Iced Tea with a kick," said one of the women.

"It's a pity we don't have a Season anymore, so many changes over time," another woman said as she generously poured the vodka into the bowl.

Maggie's phone beeped a text message. The show was over and Marie needed to be saved from going to dinner! Maggie alerted everyone that after she called Marie they would be on their way. They quieted down for her to make the call.

"Marie, hi, it's Maggie. We have a water leak under the sink in the kitchen. Ask Leona what I should do?" she said, laughing and waiting for Marie to relay the message.

"Leona said to put a bucket under it and get your butt to the restaurant!" Then under her breath she said, "Oh crap, now what?"

At this point Maggie knew Leona was messing with them, she knew! Well, not this time old lady. I have to outwit her, she thought.

"Ok, if she is comfortable with that, tell her I'm on my way," she said giggling.

Marie let Leona know that Maggie was coming as soon as she cleaned up the mess and found a bucket.

"Maggie told me to order some appetizers and drinks. She'd be here soon."

Leona looked at Marie, cocked her head, raised an eyebrow as if trying to read her mind and said, "Maybe we better get home first. We can always get take-out later after I call a plumber. Call Maggie and tell her to phone Hal. His number is in my phone book and we will head home," she said, almost disappointed.

When they arrived home the entrance was dark and quiet. Maybe my spirits got this wrong thought Leona. She was sure something was going on for her birthday, especially since no one had mentioned it.

"I'm in the kitchen with Hal, Leona. He came right over," Maggie yelled.

As she passed by the drawing room the lights flashed on and the group yelled, "Surprise!"

"Oh my, oh goodness, look at all of you! What a surprise! Thank you."

She hugged and thanked each one of them. It was a wonderful evening with good food and great friends. They each talked of how much Leona had meant to them, their cherished friendships and she in return loved them even more.

Even with all these wonderful people around her and all the love, there was a knowing. Knowing something was missing. She had felt it most of her life, a piece of her. Somehow she had to find it. She begged the spirits to send her someone to guide her to the answers. She thought it was Maggie, but now wasn't sure.

The following morning brought cooler weather, the humidity broke and it was a pleasure to sit on the veranda. That's where Maggie found Granny and Leona sitting in the rocking chairs laughing. It warmed her heart to see these two old souls enjoy each other. They were so much alike, kindred spirits she called them.

"Good morning, you old crones," she said laughing."Who you calling old, girl, why we just in our prime! Right, Leona?" Granny said, showing her Louisiana accent.

"In fact we were just planning our next outing, going over to Fort Sumter this morning. Would you like to join us?" Leona asked.

Maggie readily agreed. She hadn't been there yet and it was packed full of history. They made plans to take the harbor shuttle over at 10:00. Hopefully since it was off season and midweek there wouldn't be a lot of tourists.

"Bring your sweater, it's alway chilly on the shuttle boat," Leona reminded them all.

As they stood on the open air shuttle boat the chilly wind swept through Maggie's hair. Thank goodness she wore her earmuffs, she thought. The sea spray caught Granny off guard and she laughed as it hit her face. Oh to be young again. What she would give to know what happened to her grandparents. Her memories of them came flooding back. It had only been for a very short period of time but the warm smell of their kitchen brought tears to her eyes. She often wondered why they didn't raise her, why she went to the foundling home.

"Are you ok, Granny?" Maggie said seeing the tears.

"Yes, my child, it's the sea spray, making my eyes tear."

Maggie knew better, the look on Granny's face told her differently.

As the boat pulled up to the wharf, the Fort loomed in the distance, standing guard over the bay as it had for over a century. The boat bumped the dock several times before coming to a stop.

The women carefully stepped off onto the wooden planks, watching their steps so they didn't trip. The path was beautifully landscaped. Leona thought of Marie's talents, maybe one day she would design something famous. The women slowly made their way across the path toward the fort. As they talked and laughed, enjoying each other's company a figure caught Maggie's eye.

"Man, that guy looks authentic. They could have at least given him a uniform that fit," she laughed.

The ladies looked around to see where the man was, but they didn't see one.

"Maggie, where?" Dora asked.

"He's up there on the wall, walking back and forth, holding a long gun, wearing a tattered gray uniform," she whispered, knowing now that she was the only one that saw him.

It was as if someone hit the brakes. They all stopped at the same time, turned and looked directly at Maggie. They agreed he was there for her to see, but why. Maggie walked slowly toward the wall by herself, the others just watched, holding their breath. These apparitions usually came through as if in a dream. This was the first one that appeared looking for her.

"Please, the bundle, let them know. I saw them all, the future of my family. People thought me crazy, I'm not. Generations ahead, I see them."

As Maggie listened his image gradually faded away, then suddenly she remembered!

The bundle in the cellar, she had forgotten all about it. They were all watching her waiting to learn what she was hearing.

"Oh my, ladies, we have to go home!" she declared.

CHAPTER SEVENTEEN

Martin Harrington

Maggie ran for the cellar door, with everyone yelling at her to be careful. She remembered leaving the ladder there when Leona screamed. Climbing up, she reached for it. The bundle was wedged in tightly. She gave it a good yank, almost losing her balance when it came loose. She carefully climbed down the ladder and stood holding the bundle to her chest as she felt him, memories that needed to be told. It was as if time had stood still yet again. She slowly made her way back up to the kitchen. The ladies had made tea and were waiting for her. It was almost in reverence that she laid the bundle on the table.

"I can feel him, he's sad," Maggie said as she slowly unwrapped the dirty piece of canvas to reveal an old diary. It was brown and tattered with initials still legible that read MWH.

"Dora, please a prayer of protection from the darkness," Maggie asked as she opened the book.

Wednesday, Maybe June 1869

I am putting pen to paper, not really knowing why, only to say that maybe sometime in the future I may look back and laugh at myself. It calms my nerves to write, so be it. My name is Martin William Harrington.

Watching the house being built amazed me. There were endless wagon loads of timber over dirt rutted roads, but week by week it was coming together. After being at war and seeing things being destroyed this made me happy to watch. People thought I was simple. I guess they had a right, especially since I hadn't spoken a lick since coming home. I really had nothing to say. My family had moved up the coast while I was at war, just up and left as if I didn't exist. Now father wanted a summer home so here they were back in Charleston.

Since I was away, it was only a few short years, maybe three or possibly more I think, things had changed so much. Our plantation home was destroyed by Yankees as they marched on the other side of the Ashley River. I had returned to find it that way. She used to stand proud and majestic. Now she looked like she'd been raped, the front door ripped off its hinges, broken windows and furniture strewn all over the front veranda and lawn. My heart was broken along with my spirit. I slept there for a week, trying to get myself reacclimated to civilian life. When I felt well enough I went into town to find my father.

I found him living in a rented house along East Bay Street. It really wasn't very big but had enough room until the house on Rutledge was built. He seemed happy that I was home, although the children in the neighborhood were scared of me. I think it was my looks. I now had a horrible limp from a bullet that had pierced my thigh and never been removed. My hair was long and straggly and I really didn't care to wash it. Who could blame them, I was my own worst enemy.

My brothers and I went our separate ways long before the war. It's a shame really. I stayed with my father. Our mother died giving birth to my youngest brother, Gaylord, who was sent along with a Mammy to live in New York. They said, my mother was too old to have a child. Father couldn't care for an infant.

I was born in 1845. At that time my family was very well to do. We had a plantation that provided a wonderful upbringing. My older brother, Jonathan II was born in 1843. He fell in love at a young age with a girl who came from Louisiana. She had been visiting her grandmother in Charleston when there was talk of war. They eloped and ran away to Louisiana to escape fighting, I think he was all of 16 at the time.

I'm not sure why I'm reliving my family, but I guess it will be important along the way. You see, maybe I am simpleminded as they say. I walk the streets and watch the boats come into the wharfs on East Bay Street. Many people have been displaced, especially the old slaves. I have a friend of sorts, he doesn't speak either. His old raggedy grey shirt tells me we fought on the same side. He's a darky, maybe worked for us at one time, who knows. We sit alongside each other on the wharf some days. It has a calming effect on us who are battle fatigued.

Sunday, August 1869

Since returning home my father has decided I must inherit the family wealth since my older brother abandoned us. He was patient with me, allowed me to wander on days I needed to clear the sounds of gunpowder from my head. My friend who finally did speak, told me his name. It was Jim. His momma had been a slave on our plantation. It was at that point, sitting on the wharf, that I recognized him. He knew me all along but was aware of how frail my mind was. How could I not know the boy I was raised with, although the war did leave him with a terrible scar on his face. Father hired our now freed slaves to work for him. Some agreed to go to the turpentine farms up the coast while others stayed to build the house on Rutledge. Still others left to find their own way. The house goes very slowly, it's hard to get materials since the war. I worked alongside the men building that big old house, it was almost as if I was rebuilding me! Each month I got better. Until, finally, I realized I was having full conversations with my fellow workers and even sharing a laugh or two. Father never remarried and died before the house was complete.

Saturday, October 1870

I think it was my birthday. Jim had brought me a cake since I was now living alone in a boarding house. People couldn't understand why I didn't live somewhere grand. They didn't understand that money meant nothing to me. The only thing that mattered was the house on Rutledge. Maybe I'll live there when it's done, I don't know yet. All I know is that I must see it done. Jim and I ate the cake, it was very kind of him. I am now 25, it's 1870 and he's the only family I have. Of course, there's Jonathan, but who knows if he's even still alive. We never heard from him after he ran away.

Each month that goes by I see a completion of another project. As we go from project to project I feel stronger, able to face another day. Jim and I are happy. Learning new skills has given us strength and hope. He's a whiz at ciphering.

Monday, June 1874

Well, it's been awhile since I've written. I guess I'm getting better, not hearing those damn guns as much anymore. The house is about 90% complete not counting the furniture. It was Jim's idea to build separate front steps, he said it added a touch of class. After all you are from society Martin, he would say. I am so far removed from society that I wouldn't know how to act anymore. I've spent the last five years working, getting my hands dirty, not sipping sweet tea.

Wednesday, November 1874

I found her, she's perfect, but she doesn't know I exist. She's a nurse. I watch her some days, she's so compassionate. Her long blond hair is braided and wrapped on top of her head, her blue eyes are piercing when she looks at you. I am totally smitten. The Old Marine Hospital over on

Franklin is where she works. Jim tells me I should introduce myself when she gets off work, maybe walk her home. Maybe one day I'll get up the nerve to ask her. In the meantime, it has given me incentive to complete the house on Rutledge, for I mean to bring her there as my bride one day.

Friday, December 1874

I did it, I walked her home. I thought my heart would burst. I was so nervous. Our introductions actually came by way of the hospital doctor who I have an appointment with. Unknowingly, he introduced us as I was leaving his office. She looked at me with those eyes and I melted. Determined to see her again I sat on the front steps of the hospital until she got off work. Her name is Deardra and she lives just down the way from me. We walked home and she told me of her dreams. I can think of nothing else.

March 1875

The house is complete. It is a site, more beautiful than I imagined. I think I love it more now knowing that Deardra will be living there as my wife soon. Yes, she said yes. Against society rules Jim will stand up for me, after all he is my best friend. I've made him the foreman of my new construction company. It seems there are many society people who want homes built on the peninsula. Our future is looking bright. The wedding is set for two weeks from today. Deardra refuses to take time off for a honeymoon since they are in need of nurses. Ever since the war many are still finding their way home, even after years. We will have a proper honeymoon in good time.

September 1875

Jim jumped the broom a few months after us. She's a wonderful woman and they are expecting a child soon. Our company is growing but we have some problems with uppity whites not dealing well with Jim. I step in when I have to but times need to change. Jim's cyphering knowledge has saved our butts plenty of times. He's a whiz at putting puzzles together, which helps building these houses. The men listen to him, being the same color and all. We built a temporary office in the basement to work from. Hopefully in the next year we will have a real office in town.

December 1876

We are so excited, Deardra is expecting! It's been a year since we married and moved into the house. She now only works two days a week helping where she can. She has made our house on Rutledge a home. Beautifully decorated for stuffy people to visit but comfortable enough for me. Our child should arrive sometime during the Christmas holidays. We are already getting the nursery ready, I wanted to interview Nannies but Deardra refused. She said she will raise her own child, thank you very much! William was born Christmas Day, making him the greatest gift of all.

January 1882

We welcomed two more children, a girl named Leona for my future great granddaughter in law and a boy named Herbert for my future great grandson.

I know this sounds crazy, but no one will know this unless they read this journal. I am not crazy, I have a sight, one that sees into the future. I know that my family will go on for many generations. I know that Jonathan's family, my brother in Louisiana will live in New Orleans for many generations. Sadly, Gaylord passed away at the age of two, he will have no lineage. I also know our family will find its way back together. Until then, I am burying this journal in my cellar. I don't know which generation will find it if any, but I do know there will be much love in this house on Rutledge.

Maggie handed the journal to Leona who was weeping soundlessly. There were sniffing and blowing noses before anyone spoke.

"I have felt something for so long, since I came here, a missing piece, we now have it, how I wish Herbert was here, he would have loved this."

"What a beautiful journal, I felt for him all the way through, I wonder if we can trace the family line now that we have more names and dates?" Granny said, wondering, just for a moment if they could possibly be related.

Marie had gone into the kitchen to make tea, she brought out a tray with pastries and tea. Before she could put it down the women attacked the food, they were ravenous! Marie had broken the spell, they laughed and cried together, wondering what the hell could happen next.

CHAPTER EIGHTEEN

Life Goes On

It had been a crazy couple of months, from sea captains to Civil War soldiers, spirits of all kinds were popping up. Maggie craved some normalcy. When Allison suggested they try a four day cruise out of Charleston to Bahamas she jumped on it.

"What a great idea, Ally. Hopefully, no spirits will be out there in that air space!" she said laughing.

"Don't be so sure, there are a lot of old wrecks out there," Allison said, as they both laughed.

The girls found a cruise and arraigned their time off, it would be a much needed respite for them both.

As the day approached, Maggie set out her suitcase to pack. Leona, being a seasoned traveler came in to offer hints on getting the most into her suitcase.

Before they knew it Marie had joined them.

"I heard if you roll the clothes you fit more in," Marie said questionly.

"That is very true, my dear, I prefer the flat way. Of course it's whatever you prefer," Leona said as she piled clothes on the bed from the closet.

"Well, I really didn't plan on bringing but a few pairs of shorts, tops and a bathing suit. I'm only going for four days,"

Maggie said. Looking at all the clothes she thought, where the hell am I going to fit those.

Leona got very serious and went on to explain about cruising attire, "First you need a daytime casual, shorts or skirt for strolling the deck or sitting poolside," she eyed them to make sure they were listening as if there would be a test afterwards and continued, "Dressing for dinner is a must, everyone does it. Late evening drinks call for casual slacks and dress tops for the casino or a show."

"Leona, when was your last cruise?" Marie laughed, "The Titanic? No one dresses like that anymore on cruises. It's totally casual, heck I even wore shorts to dinner!" Leona gasped, as if she committed the biggest society blunder ever!

Maggie agreed with Marie, much to Leona's disappointment.

"How will you ever attract a wealthy man dressed like a tourist, you must present yourselves as eligible young women," Leona said as she walked out of the room in what appeared to be disgust.

The girls looked at each other and burst into laughter, the last thing she would be looking for was a man!!

Allison had hired a taxi to take them both to the port, it was so exciting. They were used to seeing the giant cruise ships docked in the city but hardly paid attention to them until now.

"Oh my goodness, this boat is huge! How did we never notice this, it's like twelve stories high!" Ally said standing in line to check in before boarding the ship.

As the line progressed the girls got more excited. Music played overhead and people were busy taking pictures of each other in front of the ship. As they walked up the gangplank they eyed the others around them, some families, others couples, then groups of young girls laughing and taking selfies as they moved along.

The girls found their stateroom and threw down their suitcases on the two single beds. Looking around they also noticed a couch, decorated with Caribbean colors, along the left side of the stateroom, a desk and a dresser to the right. A small bathroom was near the doorway. It was roomy enough for two, but when they noticed the balcony they immediately headed towards it.

"Oh my, what a view," Ally said, sliding the glass door open and stepping out.

"Can you imagine what it will look like out at sea, this is awesome!" Maggie exclaimed.

After standing out on the balcony for a few minutes they decided to explore the ship and unpack later. It was time for a celebratory adult beverage.

"Where do we start, this ship is so big?" Maggie said, looking confused.

"I say let's head up top, they have a sail away party up there. We can get a drink and help them get the party started," Ally said giggling.

They made their way up to the deck with the party, as did about a hundred of their new friends for the next four days! Dance music was blasting out huge speakers situated all around the deck. Servers were carrying around trays of exotic drinks and a DJ was up on a makeshift stage over a covered pool encouraging the crowd to dance. From the looks of things they didn't need encouragement, the crowd was revved up.

The DJ announced a countdown as the ship pushed away from the dock, the crowd ran to the railings to wave to those on land. The girls had walked up to the front of the ship as it pushed away. Toasting each other they completed the celebration by taking multiple selfies. When the ship was safely out of the harbor heading out to sea the girls suddenly realized they were hungry.

"I think there's food on the deck below, how about we wander down and find some grub," Ally asked.

"Good idea, we should have eaten before we drank," she laughed as they headed down the carpeted staircase.

As they rounded the corner with their heads down giggling about something silly, Allison bumped into a gentleman carrying a glass of champagne.

"Sir, I am so sorry," she said, looking up into his eyes.

"Oh my God, this can't be!" Boyd said astonished.

The three of them just stood there as if in shock. Then after a few seconds laughter erupted.

"Well, so much for the spirits giving us a rest," Maggie said smiling, but noticing that Boyd and Allison didn't seem to hear her, they hadn't taken their eyes off each other.

As they all ate dinner Boyd explained. The cruise was planned for Boyd and a business associate to evaluate something or other with the cruise line. The girls didn't totally understand. His business associate backed out at the last minute. He figured, what the heck, I need a vacation.

"So here I am, yet again bumping into beautiful women," he laughed, staring at Allison.

They all agreed that it was karma, meant to be, the spirits had their ways of bringing people together. Maggie knew that the two of them needed time to themselves. She could see it in their eyes.

"If you guys don't mind, I think between the excitement and drinks I will turn in early. We can catch up tomorrow," she said.

"Yes, that's a good idea. I'll go also, don't want you wandering by yourself," Allison said halfheartedly.

"Absolutely not, the night's young. Why don't you guys enjoy the sea air," Maggie said smiling at Allison and winking at Boyd as she walked away.

The girls included Boyd in their plans during the next three days. When they docked at Nassau,it was the three of them that rented motor scooters and drove all over the island before finding a seaside cafe overlooking the ocean.

"The views are phenomenal here. If I was a painter I would live here," Maggie said dreaming.

"I haven't seen a bad view in all the island," Boyd said gazing at Allison.

"Oh you guys, get a room," Maggie said laughing.

Allison and Boyd looked stunned.

"Maggie! What was that all about?" Allison said, embarrassed.

"There is no denying it guys. You guys have the hots for each other," she said looking from one to the other. "In fact, I'm going to be heading back to take a nap and freshen up before dinner. You two have fun!"

The rest of the cruise Boyd and Allison were inseparable. They tried to include Maggie but she politely declined with the exception of dinners. She spent most of her time in a deck chair reading a book and daydreaming while watching the waves play against the ship's hull. Before they knew it, it was time to disembark back in Charleston. Boyd and Allison had made plans for later that evening for dinner before they parted.

"Oh my goodness, Ally, Are you totally in love or what?" Maggie giggled as Boyd walked away waving to them both.

"I'm so sorry, Maggs, I never meant to leave you out of this trip. It just happened, like out of the blue, he's just so great," she gushed.

"Girl, it's fine, I am so happy for you. He's a great guy. See, the spirits did have an agenda this week!"

They grabbed a taxi and headed home. Allison got dropped off first, then Maggie gave her address to the driver.

"The big pink house on the corner?" the taxi driver asked.

"It's coral. Yes that's the house," she said a bit sarcastically.

"I heard that house is haunted. Aren't you afraid to live there?"

Maggie decided to have a little fun.

"That depends if you're dead or not," she said, sounding a bit ominous.

He looked at her in the rear view mirror, his eyes wide with surprise and the taxi seemed to speed up. Maggie giggled as she paid the driver.

"The spirits appear in all different forms, come visit us sometime, if you dare," she said laughing as she headed up the steps, thinking that was way too easy.

CHAPTER NINETEEN

Old Memories Come to Roost

Maggie lugged her suitcase up the steps and opened the door. It was unseemingly quiet. She looked around and called for Leona and Marie. There were no answers. After dropping her suitcase at the bottom of the stairs she headed to the kitchen, still calling out. Strange, maybe they're out back she thought. She walked out onto the second floor veranda and looked down, no one was there. Now she started to get worried. There was no note left for her, they knew she was coming home. Maybe her little joke on the driver was backfiring on her! As she headed back to the front hall to take her suitcases upstairs she heard a faint banging sound. At first she thought it was coming from outside until it got louder.

It was coming from below her. Grabbing a walking stick as a weapon, she walked back to the kitchen where the stairs to the basement were. Yup, there it was again, someone was hammering. She opened the door to the basement and noticed the light was on. Again, she called Leona and Marie, no answer. The hammering continued. She slowly made her way down the steps.

"Who's there? I have a weapon, show yourself," she said with a shaky voice.

As she got to the bottom of the steps she noticed the sound was coming from the back wall, sure, she thought, it would be the furthest part. I will never make fun of spirits again. Gathering her whits she maneuvered around the old furniture and boxes that had been stored for decades, again calling out,

"Who's there? I have a weapon, show yourself."

The closer she got to the wall she swore she heard yelling. Stopping in her footsteps she listened again, yes it was yelling.

"Who's there?"

"Maggie help us…..," a muffled voice called out.

Maggie just about fainted. She didn't mind spirits, but she liked them more if she was with another person who was breathing. It was the next scream she heard that she realized it was Marie! She ran to the wall, banging on it, screaming for Marie.

"We're stuck in here, can you get us out?" Marie yelled.

"Oh, my goodness, is Leona with you?"

"Yes, the door shut behind us and we can't get out.The key is on the table alongside the door."

Maggie found the key but the keyhole was harder to find. It was a secret door that led into a secret room. Finally locating the hole she inserted the key and turned it, the door clicked open about an inch. She had to pry it open.

There she found Leona sitting in a recliner and Marie pacing the floor. The room was beautiful as far as secret basement rooms go. It was about 12x12 in size, a beautiful Persian carpet covered the floor. The glass chandelier hung from the middle of the ceiling bathing the room in an eerie glow. The wallpaper had started peeling away in spots revealing the bare wood. There was a sofa and chair covered in red velvet, worn on the arms from continued use. A single bed with a table and two chairs rounded out the room. Maggie stood with her mouth open in stunned silence.

"See, I told you she would find us," Leona said confidently smiling.

Marie, who was visibly shaken, hugged Maggie.

"It's been hours. Oh my goodness, I had visions of dying down here."

Maggie helped the ladies find their way back upstairs after securely propping the secret door open. She waited until they made some tea and settled down into their chairs before asking what the hell happened!

Marie had been looking for a box that Leona wanted in the basement. When she couldn't find it Leona insisted on going down to find it herself. She had had another dream, *"her answer was in the box."* But she had no idea what the question was. The spirits were working in reverse this time they thought. After going through a few boxes Leona noticed a draft coming from the back wall.

"That's strange, how can a draft come through a wall. Let's get a tad closer. Marie, shine that flashlight over here."

As we moved closer, only watching the wall Marie tripped over a small box. It was wooden with an engraving on the top. As soon as Leona had seen it she knew, that's the box!

"Quick put it here, let's get a closer look," Leona said.

They placed the box on top of a dusty old drop leaf table. There was a H engraved on the top. They had both looked at each other and Leona opened it carefully. Inside the silk covering was one item, a key. As she lifted the key out the silk revealed a paper underneath. Again, looking at each other, taking a breath she had reached for the paper.

"This key will give you the answers, but first you must find the place it opens. It lays close by, not up or down. Only the one who is meant to find this will know."

Maggie looked at them both, "so what next, don't keep me in suspense."

This time Leona continued the story as Marie drank her tea. After reading the riddle of sorts Marie wanted to take the box upstairs to see if the key fit any of the doors. But then I remembered what it said "nor up or down", so we decided to search the walls for a door. It really was an easy find, the draft had led us there to begin with. We started running our hands over the wall when Marie screamed. She found it! And just like you, Maggie, we put the key in. It clicked open about an inch. It took two of us to pull it open. Marie had put the key down on the table to help me. When the door opened and we stepped inside the room searching for a light, the door slammed. Thank goodness, the flashlight was in her apron pocket.

"So, there we sat for the last four hours, waiting for you. Thank goodness, we didn't do this yesterday."

"Well, what did you find out, the answer, the question, whatever?" Maggie asked.

"Once we got stuck we forgot about why we were there. We just wanted to get out," Marie said.

"As I was sitting there, knowing you would find us, I thought maybe we could do this together, go back down and find out why that room is there. And why the spirits led me there," Leona suggested.

The girls agreed, but only after they had a good night's rest. Marie suggested they go to dinner to the Chinese restaurant down the street they all loved. Maggie knew this conversation wasn't over, even if they went to dinner. Questions would still be discussed. Leona was at it again, she thought smiling.

The following morning after tea and biscuits the women devised a plan. Armed with flashlights, water and some snacks, so they could spend the morning if needed, Marie suggested a tool box in case they needed a screwdriver or something. Armed with their goodies, they headed down to the basement.

"I've never searched for something and had no idea what it was," Marie said, as they descended the basement stairs.

"It is weird that the spirits gave you a backwards clue, Leona you have the key. Now we need the question to find the answer. Oh goodness, if this gets anymore confusing….." Maggie said, missing the last step and falling on top of a stack of boxes. "Oh crap, I swear someone pushed me. But you're both in front of me."

The women ran over to help Maggie up. She dusted herself off and started restacking the boxes when one caught Leona's eye. She gasped. It was marked Jonathan and Bertha.

"Those are my grandparents' names, what would they be doing here?"

"Did you bring some of your family belongings with you when you moved here as a bride?" Maggie questioned

"I came with only my personal possessions. My grandparents raised me, I had no items of theirs to bring," she barely whispered, as if remembering. Leona spoke, almost trancelike, "I was raised by my grandparents. My parents had died when I was barely two. I didn't remember them at all. What I did remember was not being whole. I would tell my Grandmother that often, about not being whole. My Grandmother just told me it was because I lost my Momma. We moved a lot at first. There were different cities until I was about 13. Then we settled in Savannah. Grandpappy seemed to be very wealthy. We had a big house there and I went to the best schools. That is where I met Herbert...." she looked up at them both, a tiny tear trickled down her cheek, as if the trance had broken she smiled and said, "Open the dang box girls!"

They brought the box into the secret room and placed it on the table. They looked at one another as Leona ripped the yellowed tape off the top. Inside were stacks of old musty bank statements, all addressed to Elias Harrington II. Marie and Maggie looked at Leona as if to say who's he?

"Oh, my, that's Herbert's father. Why would his bank statements be in a box with my grandparents' names on it?"

"I think we have some reading to do," Maggie suggested.

The ladies each took a handful of envelopes dated late 1970s. They decided to look for any connection to the Beaulieu's family, which had been Leona's maiden name. The first batch yielded nothing, just the knowledge that the Harringtons were very, very wealthy. As they got down to 1972, they found their first wire transfer.

"Leona, I found something. It's a wire transfer to Jonathan Beaulieu for twenty thousand dollars!!" Maggie gasped.

"Where, let me see," she said, half grabbing at it. "Oh, my....they did know each other. Maybe they were in business together. Herbert never told me, nor did my grandparents when I introduced him to them."

"More like monkey business. Here's another transfer for another twenty thousand," Marie said.

As they looked through the rest of 1972 they found a grand total of two hundred and fifty thousand dollars transferred.

"That's a quarter of a million dollars. That was fifty years ago, can you imagine what it would be worth today!" Maggie said stunned.

Leona backed up and sat down emotionless in the velvet chair. Her mind was going a mile a minute. Talk about answers to questions, what the bloody hell was going on she thought. As Marie watched Leona, to make sure she was ok, Maggie was removing the rest of the statements from the box when a smaller envelope fell out of her hand.

The envelope was yellowed from time and crinkled on one end. Written in perfect penmanship was "Leona" with three hearts drawn underneath. Holding her breath she handed the envelope to Leona who looked up at her with tears in her eyes.

"That's Herbert's writing. He always signed his notes to me that way."

Marie and Maggie slowly backed out of the secret room. They wanted to give her space and time to open the envelope. After all it wasn't everyday you got a letter from your dead husband! Leona sat up straight, took two deep breaths and opened the musty old letter.

"My Dearest Leona,

If you're reading this, then you must have many questions. I knew one day the family secrets would start to unravel, for there are many. I placed this letter intentionally in this box, I should have burned it all but there will be so many questions answered by knowing of this. You must believe my dearest that I loved you deeply, but the start of our relationship was not what you thought. We both came from families where wealth was built on alliances and to our families that's what we were bred for. You my dear were a pawn, as I also, but I agreed out of greed. You see my family was threatening to cut me off. I was 33 years old and unmarried. There was no heir to our family fortune and this was a sin in our circles. Our families needed each other's monies to enhance their own pockets. You were offered by your grandfather for a bride's price. My father found you suitable for our society and so started the lies and deceptions. Our meeting on the banks of the river was not a coincidence at all. I followed you, watched you and waited for the right moment to approach you. I wish I could tell you at what moment my lies turned to truths about my love for you but I can't. I just know that over the years your sweet nature and unconditional love for me won me over. Now that the older generation is gone you can know the truth. Our families are somehow related. They would never tell me, somehow they thought it shameful. But I leave this in your hands, my darling, and Ronald, our precious son, to put to rest the deceit that has gone on for decades.

My love for you will never die. I am with you always

Yours forever, Herbert."

Maggie and Marie heard sobbing coming from the secret room. Looking at each other they nodded and hurried to her side. She was slumped over, crying like a child. Marie quickly gathered her into her arms,

"We're here Nana, let it out," she said, gently rocking her

Leona handed the letter to Maggie and nodded.

"Read it aloud please," she said between sobs and Maggie did.

When Maggie finished not a word was spoken, each in their own thoughts. Leona's sobbing had quieted down and she was blowing her nose.

Then suddenly Leonia jumped up and said, "Holy crap!! Ladies we have work to do! Answers to questions, questions to answers, what the hell! We need to brainstorm, come up with a plan," she was rambling on faster then they could understand.

"Slow down, don't you need time to absorb all this?" Maggie said pointing to the letter and the box.

"No! I have been saying all my life that something was missing. Now I know it truly is, and by God, I'm going to find it!!!

CHAPTER TWENTY

More Missing Pieces

Walking to work the next morning took more concentration than normal. The rains had come to Charleston.The streets were filled with ankle deep puddles as she crossed carefully from one corner to another. Every now and then some dirt would wash out onto the sidewalk from a gutter. It would come off a house and splash at her boots as if to say, haha, you thought you made it without getting wet! She was wondering how she was going to tell Ally about the latest goings on at Harrington House. Too many secrets always led to heartache. She prayed there would be no more for Leona.

Ally met her at the corner deli, they both ducked inside to try and stay dry.

"So, how's my favorite lovebird this fine wet morning?" Maggie's asked.

"Oh, is it wet? I hadn't noticed," joked Ally. "We had a wonderful dinner in town the other night, he is such a gentleman. He asked me out again tomorrow. We're doing a carriage ride, he's not had the experience yet," she laughed.

They decided to take their coffee and cinnamon bun to the cafeteria. As they made their way to The Tower a huge truck came barreling down the street, hit a puddle and just about drowned the girls. Looking like drowned rats they begged the laundry manager for some scrubs while they allowed their uniforms to dry.

"Oh, my, you girls look like you went for a swim before work," Jamaica said.

"If I could find that truck driver I'd give him a piece of my mind!" Ally said.

"Yes, and make him buy me another cinnamon bun, mine is soaked," Maggie said, finally laughing.

Jamaica had worked at The Tower for decades. She knew everyone and everyone knew her. Her Momma named her for where she was born and she was very proud of that heritage, thank you very much. She found them some suitable scrubs and sent them on their way, but not before whispering to Maggie,

"You have a friend with some questions, ya? Martha knows the answer. Now git, go to work," she said, with her accent that sounded like music.

Oh, crap, thought Maggie, can we just have one normal dang day! Putting aside what Jamaica said she went to work. The girls weren't able to meet at lunch, one of Maggie's patients took a turn for the worst. She called the family and their church for a preacher that the patient had requested. Such a sweet old black lady. Mae, was 95 and looked 75. She had seen a lot over the past century. Before her decline she told Maggie stories of her childhood and her grandparents' lives. She could have listened to the stories forever but she had come to the end of her story. Her family gathered at her bedside and sang old spiritual hymns. The preacher blessed her and the family before Mae passed over. It was so peaceful and the family rejoiced. It was the greatest gift to see a family accepting a loved one's passing.

Maggie introduced herself to Mae's oldest granddaughter. She hugged her and told her what a wonderful woman her grandmother was, how her stories of their family had touched her heart. As her granddaughter hugged her back she thanked her for taking care of her grandmother. And oh, by the way, my name is Martha. Maggie almost fell over. Martha, could it be the same Martha that Jamaica told her about?

"Martha, I know you need to be with your family right now, but if you don't mind I would love to have a cup of coffee with you one day. Your mom's stories really touched my heart," asked Maggie.

"That would be lovely. I'm sure she would love it if you were able to come to her memorial service, I can text you the information if you like," replied Martha with the same beautiful smile her grandmother had.

Maggie gave her the cell phone number and hugged her goodby. Wait til Leonia hears this one, she thought. As she was making her final rounds on her patients before leaving a great sadness engulfed her when she walked into Mr McGinnis's room.

Looking down at him she smiled, "It's been a day, hasn't it. You and I always seem to feel it more. What are the spirits telling you?" she whispered, "I believe they are saying, hang in there, it's not over yet. One day we will have a proper conversation."

She went about emptying his tubes and turned him on his side; she told him about their cruise and the adventures of meeting Boyd again. Making sure he looked comfortable, she smiled,then turned to check the settings on the machine before turning off the light. She didn't see the ever so slight fluttering of his eyes.

Maggie made it home that night totally exhausted. The day was sad with Mae's passing. But it was made worse with their short staff problems. After a heated staff meeting the nurses were told there would be mandatory overtime. Instead of working three twelve hour shifts a week, they were required to work four shifts a week. Normally it wouldn't be bad once in a while but every week, that would be exhausting. The twelve hour shift usually ended up being fourteen hours,from start to finish, especially if you had an emergency with your patient. You can't just punch out and go home.

After jumping in the shower and putting on her comfy clothes she made her way to the kitchen, it was going on nine o'clock and she knew she shouldn't be eating anything too heavy at that hour. Leona and Marie always had a plate of food in the oven for her. She took the plate out and poured a glass of wine. After taking a deep breath she took a bite of salmon. She was deep in thought when Leona found her.

"Maggie, Maggie, are you ok?"

"Yes, oh sorry, Leona. I didn't see you."

"You look exhausted, honey, Why don't you go to bed, I'll clean this up."

Maggie wanted to but she couldn't, she had to explain what happened today. The spirits were working overtime now. Each episode was coming faster and faster as if there was a time limit, which scared Maggie.

She explained her experience and asked, "Do you know any of these ladies? Jamaica, Mae or Martha?"

Leona stared at her a minute, raised her eyebrows and said, "None of those names sound familiar. Again with the questions and answers, what is happening."

"I'm not sure but we definitely need a plan of sorts, an outline of what questions we need answers to. But it will have to wait til tomorrow, I'm bushed."

Picking up her dishes, she placed them in the sink turned and hugged Leona.

CHAPTER TWENTY ONE

The Plan

Marie opened her eyes to see the sun shining through her bedroom window. The blue curtains were pulled back just enough to let the sun in. She laid there a few minutes and watched the dust dance in the rays, thinking how nice it would be just to float around. Hearing Leona walking down the creaky stairs she decided to get up. When she turned her attention to throwing off her covers she suddenly felt like a flash bulb went off. She was momentarily blinded. Maggie was the first to reach her screams. Leona wasn't far behind,

"Marie, Marie," Maggie was shaking her shoulders, "What's wrong?"

Oh, my goodness, she was looking at them now, blinking her eyes, trying to focus.

"There was a flash, I couldn't see. I was in the secret room, writing something, a letter or journal of some kind. Then I was standing in front of a wall hiding it."

"Maybe that was Herbert's spirit telling you he wrote that letter," Leona said.

They agreed that's what it could be. Maggie had a feeling it wasn't but she kept quiet for now. She wanted to see where the spirits would point her next.

Leona and Maggie calmed down Marie enough for them to head down to the kitchen. They definitely needed a plan of attack now! Drinking tea they started their outline of what came first.

"We need to research the names, you know like on those websites that trace your ancestors," Leona said.

"Absolutely. Then, what does Martha have to do with this?" Marie offered.

"Then, there's the New Orleans connection that Martin's letter eluded to. That bears investigating," Maggie said.

As they finished writing down their starting agenda, they looked at each other and did a three way high five while Leona yelled, "We got this girls!!!"

"Yes, as long as the spirits point the way," Maggie whispered.

Leona decided to recruit Dora in her ancestral search. They headed to the city courthouse to see what local records they could come up with.

"Why don't you just do that internet thing the girls were talking about?" Dora asked.

"Well, first off, I'm not really comfortable using it. I would need help navigating around it. And second, there is much more information in original documents," she said, as they climbed the courthouse steps. The building was old and musty smelling, probably from years of storms and water damage.

They located the building records department and walked in. The woman at the desk turned and gave them a pleasant smile. From the look of the piles of papers on her desk she wasn't very organized.

"Good morning, ladies, how may I help you?" she asked.

Leona explained that she was looking for any documents that pertained to her house on Rutledge Avenue that was built in 1875.

"That's a tall order. If you're looking for documents that old they would be archived on the computer."

Dora laughed "Well, Leona, I guess we're going to learn about computers."

The ladies were directed to the archive room several doors down the corridor. As they walked through the door they saw a beautiful older black woman. She was dressed in a multi colored blouse, blue skirt, wire rimmed glasses and huge dangly earrings that clinked as she moved her head. She was so into her work that they had to cough to get her attention.

"I'm so sorry, I didn't hear you. My name is Martha, How may I help you?"

"Martha, it seems you can help us, how I'm not sure. Do you believe in spirits?"

She looked at them over the top of her glasses, first at Dora then at Leona. Then she stood up and stretched. Martha walked over to the window and gazed out, for a minute or two. When she turned back around she smiled,

"Ladies, let's get that question answered."

CHAPTER TWENTY TWO

A Quiet Date Or Maybe Not

Allison was so excited, her date with Boyd was tonight. She changed clothes twice before deciding on a tan mid length skirt with a yellow flowered long sleeved blouse. Before leaving the apartment she grabbed a cashmere tan cape, just in case it got chilly on the carriage ride. Throwing it over her arm she yelled goodbye to her parents and headed down the stairs to the street. The evening air was just right, no need for the cape at that moment. She made her way down King Street to Queen Street where she was to meet Boyd at Poogan's Porch Restaurant. Allison smiled as she thought, how the heck am I going to explain that spirits were at work there also!

He spotted her first, walking half way down the crooked cement slabs called a sidewalk towards her. She was beautiful, he thought, this could be dangerous for a confirmed bachelor. Her smile was radiant and genuine, his heart melted as he waved.

"Good evening, you look lovely," Boyd said, kissing her cheek with a gentle hug.

"Why thank you, kind sir," she said, with a fake southern drawl.

They made their way to the restaurant. It was an old Victorian style house that had been renovated years ago to become one of the city's favorite places to eat. Before going in Allison wanted to give him a bit of Charlestonian history.

Sitting on one of the two porches she said, "Years ago this neighborhood had gone down hill. The people who owned this house decided to sell. When they moved they left behind their dog. He existed on scraps from the neighbors until a new owner bought the house and renovated it into a restaurant. The dog had adopted the house, in particular the porch! He lived a good life til 1979 when he died a natural death. But it is said that on certain times of the day he can be seen lying on the front porch waiting for scrapes. Can you guess his name? Yup, it was Poogan, hence the name Poogan's Porch."

"Wow, that's some story. So tell me, do you and Maggie attract these spirits naturally or go looking for them," he laughed.

She explained how she didn't believe in the beginning, in fact they scared her. But the more Maggie taught her the more she accepted there was more to this world then just us.

Their dinner was awesome, but she knew it would be. Just being with him was wonderful. They could have eaten at McDonalds and she would have been just as happy. She knew she was falling for him. It would be a difficult relationship with his job taking him out of town weeks on end. For right now she would just enjoy his company. They strolled over to the stables that housed the carriage rides. The sun had just set and there was an orange glow off the bay that caught their eye.

"What a perfect night, like the stars are all in alignment," Allison said, tilting her head up to look at him.

He couldn't control himself. Looking down at her mouth he gently pulled her to him and smothered her lips hungrily with his. Her knees went weak and she stumbled.

"Oh, Allison, I'm so sorry. I don't know what came over me. I'll blame it on the rising full moon," he said, pointing to the sky.

Allison stood on her toes with her feet slightly apart to make sure she was balanced this time. She surprised him by kissing him just as hard.

"No apology needed," she laughed.

Holding hands now, they continued down the street, both feeling lighter. There was a knowing that just occurred in their relationship.

The carriage was beautiful. It was white, decked out with red roses and a driver who wore a black top hat. Allison thought, dreams really do come true as she gazed at Boyd.

"Would you guys like me to give you some privacy during the ride or would you like the history tour?" asked the driver.

They both said history at the same time and laughed. It was what they had come for, a flavor of old Charleston. He was full of stories, some Allison knew, some she imagined he either made up or embellished. Either way, Boyd was loving them. His smile and laughter made her stomach do flip flops.

"Now take this house, it's color was one of the first to be used back then. The pink came from Jamaica, some say the old slaves chose it. I do know a freed slave did help build this old house. It's said that he went on to be very wealthy himself," the driver said, smiling.

Allison wasn't smiling and she hadn't heard what he said. What she heard was, *"Find Martha, it's all theirs, I did for them."*

"Allison, Ally, are you ok?" Boyd was shaking her.

The driver stopped the carriage to make sure she was ok. Allison looked around and saw they were parked directly in front of Leona's house!!

"We have to get off now!! There's someone we need to talk to. Please Boyd, now," she begged.

He tipped the driver and helped Ally out of the carriage, still visibly shaken. He didn't question her, just followed knowing whatever it was it was important.

"Keep your shirt on, I'm coming. I heard your first ring," Maggie yelled from behind the door, wondering who the heck was ringing the bell and banging on the door.

As she opened the door Allison fell into her arms now sobbing. Maggie looked over her shoulders at Boyd.

"What the heck, Ally. Calm down, did he hurt you? I'll knock him out."

Boyd, who by this time looked totally terrified, tried to explain. They were all talking at the same time when Marie and Leona ran into the foyer. Seeing the total lack of control Marie placed two fingers in her mouth and whistled. Everyone stopped and looked at her. Leona brought them all into the drawing room, made them sit and told everyone to take a breath. She asked Marie to bring the bottle of bourbon from the kitchen with five glasses.

No one spoke as the bourbon was poured and she said, "Now everyone, like it or not, take a gulp, breath, and we will start this all over again in an orderly manner. Marie, hit me again, Anyone else?" Boyd raised his glass as Marie poured, "I'd like to start if I may," Allison said, Leona nodded.

"We were on a carriage ride, all was fine. Then the driver started telling a story about this pink house….."

"It's coral!" Maggie and Leona yelled at the same time.

"I heard it," whispered Allison.

They all looked at her. They could barely hear her. Her face was white with a far away look in her eyes. Boyd told them that's what happened in the carriage. Maggie got up and knelt down in front of her friend,

"Ally, sweetie, what did you hear?"

She gazed up at Maggie, "The spirits spoke to me Maggs. I really didn't believe it until now, I heard him."

Allison took another gulp of liquid courage and told them what she heard, "It was a man, a black man. I heard the slight accent, Jamaican. He said, *"Find Martha, it's all theirs. I did it for them."*

She looked at Leona as if to say what does it mean? By this time Boyd had made his way over to Allison and had his arm around her. What had he gotten himself into, he thought, but only for a second as he looked at Allison's ashen face.

"I think I should probably take her home. She's been through enough for one night," he said boldly.

They all agreed and Marie went to call a taxi.

"I think I'd like to walk if it's ok with you Boyd? I could use the fresh air."

CHAPTER TWENTY THREE

Some Answers to Some Questions

Leona needed a pen and paper to keep this all straight. Too many things were happening at one time to keep track. Maggie brought her tablet and they started by reviewing their outline. They felt confident connecting Martha in Allison's experience to the Martha they found at the courthouse, who also happened to be Mae's granddaughter.

While Maggie had attended Mae's memorial service, Martha had told her she worked at the courthouse.

Martha had some pretty interesting information for Leona and Dora during their visit. Leona explained to Maggie and Marie, "It seems that Martha's great great grandfather grew up on a plantation across the Ashley River. She assumed he was a slave. The family plantation was owned by the Harringtons. But once the slaves were freed she lost track of him. There was no way to find a freed slave with only a first name." There was an audible gasp from the girls.

Leona looked at them and smiled, "Here's the kicker, girls, his name was Jim!!!"

"No friggin way!" Maggie said, followed by Marie's, "what the hell!"

Jim had been Martin Harrington's best friend, they were sure of it. But what did this message mean? By answering one question, it caused another.

They decided to invite Martha to brunch on Saturday. Maggie, Dora and Allison were asked to attend also, they would need everyone's input on this riddle. Maybe if they all put their heads together they would find an answer, in the meantime they prayed the spirits would leave them be for a while.

Saturday turned out to be one of those summer days that you lived for, no humidity, a breeze off the bay and a temperature of 78 degrees. The ladies thanked the spirits for the weather as they set the table out on the second floor veranda. The view of the bay was partially blocked by the blooming Magnolia trees, which led to its overwhelming fragrance.

Martha arrived right on time, she brought with her a bottle of Sweet Carolina Wine that she handed to Leona, as she hugged Maggie, "Good to see you again my friend," she said.

"Welcome to our home, Martha. I'm so glad you could join us, we have much to talk over," she said leading her through the foyer and kitchen to the back veranda.

Martha walked out to the railing and took a deep breath. She wore her dreadlocks down today, they cascaded over her shoulder to her breast. As she swept them back over her shoulder she turned and said, "How wonderful this house is. I almost can feel it breathing. It's a happy house but has many secrets."

"And that is the jist of our little get together today, my dear. I hope we can help each other solve one or two," Leona said with a wink.

The ladies sat down to the black wrought iron table complete with a glass top for brunch. Maggie, Allison, Dora and Marie had prepared the menu of finger foods along with some chicory coffee and Martha's sweet wine. They came out to greet their guest carrying the food.

Martha hugged them all, stopping at Allison she said,"He spoke to you."

"It was a he, I don't know who he was," she stammered.

"Tell me, child, the exact words. I need to hear them."

"Find Martha. It's all theirs, I did it for them," Ally whispered. They all looked at Martha, as if she had the magical answer. She didn't. She just looked as puzzled as they did. Leona broke the spell, she took Martin Harrington's journal from her apron pocket and handed it to Martha.

"This may answer a few questions for you Martha."

She read it in silence, every now and then raising an eyebrow, she finished reading and handed it to Leona. She had found her great great granddaddy.

Now that question was answered. The next question was what happened to him after the house was built and what surname had he taken. Brunch went fairly well, the ladies enjoyed the company and the food. Martha's sweet wine bottle ended up empty. They agreed that more digging was in order.

"There must be documents on file with the other houses that Martin's company built, if he made Jim his foreman, his name should be on those papers, don't you think," Dora suggested.

"That's an excellent idea Dora. We can start Monday morning. Martha, which department should we visit?" Leona asked.

"I would think Building Permits and Taxes. But that was so long ago, did they even have permits back then?" Martha replied.

"I guess we'll find out, won't we," Leona laughed.

Monday brought a wet morning. As Marie stood at the veranda railing drinking her coffee, she watched the fog roll in off the bay. She was daydreaming again about nothing really when it happened again, a flash blinding her. Then seeing him writing at the desk in the secret room and putting something in the wall. Only this time she saw him! There were no screams this time, just a knowing smile. She looked up to the sky and thanked her spirits. She found Leona and Maggie in the kitchen, one sitting at the table drinking coffee, the other frying up some eggs.

"Good morning, ladies. I think I have another answer, but I fear it leads to another question, as usual!" Marie said.

They both stopped what they were doing and let Marie explain. She had another of those flash bulb moments.

"Oh, Lordy, are you ok?" Leona interrupted.

She assured them she was quite ok. This time was just a bit different, she had seen the man. He was very large and very dark. It was Jim. She felt it just as sure as she was standing there. They had almost forgotten about Marie's first experience, never connecting it to anything really. But now, they had to search that room. Leona quickly got up to find her cell phone.

"I'll call Martha. See if she can get the day off and help us search. She should be here, after all it's her great great granddaddy."

Martha was already at work when Leona called her. She couldn't just up and leave so they both decided that Martha would do some searching there while the others searched the secret room. Maybe, just maybe someone would find something.

The ladies finished their coffee and eggs and cleaned up the kitchen. They went up to finish getting dressed, agreeing to meet back in the kitchen at nine o'clock.

Allison knocked on the door just as Maggie was walking down the stairs to the foyer.

"Good morning, That was good timing Ally," she said, noticing Ally wasn't her usual bubbly self. "What's wrong, girl, you look like you lost your best friend."

Then realizing what she just said she clapped her hand over her mouth and said, "Is it Boyd, did he break up with you?"

Allison looked at her as if they were in high school. Breaking up with me, Lordy, they were not going steady. She laughed. She was worried, however, that this spirit stuff would scare him away. He had been so kind and worried about her on their walk home that night. He did tell her that business would take him to Cincinnati that week, but he'd call her and he hadn't yet.

"I'm sure it's ok, hopefully, if it's meant to be he'll understand. After all his mom had the sight," Maggie reminded her.

They met up with the others in the kitchen. Maggie jokingly asked if they were ready to go into the belly of the beast. But no one laughed. This crowd was too solemn, she thought.

"Come on, ladies. It's going to be fun, another answer. Why the long faces? It's only a cellar with over a hundred and fifty years of secrets hidden in it….." she laughed like a ghoul.

That broke the ice. As they laughed with her, she led them into the belly of the beast! The basement was dark and musty smelling. They found a few hanging light bulbs and turned them on. One popped, blew out and scared the poop out of them. Marie went upstairs to find a few extra bulbs just in case these old ones decided to blow out also. In the meantime, flashlights worked very well. They navigated around piles of old boxes and furniture to get to the secret room. The door was still propped open just as they left it. Leona went in and found the hanging chain to the light bulb and pulled it. The room had a different glow this morning, almost welcoming. They hadn't been back down here since they found it a week ago.

Marie found them all waiting for her in the room. She really didn't want to come back down here, the thought scared her. But now, there was nothing scary at all. The warm glow filled the room and put her at ease.

"Now Marie, where exactly did Jim put whatever he put in the wall?" Leona asked.

"I really don't know the location. I just saw a wall and him removing a brink to put something behind it."

"I doubt these old bricks will be easy to move after all this time. But maybe if we start shoulder height all around the room, just shaking one brick at a time, we might get lucky," Maggie suggested.

They each took a wall and went to work. The years of dust and an occasional spider was all they found the first hour. Leona sat down on the velvet chair thinking what it was like to be Jim. Why was he down here to begin with, in Martin's home? But of course the spirits don't answer on demand. She smiled to herself and offered to go get a few bottles of water.

While Leona was upstairs Martha called her, she had a lead. There were some old documents on microfilm in the archives. She was going to try and get to them this afternoon. Hopefully that would have Jim's surname. At least she was getting somewhere, Leona thought, as she made her way back downstairs. As she passed a pile of old boxes something caught her eye. It was labeled Newspapers. Why would anyone save old newspapers? It might be fun to read them one day, just to see how life was back then. They really needed to be donated to a museum or something she thought.

She arrived with the bottles of water just as the girls were sitting down taking a break. Leona told them of Martha's phone call. They agreed that maybe she would have more luck. These bricks weren't going anywhere. They had completed three rows shoulder height all around the room.

Then Marie remembered something,"He was very tall, we aren't, maybe the brick is higher than our shoulders!"

"Great idea Marie!" Ally said, as they all went back to work on the wall.They worked for another hour or more with no luck. It was time for lunch as they headed up the stairs bummed out that nothing was found.

"Maybe the spirits are trying to tell us something different and I'm just not seeing it," Marie said in desperation while they made sandwiches at the table.

Leona assured them that whatever signs the spirits were sending they were seeing correctly. "Spirits very rarely send you on a wild goose chase. Spirits led Maggie to a woman named Jamaica, Jim was from Jamaica. Spirit led Maggie to Mae which led to her granddaughter, Martha. We will get our answers, just not on our time, in spirit time. Remember, girls, these secrets are over a hundred years old, they need coaxing out."

Just as they were finishing lunch the phone rang. Leona saw it was Martha and alerted the others. They all huddled around the phone as she answered.

"Martha, good afternoon. I hope you had better luck then us."

As it turned out she did.

"There was an old blueprint of a house on Tradd that Martin's construction company had built. At the bottom barely legible was a signature and it wasn't Martin Harrington's," Martha continued, "Years ago slaves had no surnames, so they usually took their owners' names. After the war the freed slaves took many different names. Most chose their own. I think my great great granddaddy loved Martin but didn't want the name. He did, however, keep part of it in his new name, James Harris!"

There were whoopies and happy dancing all over the kitchen. Leona invited Martha to dinner that night to celebrate. She accepted.

CHAPTER TWENTY FOUR

Relax and Recharge

It had been a crazy couple of days, finding Jim's name, searching the basement. The girls needed some time off from spiriting. Maggie was working the next few days as was Allison. That left Marie and Leona on their own. Dora phoned and invited them to lunch at The Charleston Grill, a very exclusive restaurant. They agreed to meet at twelve thirty but wondered what warranted a lunch at such an expensive place.

Marie and Leona dressed as proper southern ladies did for lunch at that restaurant. Leona had her white gloves and hat on, while Marie took a more modern approach. They found Dora at their table as the maitre d seated them. Kissing each other on the cheek they sat. Dora has already ordered Mamosias to drink for them all. Leonas eyebrow turned up as she looked at Dora,

"What's going on with you? This is highly irregular, even for us," Leona asked.

Dora explained that it had been far too long since they were out in society. They needed to be seen more, this new generation will forget what Charlestonian society means. And there was another motive, Gregory Barnwell usually luncheoned here.

"Who the heck is Gregory Barnwell, Dora?" Marie asked

"Why, darling, just the most eligible bachelor in Charleston!" she said, looking directly at Marie.

"Is that what this is all about? Oh Dora, I don't need to be set up with that kind of man, you must remember, I'm down home, not society," she said, with her eyes pleading with Leona.

Their waiter interrupted the conversation just in time. After taking their order the ladies decided to change the subject. Dora spoke of her new flooring she put in the bathroom, complete with heat under the tiles, no more cold feet in the morning. Leona had gotten some new plants that she planned on finding a home for them in the courtyard. Then they looked at Marie, expecting her to chime in on her latest interests.

"Ladies, I'm just trying to study for my finals and be done with this semester. No big story here," she was still a little miffed that Dora was trying to set her up.

They finished their lunch, which now seemed a little awkward. Dora apologized over and over for interfering but they all knew she'd do it again, it was just part of her personality.

Dora walked to her car and offered them a ride. Leona and Marie decided to walk, it was such a beautiful day and not far from home. As they walked Leona asked Marie what her plans were after graduation next year.

"Nana, I'm not sure. I want to stay right here with you, after all we just found each other," she said smiling.

"You are welcome to stay as long as you want. It is, after all, your house also."

They walked along the streets each in their own thoughts. The bay breeze had kicked up a bit and Leona noticed a few dark clouds. They picked up their step enough to get them into the house before the heavens opened up. It came down in a deluge.

With full bellies and a steady rain outside Leona decided to take a nap. Marie went into the drawing room and sat by the window. She loved days like these, they were comfortable and safe. Before she knew it she had drifted off into a peaceful sleep.

Her dreams were far from scary. She dreamt of growing up in New Orleans and the bayou. Scenes from her uncle's fishing boat floated by and her cousins playing in the yard. They were happy memories even though she had no parents. To her it was normal. Then suddenly her dream brought her back to the house. She was with Jim, he was so kind. They sat together in the courtyard. He wanted Martha to know that he had truly loved Sadie but couldn't be with her. Martin could explain. Then she woke up with a start, sitting straight up, thinking who the heck was Sadie? Seeing the clock was close to four, she decided to start dinner. She stood and stretched, noticing the rain had stopped, Outside the window there was a beautiful rainbow. She smiled as she made her way into the kitchen.

It didn't take long for Leona to join her. As they stood side by side peeling potatoes Marie asked if she knew a Sadie. No, she hadn't. Marie told her of the dream. Somehow Jim, Sadie and Martha were connected, but Martin? More questions with no answers. They cooked and ate, deep in their own thoughts. Once in every couple of bites Marie would smile and say the food was good. Leona would nod. Then back to their thoughts. Cleaning up was just as quiet.

"I'll make a plate for Maggie," Marie said.

"Good, good, I think I'll phone Martha. See if that name rings a bell."

Martha's phone went directly to voicemail so she left a message. The evening sun was just going down when Leonia decided to take a glass of wine out on the veranda.

That's where she found Marie, "Did you want a glass of wine my dear?"

"No, thanks Nana, school tomorrow. Do you mind if I ask you some questions?"

"Of course not, what is it?"

"Could you tell me of my father's childhood? I dreamt of mine this afternoon and I know his was totally different."

Leona smiled as she recalled Ronald growing up. "He was a quiet boy, always thinking and very caring of others. When he was eight he started following his father to house calls. They were a thing of the past but my Herbert always took care of his friends. During his teen years he studied hard to keep his grades up. His dream was to follow his father's footsteps. When Herbert died, Ronald blamed the medical establishment. He couldn't understand how his father saved so many people yet no one could save him. I think that's when he met your mother." She sat silent for a few minutes, in her own memories.

"He had the sight, he just didn't understand it. If only he would have come to me. Oh well, water under the bridge so to speak."

The phone rang and Leonia thinking that Martha was calling back quickly got up to answer it.

"Hello, how are you? It's been too long," Granny said.

"Oh, Flo, I'm so happy to hear your voice. I was thinking about you today."

"I felt your vibrations, so what you say, we come for a visit? My Geraldine is missing Magdalene," she asked in her Cajun accent.

"We could use a little fun up here and some spirit help. By all means please come."

They made the arrangements for them to arrive in two days and Leona hung up, happier then she'd been in a while. Marie noticed the change in her as soon as Granny was on the other end of the phone line. It was as if she was renewed, her energy field glowed.

Maggie came in from work looking tired, then again she always looked tired after work. Today she had a particularly stressful afternoon. Her favorite patient, Mr McGinnis, took a turn for the worse. She hadn't been caring for him that day but helped respond to the emergency. The doctors were able to stabilize him after a few hours. She volunteered to sit with him while his nurse for the day, Carol, went to check on her other patients. Her conversations with him were one sided but she always felt better after them. Arriving home, she heard the others in the kitchen chatting excitedly. As she made her way through the foyer she heard Grannys name.

"What's going on here? You two are cackling away like a couple of excited birds," she laughed.

"That's because we are excited. Flo and Geraldine are coming for a visit in a few days," Leona smiled.

Maggie was so happy to hear the news she hadn't realized how much she missed her mom. She took her plate of food out of the oven, sat down with the others and inhaled the food. It seemed the whole house turned happy that night.

CHAPTER TWENTY FIVE

Granny and Mom, Road Trip

Geraldine decided to make a road trip out of their visit instead of flying. There was so much country she hadn't seen, this was a good chance to see it. They got in Grannys old Toyota van, crammed with suitcases and snacks.

"You ready to roll, Mamma?" Geraldine said looking over at Flo.

"Just as soon as the spirits give us the green light," she winked.

The first night they stopped in Pensacola, Florida at a cute B&B on the ocean. The cottage was two stories with a balcony on the second floor facing the ocean. It was painted a pale blue with white shutters. You entered the yard through a gate with an archway filled with green vines. It would have been magical except it was nestled in between two high rise hotels.

Flo swore the spirits led them when a woman opened the door, dressed like a gypsy! After showing them to their rooms she invited them downstairs for tea in the parler, which had been tastefully decorated in beach decor. Flo thought it definitely didn't match the woman who answered the door, maybe she just worked there.

When they came downstairs the tea pot had been set out with matching cups. All had beautiful flowers painted on them. The woman sat in one of the overstuffed chairs and pointed to the other chairs for the ladies. She introduced herself and gave a little of her background. Mary was about fifty five but looked seventy, she had a hard life. Her sister had owned this place but passed on with no heirs. So here she was, a gypsy turned capitalist, she laughed. She asked their destination with a cocked head.

Before they could answer she said, "You will find some answers, but more questions," smiling she continued, "From one gypsy to another."

The spirits had a way of leading gypsys to each other. They could recognize kinship in each other's eyes. Mary knew right away Flo was one of her clan. As they enjoyed their tea, Flo and Mary reminisce about places they had seen and silly things the spirits had them do. Geraldine excused herself.

"It's been a long day for me, I'm not used to driving that much. I think I will head up to bed. Thank you, Mary, for your hospitality. See you in the morning Mamma." Blowing them a kiss she headed upstairs.

"Your daughter has the sight, ya?"

"Yes, as does my granddaughter, that's where we are headed, to Charleston. But first we might stop in Savannah. I've always been drawn to their history."

Mary's eyebrows shot up and her eyes bulged out, "There's some strong juju in those cities. Cover yourself sister, there's dark spirits at work there. May I ask you a question?

Before Flo could answer, Mary said, "Do you think my decor matches my personality, I've been thinking about making some changes."

Both ladies looked at each other and burst out in laughter,

"Oh, Mary, please do change it, it's too conventional for you. Make it your own, sister, more will come."

The sunlight, reflecting off the ocean waves, danced on her closed eyelids waking her up. Geraldine stretched and thought how nice it would be just to sit on the beach for a few hours. But they had places to go. She washed, dressed and repacked her suitcase. Dragging it down the stairs, where she met Mary,

"Your mom's enjoying tea and scones on the back patio. Please join us before you have to leave."

"That sounds great, do you happen to have coffee. I'd love a cup or three," she laughed.

"Absolutely, I always have coffee ready. I'll meet you out back."

After thanking Mary and promising to stop back when they headed home, Florence and Geraldine were on their way. They took I-10 East towards Jacksonville. The traffic was minimal for midweek which allowed them to enjoy the ride.

"Mary was some character, she had your number right from the start."

"I like her, she's genuine. We both could use a beach getaway now and then. She's going to make it her own, I can't wait to see that," Granny laughed.

The traffic got much heavier the closer to Jacksonville they got. Instead of the normal I-95 N route to Savannah, they decided to take the longer more scenic way, Route 17. Driving along marshlands was way more relaxing than fighting the crazy drivers on the interstate.

They stopped for a late lunch in Yulee, Florida. There wasn't much to the town, being off the beaten path. At one time years ago, before I95, it was the main thoroughfare to Florida's east coast cities. They found a small cafe called The Spiral Way that looked interesting. The colorful eclectic window designs drew them in. When they walked through the door they looked at each other,

"The spirits led us here for sure," Granny laughed.

The walls were painted in swirls of vibrant colors highlighted by a black light hanging from the ceiling. The hostess who was dressed like a hippie from the sixties greeted them.

"Welcome, fellow travelers, we have food to fill your belly and peace to fill your soul. Follow me."

The ladies giggled and followed the young girl who seemed to relish her part in this act of sorts. When they were seated an older woman came to take their order. She looked tired and worn, her back slightly rounded as if she had worked hard all her life. She had suggested the special, which was a bed of greens piled high with avocados, tomatoes, cucumbers, strawberries and nuts. They agreed that sounded good and added two sweet teas to the order.

As they waited they admired the different artwork that hung on the wall. The pictures were made up of swirls of colors that they realized could be interpreted in different ways. One in particular caught their eye. It was filled with purples, reds and black. In the swirls Geraldine saw a woman holding a child, where Granny saw pain and heartache. As they discussed what they saw the woman brought their food.

"You like the painting?" she asked, as she was placing the plates down in front of them.

"Yes, they are intriguing. Did you paint them?"

"No, my late husband did. He was a seeker, he had the sight. But left me way too early. He told me these paintings would help support me one day, I laughed, but he was right," she stated.

"Are they for sale?" Geraldine asked.

"They are, and it takes a person with the sight to see them. You both saw something different, am I correct?"

Granny and Geraldine both said yes at the same time. She went on to explain that over the years spirit had brought people here to eat but then they saw a certain painting and had to buy it. Her husband had been correct, it did help support her. His unusual way of painting lended to people looking at it to see what was there for them and them only. The ladies bought the picture!

Back on the road they praised spirit for their wonderful experience with a new friend and headed to Savannah, Georgia. It was only two hours down the road, they would get there while the sun was still up. It was always better to navigate a new city in the daylight. The drive was beautiful and they enjoyed a rather unconventional discussion about their new painting and their interpretations. Before they knew it they were in Savannah. They followed the signs to the historic district and let the spirits guide them to a small family owned hotel on the river.

The Rebel Family Inn seemed appropriate, after all they were rebels in their own right. They settled into a small but comfortable room with two queen beds. There was a view of the Savannah River from the window. The clerk had suggested a walk along the river for the evening. It was a tourist draw but also held many spirits. Having just eaten a few hours ago, they decided a walk would be a good way to stretch their legs a bit.

They walked along the sidewalk until they saw a sign which pointed to a set of stairs leading down to the river. The steps were made up of a steep stone staircase that looked very unsteady. The width of the steps was a mere eighteen inches wide and iron railing was the only support. They were built alongside a stone wall that divided the upper land to the river.

"Well, I'm game if you are," Granny said.

"Let me go first, it looks very steep."

The ladies made it down to the bottom very slowly laughing, when a gentleman who was walking by said, "I suggest you take the elevator up when you finish your walk ladies, it's in the hotel over there," he pointed, laughing as he walked away.

They looked at each other and laughed even harder.

"Thank you, sir, but where's the adventure in that," Flo yelled as he just kept on walking.

As they enjoyed the shops, a riverboat filled with revelling diners heard down the river as jazz music filled the air. By this time their stomachs told them to get a bite to eat. They were passing Wet Willies, it looked intriguing and they decided, what the heck. The whole wall on the left side as you walked in was filled with every kind of flavor frozen daiquiri you could think of, rolling around in what looked like giant tumbling dryer doors. Each armed with a spigot to fill your glass with whatever flavor or combination of flavors you desired.

"Wow, does that look yummy? how do you decide?" Granny said wide eyed.

"We will definitely indulge. But I think some food first Mamma, or we'll be like drunken sailors trying to get back to the hotel."

They found a table and ordered typical bar food, burgers and fries. The fun part came trying to decide what to drink. The server suggested they each try something different then they could share. Geraldine ordered a Monkey Shine, which was made with a banana daiquiri and Bacardi rum. Granny ordered Sex on the Beach, since it had been such a long time since she had the real thing. It had raspberry, peach, cranapple and vodka. They weren't disappointed when their order came. Like two school girls they traded their drinks back and forth. The server asked them if they'd like to try another combination.

"I don't think so for me. If I was ten years younger I'd indulge in another, these were so good," Granny said.

"Just wait til you stand up, that's when they hit you, I'll bring you ladies the bill," she said walking away.

And she had been right. They decided to take that stranger's advice and ride up the elevator to street level.

They had another beautiful day for driving. The skies were clear and there was a slight breeze off the river as they drove over the expansive bridge leading out of Savannah. They headed up Route 17 passing by the small towns. Wondering how these places still existed without Wal Marts and other big box stores. The never ending marshland showed off its billowing tall grasses with an occasional osprey standing tall on the side of the road.

"Why don't you text Maggie and Leona and let them know we're only about two hours away," Granny said.

"Good idea, maybe we can pick something up for lunch."

CHAPTER TWENTY SIX

Granny and Jim

Arriving in Charleston almost exactly at noon they parked the car in the rear alley and grabbed their bags. They headed for the kitchen door just as it burst open spilling out the happy group of ladies. With greetings of hugs and kisses there were four different conversations going on as they headed inside.

"Please just leave those suitcases here for now. We have a buffet luncheon ready for y'all in the dining room," Leona said proudly, since the joke was that only royalty dined in that room.

"That sounds great, but I have to pee. I'll be right there," Granny said.

She headed for the half bath off the back kitchen. While she was washing her hands she heard him, *"They need your help. It's all for them, the family I was robbed of."*

Oh my, she thought, I'm not even here an hour and the spirits are talking to me.

The dining room was decked out with Leona's finest china filled with all sorts of delicious foods. The crystal glasses were filled with Carolina Sweet Wine brought by Martha, their favorite now.

Leona raised a glass to toast her friends, "To family, old friends and new friends, may the spirits guide us always."

Granny looked around to the ladies in the room, how blessed she was to know them, Geraldine, Maggie, Allison, Marie, Leona, Dora and now a new member of their spirit led group, Martha. She wondered driving here what adventure spirit was going to send them on this time. Now she knew. The question was, who was that man?

When they finished eating they remained sitting around the table chatting, Granny thought it time to ask.

"Who's your resident male spirit?"

Everyone stopped talking, turned and looked at Granny. Leona looked at Maggie, as if to say she hadn't said anything to Flo. Maggie gave a "no" nod back.

"It's Jim. I guess we need to catch you and Geraldine up on our Harrington House Mystery!" Leona laughed.

They spent the next hour rehashing their experiences surrounding Jim.

"So let me summarize, Jim was a slave who became Martin's best friend and helped him build this house. Later he became foreman of Martin's construction company," Granny paused to think. "But now he's appearing in a secret room you've found in the basement. Do I have it right?"

Maggie and Leona nodded at the same time that Marie said, "Yes, now tell the others what he said to you?"

"How did you know that he spoke to me? Granny asked.

Marie explained that anytime Jim spoke or appeared, she heard. So she knew this whole time what Granny had heard in the bathroom. Granny looked at her with a smile of gratitude for not speaking out until she was ready,

"They need your help. It's all for them, the family I was robbed of," she whispered. Now the questions started, everyone had one. They really needed to organize their search once again, update their outline. The new information that was learned today was that Jim had somehow been robbed of his family. Martha had been quiet all this time, just thinking.

"Maybe, now that we know Jim's last name we could trace him in city records?" she questioned.

"That's an excellent idea, see if he married or had children, which we know he did since you're here Martha!" Dora said excitedly.

"But we need to confirm that he really is my kin," Martha said hopefully.

They agreed that since Martha worked in the courthouse she would be the one to start that search. Granny and Marie volunteered to go back down the basement to the secret room, to look for clues or maybe hear from Jim himself. Maggie and Geraldine decided to separate old boxes, see if any had Jim's name on them. Allison had promised to help out her parents so she couldn't help the next few days. That left Leona and Geraldine who offered to organize what information they had or where to find. They would start their searching tomorrow, today was for renewing relationships. Once they all had their assignments, the ladies stood up, filled their glasses one more time and toasted their next adventure.

"Here's to you, Jim, may we solve your problem so you may join your loved ones on the other side," Leona said.

Allison, Dora and Martha decided to leave around three that afternoon. The rest of the ladies spent the afternoon reminiscing adventures they had been through. When it came time for dinner they decided to finish off the leftovers from lunch which led to a few more glasses of wine, leading to an early bedtime.

CHAPTER TWENTY SEVEN

Leads, Leads Everywhere

A storm was coming, the sky was dark and the tree leaves had turned up just the way they did before a gale. Martin stood on the veranda staring out, but seeing nothing. How appropriate this storm was he thought. Lives would be changed forever just as a wind changed the landscape. I must save him, there's no discussion, the die has been cast. How could I explain this to Sadie,to his family, I know they will be searching. I must be very careful, if this information falls into the wrong hands we will all suffer.

Dreams came at all times, most times sleeping. But to seers, they could appear at any time, a room, a smell, a feeling could trigger an awake dream. This was an awake dream. Geraldine stood at that exact place on the veranda and felt him and felt his anxiety. She was afraid to breathe, and didn't want to break the spell. Then Marie spoke,"Good morning, did you sleep well after all the excitement yesterday?"

He was gone, just that fast. She turned and faced her.

"Ah, Marie, yes, just getting some fresh air before we go to work on our next adventure."

"I've brought a pot of coffee and two cups. Would you like one?"

She smiled, knowing Marie would ask her about the conversation with Martin. She would wait, let her take the lead.

"I'd love a cup, thank you," Geraldine said, as she sat on the wrought iron chair.

She listened to the leaves rustling and an occasional osprey call to its mate. How peaceful it is before a storm, but there was no storm in sight.

Marie looked at her, cocked her head and raised her eyebrows, she was waiting. It seemed that Marie had patience. Geraldine sipped her coffee, now it was a battle of the wills. A crow, black as night, flew over and landed on the railing. It looked at both of them as if it had a tick in its neck, back and forth. Then after a loud caw it flew away. Marie and Geraldine looked at each other and burst out in laughter.

"I guess he told us!" Marie laughed.

"You know don't you?"

"Yes," she whispered.

"We have a new lead now, another name, Sadie!"

They quickly phoned Martha at the courthouse and gave her their new lead, hopefully this would turn up something new.

Geraldine headed down to the basement joining Maggie in going through old boxes. She filled her in on their latest find, Sadie. The dankness and dust of the cellar gave Maggie a fit of sneezes. The stone stacked walls showed some weeping at points, the water level being what it is, but the cellar never showed old wounds of being flooded. They divided up the boxes not related on the right side wall, boxes that might be related on the left and boxes to rummage through now, smack in the middle.

"Over the ages this family saved everything, at least they were organized and labeled them. That helps," Maggie stated.

"Dividing them certainly helps but I have a suspicion that we'll end up looking through them all.

The hours flew by when they heard Granny call down to them,"Come on up here, ladies, it's time for lunch, I've set out jambalaya."

Hearing that, Maggie and Geraldine didn't waste a minute getting up the stairs. The table had been set for six, but only five were here.

"Mamma, who else is coming to lunch?"

"We set a place for Martin, he's made it a point to let us know he's here."

They all laughed and agreed, he must be included, who knows maybe he has more to offer.

CHAPTER TWENTY EIGHT

The Old Slave Market

After two more days of searching through dusty boxes the ladies decided to take a day off, clear their heads so to speak. They needed some positive juju.

Granny said, "Let's do the tourist thing, Geraldine suggested, but not too far, maybe something local."

Leona had just the thing, local, with lots of shopping and food! The Old Market on Chalmers street. Some used to call it the slave market years ago. They could take their time and just stroll through the multiple buildings.

"That sounds nice, plus it's not that far. We can walk to it if y'all are up to it."

They decided to walk along Broad to East Bay and enjoy the sea breeze. The day was lovely and there seemed to be a lot of others enjoying the day also. There were so many dog walkers in Battery Park that they joked that the Dog Show must be in town. Turning down Chalmers Street you could see the Market, openwalled brick buildings standing in a row, one after the other. The arched openings drew your eye architecturally, being built back in the 1840's, it was quite an accomplishment.

As they entered the market there was a pedestrian walkway down the middle with vendors on each side, right and left. They sold everything from leather products to hats, tee and sweatshirts, paintings, carvings and blown glass items, mostly depicting beach scenes. At the end of each building, the sweet grass vendors sat in the sun weaving the billowing yellow stalks into beautiful baskets.

"Those are gorgeous, how fun that would be to learn," Maggie said.

"Thank you, lady, you are a seer, there is much for you here. Make sure you stay open as you walk through," the vendor said as she continued weaving.

Maggie said to herself, I thought this was a day off spirit. I guess not, bring it on!

As the ladies walked on, one or two of them picked up small trinkets that called out to them. Granny found a vendor who sold chicory coffee and had to get one. Geraldine joined her, enjoying a touch of home. Maggie walked ahead to a vendor selling carvings from driftwood. The figurines were beautifully displayed.

"Hello, can I help you find something special?" a young woman asked.

She was dressed in a traditional African dress including a wrapped headpiece. The colors were more muted then gypsies but just as beautiful.

"Are these your carvings?"

"Yes, madam, my great grandfather taught me the trade."

She went on to tell her how they would walk the shore out at Folly Beach searching for pieces of driftwood. The storms brought in the best wood, sometimes they even found pieces of sunken boats that had broken up. She called him Ggdaddy.

He looked after her after her own father died in a shrimp boat accident. Now he's teaching her daughter, but she doesn't like tradition. Young people these days don't understand.

Maggie bought a piece that called to her. The wood was formed with what looked like angel wings, it was perfect.

"Thank you so much for your story. I hope your daughter finds that following tradition is a timeless investment," Maggie said, as she walked away thinking, if spirit was going to show me something that woman would have been perfect.

She caught up with the group and showed them her driftwood carving. They all agreed it was beautiful. A small outdoor cafe was on the street side of the market. Granny suggested that they take a break and sit for a while, maybe indulge in something sweet. Sitting, drinking hot chocolate and eating Benne Wafers, Charleston's favorite cookie, Maggie relaxed. As if on cue, spirit spoke.

She said, "I stood here one day. It was a long time ago, I was so young, so scared. We were crowded together. I remember they took our whole group and put us in a wagon. We traveled over a river to a new home. After the men and women were separated into different cabins the master came to see us. We were to work for him. He would give us a place to live and food. He didn't believe in beatings unless you committed a crime against another."

"Years went by and I ended up pregnant at fifteen. When the baby was born the master's wife allowed me to care for him but in her house. I think she knew that the master had taken me and that my baby was his. She had a son that needed company, my son was to be his companion. I became a house mammy to them both. It was the winter of my son's second year and there was a diptheria outbreak. I contracted it from a field slave. There were four of us that were sent away. We all died. I can't leave this earth plane until I know if my Jim survived and how he lived."

Maggie listened, feeling her pain. Telepathically, she asked the woman what her name was and if she knew what plantation she worked on.

"My given name was my grandmother's, Kauchee. I thank you for asking. I lived across the river at Harrington's Plantation."

Once that was communicated she was gone. Maggie sat stunned. This can't be, Harrington's! The others noticed how quiet she had become and the far away look in her eyes. They knew and waited silently until she was ready to explain.

"Why are these spirits coming so fast now? We barely have adjusted to one than another appears. It's almost like they have a timeline to follow," she said, knowing the others would understand.

"When you're ready, child, tell us. It's ok," Granny said, reaching out to hold her hand.

"Leona, I fear your husband's lineage left many spirits behind. I've found another and she's the oldest one yet! Her name is Kauchee. She was a slave on Harrington's Plantation and I believe her son was a half brother to Martin!"

The story brought tears to a few eyes by the time Maggie was done telling them her story. It was time to see what information Martha had found. Maybe, just maybe they could get some answers.

CHAPTER TWENTY NINE

Martha

Martha started her day just like any other, a strong cup of coffee and a cigarette. She sat at her small kitchen table flicking her ashes into the ashtray thinking, the spirits sure do have a sense of humor. Her being a civil service worker down at the courthouse cavorting with the likes of Leona Harrington! Now that was a hoot! She smiled to herself, who was she to question spirit. She finished her coffee and dressed for work, checking the clock so not to miss the bus. The CARTA bus system ran right past her house which made it convenient for her not to own a car.

Her apartment was way uptown, past the interstate. The old Victorian home was converted to four very small apartments. Hers was on the second floor. She preferred being upstairs, less chance of anyone breaking in. Her belongings were few but she liked it that way, no attachments. It made it easier to move when they hiked the rent up and they always did. She often wondered why she made herself live like this. Her job paid well, she had no dependents and her bank account grew over the years to where she could live anywhere. She had this mortal fear of never having enough, so she saved, saved every penny. There was one indulgence that she would allow herself and that she shared with her new friends, Sweet

Carolina Wine. She would never have more than two glasses, after seeing what "the drink" did to some of those she grew up with. It scared her. But she did like the taste, that and a cigarette were her weaknesses.

This morning she didn't have to run for the bus. She stood under the sign marked "Bus Stop" with a picture of a bus under it. The sun was coming up over the tall buildings and warmed the chilly corner. She thought about the records she could go through today. They must find James Harris and his family, if he even had any to begin with. She hoped she could connect herself to him.

By the time Martha got to the courthouse it was time for another cup of coffee. She stopped at the vendor outside the steps before going into work. Anything she did was done with purpose, and always done in the same order. She took off her light jacket and hung it on the tall coat rack that stood behind the desk. Next she turned on her computer and opened the window behind her just enough to let out the cigarette smoke as she lit the second one today. She had realized years ago that she had OCD, but never sought treatment. She liked organization, that's what made her so good at her job. Finishing the cigarette she carefully snubbed it out and threw the butt away, making sure it wasn't hot by touching the end.

The bell above the door jingled as her first customer walked in for the day. That was her signal to stop daydreaming and start working.

Smiling, she turned and asked, "Good morning, how may I assist you today?"

There were many customers this morning. The end of tax season always brought out the procrastinators. But it kept her busy and she liked it that way. Keeping busy helped her not think of losing her Gran, Mae was more like a mother to her as hers had left years ago. She would have to make time to stop by the assisted living facility that Gran lived in. They had called to tell her that the things she left behind had been boxed up and were ready for her to pick up. Normally that task would have been done immediately, but her heart couldn't bring her to go there yet. Just one more day, she thought, then I can handle it.

Her lunch break came at 11:30. After helping the last customer she put the sign, 'out to lunch' up and slipped on her jacket. She headed to the municipal building on the next corner.

The lady's name tag said Cindy. Strange, she thought, she didn't look like a Cindy. She had beautiful caramel colored skin often seen in mixed marriages. Her hair was braided to one side and her eyes had a slight slant to them.

"I'm looking for a possible marriage record, can you help me?" Martha asked.

"I can try, do you have the names and date?" Cindy said rather sweetly, another trait that didn't match.

"All I have is the man's name, James Harris, born on Harrington's Plantation about 1845. Possibly married about 1875."

"I'm so sorry, our records only go back to 1890. There is a possibility that it might be on church microfilm, that is if you know the church."

"I doubt there was a church, they were freed slaves."

"Oh yes, jumping the broom," she smiled, "Such a beautiful tradition. The Old Slave Market Museum might have information that could help you," she suggested.

Martha thanked her and started to leave, then remembered that she also wanted to find out who Martin married. She turned back around to ask Cindy and there was no one there.

"Hello, Miss Cindy, are you here?"

A older woman came out of the back room,

"I'm sorry, I must not have heard you come in. I wish they'd fix that bell, how can I help you?"

"I was just speaking with Cindy about a marriage record."

Before she could continue the older lady interrupted her,"I'm sorry did you say Cindy?" looking rather gray.

Martha told her of the conversation as she grew paler and paler. It seemed that there was no Cindy that worked there now. There had been many many years before but she was long gone now. Cindy was their resident spirit. She hadn't been seen in over a decade, many thought she has crossed over. She seemed to appear when people needed special directions, other than city records. Not one to disobey the spirits, Martha decided she would head to the Old Slave Museum on her day off tomorrow. Smiling, she thanked the poor pale old lady and left.

CHAPTER THIRTY

Martha's Results

After her morning coffee and cigarette, Martha once again boarded a CARTA bus. But this time she wasn't going to the courthouse. She was headed towards The Old Slave Museum on Chalmers Street. As she stood on the cobblestone street approaching the building a chill ran through her body. There was a heaviness in her soul as she walked through the arched entrance flanked by two huge wrought iron gates. The words worn by time in the arch said Old Slave Mart Museum. It was a somber place, hard to think of the number of men and women that passed through these gates not knowing their fates.

"Is there something in particular that I can point you to?" a woman with a Jamaican accent dressed in traditional African dress asked.

"Yes, thank you, it's just, I didn't think I would have this visceral reaction to seeing all this," she whispered.

"It can be overwhelming, especially if you are sensitive to our ancestors."

"I am looking for a man and his family. He was a freed slave from the former Harrington Plantation. Do you have any records on marriages?"

The woman regrettably did not, the decade after the war ended record keeping was scarce. But there was a group of older women that were trying to put together an ancestral book of lost peoples. She gave her their numbers and wished her luck.

Martha found an outdoor cafe and sat down for a cup of coffee and cigarette. As she fiddled with the paper given to her, she thought, how many generations had come before her, what were their stories. How many suffered and survived the ostracities for her to be alive today? Taking out her cell phone she punched in the number of Miss Faith. After two rings a pleasant voice answered,

"Hello."

"Miss Faith, my name is Martha. I am searching for my possible family. A woman at the Old Slave Mart gave me your number."

"I would love to help you, is it possible for you to come by? I live at the assisted living facility in Mt Pleasant."

Martha almost dropped the phone, Mt Pleasant! That's where her Gran had lived, that's where she had to go for her belongings, this was too much. Martha made arrangements to meet her after dinner, thanked her and hung up, she called Leonia.

"Leonia, I need a favor, we might have a great lead. I need to go to Mt Pleasant after dinner but there's no bus that runs that way at night. How would you like to drive us over to speak to an elder doing slave family research?" she said all in one breath.

"Martha, slow down, of course I'll help but you need to explain."

Martha told her of the trip to the Slave Market and the phone call to Miss Faith. But what she didn't tell her was about her Gran, that was too personal. They made arrangements for Leonia to pick up Martha on the way out of town.

Leonia found the address where Martha lived by using her GPS. It had been a few years since she had driven and Charleston had grown. There was a time that she knew all the streets, but then again those were the streets on the peninsula. Martha was waiting on the portico and waved as she pulled up. Getting in she thanked her for going with her.

"Thank you, Leona, hopefully we'll find out more information. What a beautiful day for a drive."

They drove over the Cooper River on the Arthur Ravenel Bridge. The six lane expanse was a big change from the old bridge. Leonia thought back to the old two lane rickety bridge that stood for years, many refused to drive on it. They would drive out of their way around to bypass it. They entered Mt Pleasant on the other side of the river, the tree lined streets were quieter and a tad slower than downtown Charleston. The assisted living community was a mile down Highway 17 to the right, towards the ocean. The ladies pulled in and parked.

"Martha, we need to get our stories straight. What questions do we need answers to?"

"I agree, we don't want to overwhelm her."

They made their list of questions but also realized that the spirits would be giving them more. The lobby of the building was shaped in a triangle with two corridors leading off to private rooms. A desk sat in the middle with an elderly gentleman manning the telephone.

"Hello, ladies, how may I help you?"

"We are here to see Miss …".before she could finish a tiny old black woman appeared behind her and tapped her shoulder.

"I'm Faith, you must be Martha," she said, taking her hand, "And your friend is?"

Martha introduced Leona as Miss Faith guided them to a sitting area. There were three overstuffed chairs in a bright floral pattern material, two end tables stood between with wrought iron lamps. The area was bright and welcoming, a space that made you relax.

Martha explained that she was searching for Jim Harris, who lived on the Harrington Plantation before the war. They knew that he worked for Martin Harrington after the war but then lost his trail after 1877. There was one other name that they found, it was Sadie. Miss Faith had a loose leaf binder filled with papers, she thumbed through it humming. Leona and Martha sat patiently looking at each other. They weren't volunteering any information the spirits had given them.

"Did your Jim work for Martin Harrington building homes?"

"We believe so, yes, they were very close, best friends," Martha stated.

"They weren't well liked, white man and black man being friends and all. But people liked their houses. I have an article here about their undignified relationship the newspaper wrote after the governor had them build him a summer home on the peninsula," she said, as she rummaged through finding the article and handed it to them.

Not only was there an article but it also had a picture of the two of them! Martha stared into the face of her hopefully great great granddaddy and thought, is that you? Did we find you? What secrets are you keeping?

"Unfortunately we have very few records of freedmen and women jumping the broom. Those are usually handed down from family to family. It's too bad you didn't come sooner, one of our oldest ladies just passed away. She held a lot of knowledge about local families. She was a treasure, could sit and talk all day long. Sometimes I think she embellished a bit but that was ok because her stories were so good."

"May I ask, was her name Mae?

Miss Faith looked shocked, "Yes, did you know her?"

"Actually she was my Grandmother, she raised me. She refused to tell me stories of the old times. She told me I was to grow up a strong black woman with no baggage, make my own history," she said as a tear rolled down her cheek. "I was going to pick up her belongings while I was here."

Miss Faith was looking tired and Martha felt like a mule had kicked her. Leona suggested that they head home. The gentleman at the desk helped them with Maes belongings as the ladies hugged Miss Faith and thanked her for her time and information.

CHAPTER THIRTY ONE

Newspaper Search

Leona and Martha were both deep in their own thoughts on the ride back to town. It was almost at the same time that they both remembered.

"Oh my God, the box….." Martha said.

"Of newspapers!!!!" Leonia yelled, almost stopping the car. It was a good thing there was a red light. She pulled over on the next street and stopped.

"There was a reason they saved all those boxes of newspapers. Maybe we can even find that article Miss Faith had to show the others," Leona said.

'Well, it's the weekend, I'm not working. Is Maggie off?" Martha asked.

Leona dropped off Martha with plans for her to pick her up in the morning. They would spend tomorrow going through newspapers.

When Leona got home it was close to 8:30. The ladies were in the kitchen playing cards as she walked in. After filling them in on the information they had recovered she joined their game. Of course, every bit of conversation in between playing a card was about what they could find tomorrow. It was after 10:00 before they finished playing and headed to bed.

"Maggie, can I see you for a minute?" Marie said as the others headed up the stairs.

"Sure, what's up? Are you ok?"

Marie assured her she was fine, but had something she wanted to discuss, "I am feeling Jim more and more, almost like he has an expiration date. Which is crazy! But that's the feeling, like if we don't solve this soon, it will be too late."

"That's exactly what I was thinking, the spirits are giving us clues faster and faster. We just about get one question solved and another pops right up."

They agreed that the newspapers must have the answers. After locking up the doors they also headed to bed.

It was a large clap of thunder that woke Maggie. Getting up to close the window, a bolt of bright lightning lit up Colonial Lake as she gazed out. What got her attention was the man on the sidewalk peering up at her. He was dressed in an expensive looking suit of old, complete with a top hat. His eyes held hers, in a flash she knew it was Martin!

"Time is short, you must find it, it's all for them. His ancestors. He paid a price for something he didn't do," she heard telepathically.

She blinked and swore he tipped his hat before disappearing. Looking over to the clock she noted it was 5:30. No sense in going back to sleep now, she thought, putting on her slippers. Sneaking down creaking stairs wasn't easy, but she didn't want to wake anyone else. First the right foot gently to the far side of the step, then the left foot. She was concentrating so hard on not making a sound that she didn't notice Marie standing at the bottom of the staircase giggling to herself.

"That does take talent, Maggie, but I prefer sliding down the banister!"

Maggie looked up to see Marie and they both fell into a fit of giggles, trying to be quiet, muffling the sounds with their hands as they made their way into the kitchen.

The tea pot was put on the stove and Marie pulled out some Benne wafers from the closet.

"Why are you up so early?" Marie asked.

"The thunder and lightning woke me," she said, not volunteering anything else.

"Thunder, what thunder? I've been down here since four and didn't hear any thunder."

Realizing what had happened Maggie felt compelled to confess the rest of her story. Just as they spoke of last night, more clues, but clues to what. The tea kettle whistled, it was ready. The girls poured themselves some hot water into their cups and added the tea, Maggie liking green tea while Marie preferred the loose leaves. As they waited for the tea to seep they decided to start in the basement when they finished instead of waiting for everyone else.

"We can do some organizing, there's so many different boxes down there. Who knows what's in them," Marie offered.

"Great idea, I'm eager to get started anyway," Maggie winked "But I suggest we put on more appropriate work clothes," laughing after realizing they were still in their pajamas.

It only took them ten minutes to change once they cleaned up the kitchen. The basement stairs creaked worse than the ones upstairs. They made their way down turning on the light half way down. Somehow it smelled mustier this morning, and chilly,

"I should have worn a sweater, but once I get working I'll warm up," Marie said

"Do you feel it? The chill is almost spooky. I hope we don't have spirits with bad juju working against us," Maggie stated as she made her way past the first group of boxes.

They agreed it would have been convenient if the boxes had dates on them but that would have been too easy. They moved a few boxes into the secret room. It was more comfortable and had better light. As Maggie went to open a box a spider ran across the top. She immediately dropped it and jumped back,

"Oh God, I hate spiders, maybe we need gloves," She laughed half heartedly.

Making sure there were no more spiders on that particular box she ripped the yellowed tape off the top and opened it. There were piles of yellowed papers from The Charleston Gazette.

Sitting down on the bed she took the first one out and gently opened it up to read. Marie took one and sat down in the overstuffed chair. They sat in silence for a long time before either spoke,

"These should be in a museum or something, so much history. We should really have a pad and pen to jot down anything we find interesting."

"How about we set the ones we find information in aside right now. When the others get here we can ask them to bring them down," Maggie said.

Granny opened the basement door and hollered down, "You guys are up early, Your mom and I are going to have a cup of coffee then be down, Leona left to pick up Martha, then hail hail the gang will be here," she sang laughing.

By the time they had finished their coffee, Leona and Martha arrived carrying a box of cinnamon buns from Maggie's favorite deli. If anything could coax Maggie upstairs it would be them. When Maggie and Marie heard cinnamon buns they decided to make their way upstairs and report their findings, which were nil.

"So far we haven't found anything connected to the family or Martin's business," Marie said, "But Maggie had a visitor this early morning," she said, looking at Maggie.

Everyone looked at her, waiting patiently as they ate their buns for her to speak. She told them if the thunder and a man she thought was Martin.

When she repeated his words Leona said, "There it is again, like we're on the clock, the spirits are getting desperate."

With the cinnamon buns gone the group headed back down the basement, this time armed with paper and pens. Since there were so many boxes they decided each person would pick a box, find a comfortable spot and go to work. Maggie and Marie went back into the secret room along with Granny. Geraldine and Martha sat on boxes and stayed in the main room. Every now and then you'd hear a giggle or laugh, it was fun going back in time. It was Granny who found the first article related to their search,

"Look here, girls, it's an advertisement for Martin's Construction Company, it even gives this address as their office, so it must have been early on."

"What's the date on the top of the page?" Maggie asked.

"October 20, 1877."

The advertisement didn't offer any other information other than they offered luxury homes built on the peninsula. This small clue got them excited. Once more, the pages started turning and you could hear the rustle of yellowed newspapers.

They worked for another hour before Leona said, "I found a birth announcement, it's Herberts great great granddaddy, William!"

She read it outloud: "Master Martin William Harrington and his wife Deardra announced the birth of their son, William, on June 21, in the year of our Lord,1876. The child was born at home with a doctor and wet nurse in residence. Mother and child are reportedly doing well. A private baptism will take place later in the month at St Philips Church. The family will receive guests at a later date to be announced."

The family tree was fanning out! Leona sat and read the announcement in silence, almost like she was willing more information out of it. With renewed excitement again the ladies continued for the next hour.

"I don't know about you girls but I need to stretch my legs. I'm going upstairs for some bottled water, anyone interested in some?" Geraldine asked.

"It's 11:30, why don't we all take a break and have a bite of lunch," Leona suggested.

"That sounds like a good idea, I really feel like I need to wash my hands. All this newsprint has made them blacker," Martha said laughing.

As the ladies unfolded themselves to get up, you could hear all sorts of groans and moans. Someone said they sounded like an old haunted graveyard!

After a light lunch and a few Tylenol they headed back down the basement. Marie had finished her box and found another. Removing the yellowed tape gave her chills down her spine, she opened the flaps.The smell of mildewed paper hit her nose first as she gazed inside. The front page read "Great Earthquake kills 100" with a picture of a collapsed building.

"Oh, ladies, oh, my God," there were tears rolling down her cheeks as she held up the headlines "Earthquake Destroys City."

They all gathered around the paper as Marie read the disastrous details. It happened on August 31,1886 at 9:00 at night. There were different stories of families who had lost family members, store owners who lost their buildings and homes that were leveled. Knowing that it happened in history was very different than reading first hand accounts from a paper written the following day!! That box was filled with papers from that time period, no one wanted to relive it so they placed the box to the side for last. The mood had sobered considerably.

The afternoon wore on with no further valuable information. Feeling depressed the group dredged upstairs to the kitchen. The sun was setting past the trees line which meant it was time for dinner.

As they all sat at the table, Geraldine said, "So, today was a bust. We're not done yet, there is more in those boxes. It will just take time. How about pizza and beer for dinner?"

The idea sounded great to everyone except Martha, she had a date with a friend for dinner. Leona and Maggie volunteered to take Martha home and pick up the pizza on the way back. Marie checked the refrigerator to make sure they had beer. She answered with a thumbs up.

CHAPTER THIRTY TWO

Maggie and Allison

They met at the cafe, just missing the line forming behind them. The morning was starting off well, thought Maggie. The chill in the air told her that autumn was here. She really hadn't noticed until this morning. She walked down Rutledge to the cafe, noticing how the colors looked more vibrant, the dew glistening off the oranges and rust colored leaves as the sunlight played in between branches. She felt a lightness, almost like a relief from a problem had been solved. Funny, she thought, this feeling was far from the truth. They still had Jim's mystery to solve.

The girls thanked the older woman behind the counter for their coffee and cinnamon bun and headed out the door. There were small wrought iron tables outside on the sidewalk, usually they were full, but this morning they were able to find one that a couple had just got up from. Sitting down Maggie took a deep breath, closed her eyes and looked to the heavens. Silently she said a prayer to the spirits for Jim. Opening her eyes she saw that Allison was looking at her with her head slightly cocked,

"I never saw you pray before eating, something new?"

"I felt the need to ask the spirits for help. Jim seems to be on everyone's mind. We need to solve his dilemma."

Hopefully the others would be working in the basement today while Maggie and Allison were working at The Tower. The girls drank their coffee and ate their buns in silence while watching the traffic. There were delivery trucks and cars all rushing to get somewhere. The one way traffic street was tight especially if a car was parked on the curb, which there were plenty of.

"You done? Time to hit the bricks," Allison laughed.

"Ready when you are," Maggie said as she got up to throw her trash away.

Turning to face Allison she almost bumped into Boyd.

"We really have to stop meeting like this," he laughed.

He had surprised Allson by showing up two days earlier than planned. Allison was beside herself with joy, but now she had to work twelve hours! Maggie hugged Boyd and made an excuse that she had an early meeting and made plans to see them both later. Winking at Ally, she walked away giving them some private time.

Maggie texted Ally around 11:30 to see what time she was taking lunch. They agreed to meet at the cafeteria at 12:15. Maggie made her way down on the crowded elevator to the first floor. The lobby seemed to be busier than normal, she hoped that they would get a table. The line into the cafeteria was relatively short when she saw Allison waving to her from a table. She had already gotten her sandwich. Waving back she took her place in line. It was then that she saw him, standing behind Ally. This time he smiled while tipping his top hat. She blinked and he was gone. Suddenly she wasn't hungry, she had to call Granny! Leaving the line she hurried over to Ally hardly able to contain herself.

"He was here, right behind you, right here Al. He smiled at me, tipped his hat."

"Woah, slow down girl, who was here?"

Maggie told Ally what she had seen. She had to call Granny. They must be close to discovering something in the basement! That's why he was smiling. The girls decided that the phone call was better off done outside, away from other people who wouldn't understand. They got a to-go container for Ally's lunch and headed out to the public seating area. Maggie called Granny and explained what she had seen.

"Oh, child, thank you. We were losing faith down here. Just hearing you say Martin smiled, I know we're close. I will keep you updated, thank you!"

Maggie and Allison were too excited to eat. They still had twenty minutes left until their lunch break was over. They decided to walk, heading down the magnolia lined street now filled with cars parked on either side and bumper to bumper traffic. They discussed Martin's appearance.

"It kind of freaks me out that he was standing right behind me," Ally stated.

"I think he needed to get my attention, and boy did he!"

Each spirit clue seemed to be leading them to an answer, hopefully it will be a happy one. Heading back up the entrance steps they agreed to put their excitement aside until the end of their shift. Ally had a date with Boyd tonight and Maggie would be rushing home just as soon as she could. But not before she stopped to see Shamus. She stopped using his proper name, Mr McGinnis a while ago. She felt as though they were friends now, caring for him on and off these past months. Maggie made it a point to sit with him for a few minutes at least once a week if she hadn't been assigned his care. Allison joked that he had become her Father confessor. She didn't realize how right she was.

CHAPTER THIRTY THREE

What?

The phone call from Maggie couldn't have come at a better time. When the cell phone rang Granny was sitting in the overstuffed chair in the secret room, her head leaning back with her eyes closed. She had been thinking, how are we ever going to solve this? Geraldine had curled up on the bed and was staring at the wall thinking the same thing. Leona had just finished a box and was folding back the flaps, looking at the next box in the pile. Marie had gone up to the kitchen to start lunch, all the ladies had lost their excitement.

"We're close, I know it! Martin wouldn't be smiling, he's telling us to keep going!" Granny said with renewed enthusiasm.

"I agree, let's have lunch and then resume our search. But this time with a positive attitude, I think our negative outlook has slowed us down," Leona said smiling.

The ladies headed up the stairs with a bit more energy than they left down in the secret room.

Marie had decided that they should eat lunch on the second floor veranda outside the kitchen. Plates of fruits and salad were set out with bottles of water. The weather had been cool but they needed the air after being held up in the musty basement all morning. As they ate they watched the foot traffic that seemed to be unusually high this morning walk past the house. Then they heard him, a tour guide telling his group the history of area homes.

"This house shared a strange relationship, master and slave so to speak. Their friendship went so far as to become partners in a business, highly condemned by their peers at the time. The pink color comes…."

At that moment the ladies, in unison all yelled from the veranda "it's coral!"

The tour group looked up at the ladies now in a fit of laughter and the gentleman speaker smiled and tipped his hat. With that the ladies stopped laughing and looked at each other in a stunned silence.

"The spirits are really screwing with us now, sending the same message twice in one day! Finish up ladies, we have a mystery to solve!" Leona said.

Once the ladies were back downstairs, they gathered together in a circle. Granny had suggested that they ask the spirits to guide them to the right boxes. They let their intentions be known and took a minute or two to allow the intention to marinate, so to speak. Separating they each found a box and started searching, but this time their positive attitude led to humming as they worked.

It was in a box marked "1880". Geraldine gasped, then looked at the others.

"Please stop, you have to hear this. It isn't good," she said, visibility upset.

The ladies quickly gathered around her wide eyed and waited. The Charleston Gazette editorial read,

"Martin Harrington's business partner has been accused of the unthinkable.

Making unwarranted and sexual advances to a white woman. We warned Mr Harrington of making alliances with a darky had the making of a disaster. To this writer the two races don't mix in business or pleasure. The war of northern aggression may be over but our values haven't changed. People need to know their place. The arrest is pending on the sheriffs interview with the wounded woman who was put through this horrific event."

They all looked at each other, what they had learned of Jim didn't fit. The spirits wouldn't send them on a quest of someone who had hurt another. In total unbelief they agreed, the answer was still out there somewhere. More questions now, who was the woman? What ever happened? What about his family? Again, they got an answer but it led to more questions. After drying some of their tears they each took a newspaper from that box and continued reading. It only took another ten minutes, Leona found the article.

"Miss Penelope McKenna has asked the local justice to investigate the Martin Harrington Construction Company. While building her home the foreman made certain sexual advances toward the woman. The foreman, James Harris, who is a freed slave, was working at the site the day the accusations were made."

Now the two articles were starting to form a story. It would make more sense if they found the articles in order but they'd take what they could get. Moving on they continued to read. Marie had an idea.

"Why don't I go get my laptop. Now that we have names and dates it might be faster then going through all these newspapers!"

"Oh, my God, you're right!! We're wasting time when all this information might be available online. It took a youngster to think of that, thank you, Marie," Granny said.

The ladies wrote down the names and dates they had found and headed upstairs.

Settling into the drawing room the ladies waited for Marie to get her laptop. You would think that they would be relaxed. But each one of them were on edge as if on the verge of making a great discovery. The room was warm with the sunlight streaming through windows, every now and then the shadows of branches danced on the walls. There was an eerie silence until Marie came into the room bringing renewed enthusiasm.

"I've got it. Holy crap there's a bunch of information here," she said sitting down on the settee as the others came closer....

"Before we run down a bunch of rabbit holes, why don't you read as much as you can Marie. Then you can summarize it for us. How does that sound ladies?" Leona suggested.

They all agreed as they gave Marie room to sit with a pad and paper to do her reading. It didn't take long before she was writing all sorts of information on her pad. The ladies waited, but not patiently. Geraldine paced back and forth stopping periodically and staring out the window thinking Maggie should be here. She would be so excited. Thinking of Martha also, Geraldine texted her to see if she could come by after work. She answered immediately. She had just left the courthouse and would come by. As Granny and Leona joined the others in the drawing room an hour later, Marie told them about the text messages to Maggie and Martha. The group unanimously agreed to wait for the other two to get home before revealing the information Marie had found.

As Marie continued her deep dive of Martin Harrington and Jim Harris the ladies started doing other things, mostly out of boredom. Just sitting around made them all antsy. Granny and Leona decided to take a walk across the street to Colonial Lake, where they sat for a bit in a lakeside swing. Geraldine finally settled on a window seat with the book she had been reading. As the clock ticked it got closer to Maggie being home.

Maggie watched the clock closely, it couldn't go fast enough for her. Her final rounds on her patients went well. Everyone seemed to be resting comfortably, two needed pain medication and another wanted to walk in the hall. Having completed her duties she reported off to the oncoming night shift nurse who was more interested in having a conversation about staffing then her patients. Grabbing her sweater she headed to the elevator, as the doors closed her cell phone dinged a text message from Marie.

"Come right home, big news, all here waiting," followed with an emoji of a heart.

Maggie and Martha met at the bottom of the front steps laughing at each other,

"We couldn't have done this if we planned it. Did you get a text also?" Maggie asked.

"Yes, I had just walked out the door. I'm glad I hadn't grabbed the bus home."

They both ran up separate steps and went through the door breathless, laughing. The others didn't need to question who was there, their laughter told them who had arrived. They made their way into the drawing room to find four faces looking directly at them with the most serious looks.

"Oh boy, you guys are scary looking. I was going to ask if someone died, but I already know that," Maggie said, trying to lighten the mood.

"Sorry, we've just been waiting for all of us to be here and the suspense is killing us," Geraldine said.

Marie stood, fiddled with her pad, then explained what she found online.

"First, before I start I need you to know there is more to find. I have information that will answer many of our questions but the mystery of the secret room has not been solved." Several groans could be heard from the ladies, Marie continued, "Martin and Jim were indeed partners in the construction business. They were very very successful. So successful that many white Charlestonians could not accept the fact that they had a rich ex slave in their community. The McKenna family was the most outspoken in town and at one point tried to arrange a lynching of James. When that didn't work Penelope came forward with the story and accusations of sexual advances. An arrest warrant went out for James, but he disappeared. When the sheriff went to his home he was gone. It was quoted that his wife and daughter were questioned for hours until Martin Harrington intervened," Marie paused and waited.

"Do you have names of Jim's wife and daughter?" Martha asked.

"I do, Martha," she whispered, "His daughter was Mae Bell."

At that point all hell broke loose. Everyone was shouting questions except Martha. She thought, could this be her great grandmother? What had just happened? Suddenly she felt lightheaded, as she stood to clear her head everything went black.

CHAPTER THIRTY FOUR

Answers

Martha was watching a movie. No it wasn't a movie. It was them, in real life! They were arguing, Martin and Jim, both in the secret room which wasn't old and musty. It was beautifully decorated in a masculine tone of rich leathers and mahogany woods. Martin was trying to convince Jim that he couldn't win this fight, it was trumped up against him. They would never believe a black man over a white woman. Jim was adamant about his family, this would ruin them, lose their standing in the community. He had worked so hard for them to live free and in relative comfort financially. All his hard work, it was all for them, he yelled at Martin. Martin was promising him he would care for them. They would be fine. He would find a place for them up north, more acceptable of black families with wealth.

Martin and Jim were now sitting quietly drinking what looked like brown liquor. Martin suggested for the time being,until things quieted down and they stopped looking for him they have him live in the basement office. Jim looked at him laughing. The law will search your house Martin, he had said. They will find this room, it's not exactly secret. With that they both looked at each other, a secret room, that was the answer. They had built many houses. They felt sure they could build a door to this room that no one would find unless they knew it was there.

Jim was in the room now by himself, the door closed, sitting at the table with papers in front of him. Looking at them he said aloud, these were for my baby girl, her wedding, and the home I would build for her. I will never see that day. Tears rolling down his cheeks he slowly put the papers in an envelope. He stood and walked over to the wall, removed a brick and shoved the envelope in before taking off his wedding band and putting that in also. He replaced the brick and grabbed a handful of dirt from the floor, packing the dirt around the brick made it look as though it had never been touched.

Martha opened her eyes to see everyone looking at her, she was lying on the floor. Maggie was feeling her pulse, Geraldine had a cool compress on her forehead and Leona was crying as Granny held her. She didn't remember passing out. But she did remember her dream, or was it a dream.

"Martha, thank goodness you're awake. Are you ok? Does anything hurt?" Maggie asked.

Gathering her whits she replied,"What just happened? I saw them, they were here, I know where it is!"

She wasn't making any sense and Maggie thought maybe she took too hard of a hit to her head when she fainted. Being the nurse that she was she started feeling Martha's head for any bumps or bleeding. Martha wiggled away and sat up, took a deep breath and told them she knew where the brick was. Once again everyone had a question until Marie put her fingers in her mouth and whistled, they all stopped and looked at her,

"Please, we have to have some kind of order ladies. Let's get Martha up to the chair, give her a glass of water and take a breath. Then she can explain."

When Martha finished explaining there wasn't a dry eye. In this day and age they couldn't fathom what that could have felt like. It all was making sense now, the spirits led them to Martha for a reason, her inheritance as Jim's great granddaughter was behind that brick. Making sure Martha felt good enough to go downstairs, they all headed that way, each feeling like they were intruding on something very personal.

The door was still propped open and for a split second Martha swore the men were standing there smiling. She walked into the room while the others stood at the doorway.

"Y'all better get in here, cause if there's a snake in that hole I'm gonna faint again," she laughed trying to break the anticipation of what they would find.

The others gathered around her. Granny said a prayer of protection from the dark spirits as Martha located the brick and attempted to wiggle it out. It didn't move. Geraldine handed her a screwdriver to chisel around the dirt. After removing dirt from all sides she wiggled the brick again, this time it did budge. She turned and looked at the others as if to say, should I? They all nodded and held their breath.

The brick finally slid out revealing a dark hole. Martha closed her eyes and carefully put her hand in. Feeling around she located the wedding ring. She pulled it out and held it out in the palm of her hand for the others to see. There was a hush and feeling of reverence before she continued on with more vigor to find the envelope. It was bigger than she expected and yellowed from time. On the front of the envelope in beautiful script handwriting was the name Mae Bell. Carefully opening it she pulled out a letter and five large deeds.

"Oh my goodness, someone read those deeds, while I read this letter." Martha said.

"My Dearest Mae Bell,

Before I go any further I must tell you how much I love you. You were cherished and loved by both your mother and myself. I don't know where life will take you, but you must know I am innocent of the charges put against me. I had to disappear or your life would have been very different, they would have taken it out on you and your mother. I pray that one day our family will reunite and be able to put the past behind us, but I don't have high hopes for that.

Your Uncle Martin will care for you and your mother, I have full faith in his promises. Remember they are your family, I must tell you now that Martin is my half brother. We have the same father. Even though our circumstances were the worst, we made it the best. Please remember that we are all brothers and sisters in this world. Martin and I never saw color. We only saw each other and what good we could accomplish together.

I had big plans for the day you were to be married. My gift was going to be building you and your husband a house on the peninsula. But alas, this will not be. So I have enclosed five deeds to land that are now yours. Do with them whatever you want. Hopefully, you'll build yourself a home and fill it with many children. All I ask is that when you tell the grandchildren our family story, you do it with the love of two brothers who tried to change their part of the world.

When the time is right I will be relocating again. I don't want to put Martin and his family in any more danger then they already are in. I pray our paths cross again if not in this lifetime than in another.

Your Pappy loves you with all his heart"

By the time Martha finished the letter she was sobbing. Without realizing it the women had gathered around her as she was reading. They were hugging her now and crying along with her.

She turned to them saying,"I can't believe this, it's almost unbelievable. Leona your Herbert was my cousin!! I just can't wrap my head around this," Trying to laugh through her tears.

"Well, if you can't wrap your head around that wait til you hear the address on these deeds!" Maggie said.

CHAPTER THIRTY FIVE

Deeds

Leona found Martha the best real estate attorney in Charleston, an old family friend and pulled some strings. She was able to send photocopies of the deeds ahead so he could do the research before their meeting.

"Don't be nervous. Donald is an excellent attorney and will help us sort this whole thing out," Leona said, smiling at her friend as they drove to his office.

"I can't thank you enough. This all seems so surreal, you and I, related by marriage. It's kind of funny when you think about it."

Walking into the plush office there was a beautiful gold plaque on the wall. It read, Donald McKenna, Real Estate Attorney. They both realized something, almost simultaneously.

"Oh my goodness, he's a McKenna!" they said in unison.

"Do you think he knows?" Martha whispered.

"I highly doubt it, although us southerners love our family history. Let's not rock the boat right now," Leona whispered back.

The receptionist led them into his office, even Leona was impressed. The dark oak walls and rich leather chairs told them a man worked here. The desk was so big two could work at it without touching elbows. The receptionist asked if they would like a cup of coffee or bottled water. The ladies declined, smiling. In truth they were too nervous to touch anything with liquid in it.

"Leona, my dear, it's so good to see you," he said, extending his hand. "And you must be Miss Harris," shaking her hand also.

"Actually it's Miss Edwards. I never married and that was my daddy's name, but my momma never married him…." she stopped realizing she was rambling.

"Please ladies, sit, make yourself comfortable. We have much to discuss. Leona, how may I ask, did you acquire these deeds?" he asked.

There was no way Martha and Leona could tell him how the spirits led them to the secret room in the basement, then to the brick hiding place. He would call the men in white coats! The ladies had come up with a story, Leona had found some boxes in the basement as she was making room to store some unused furniture. When she realized how very old they were she contacted the courthouse. That's how she met Martha. She did part time historical preservation, so she hired her to go through the boxes and take what needed to be saved. Being a responsible Charlestonian, she wanted to preserve the precious history they might have hidden in them. While Martha was dividing the newspapers into piles of importance an envelope fell out of one, in it were the deeds. Finishing the story, they sat there, hands folded in their laps and Cheshire Cat smiles on their faces.

At that point Donald raised his eyebrow and cocked his head.

"Really, Leona, you have woven quite a story here. You had me up til responsible Charlestonian," he laughed, "Either way you are in possession of deeds that hold some of the most expensive land on the peninsula," he let that sink in a moment.

The ladies looked at each other, their eyes wide open, then looked back at him,

"And so? It sounds like there's much more to this story," Leona said.

Donald went on to explain, "In researching these deeds it has come to light that they have been lost for over one hundred and forty five years! The importance of this is that there is a one hundred and fifty year clause to any unclaimed deed in Charleston. If the property has not been claimed in that time frame it reverts back to the city. The reason for the one hundred and fifty year clause is after the war many families were scattered. The deeds went with them or were hidden. We have had two or three generations removed come to claim land in the recent past."

"What happens now?" Martha interrupted nervously.

He continued, "The name on the deeds goes to Mae Bell Harris, now we know she is no longer alive. You, Miss Edwards, will have to prove that you are her kin. Since you have possession of the original deeds there should be no problem transferring them into your name once you prove your relationship."

"Donald, may I ask, how much money the estate would be worth to Martha?"

Without even blinking an eye he said "Hundreds of millions!"

CHAPTER THIRTY SIX

The Proofs in the Pudding

Lunch with the ladies took on a whole new meaning that Wednesday afternoon. Leona and Martha set about calling in the troops. They met at a small cafe on Queen Street, Leona was good friends with the owners. As they staggered in one and two at a time, the waitress directed them to a back room, usually used for the owners family gathering. It was all very clandestine they thought. The ladies ordered their drinks and baskets of bread arrived at either end of the large table. As if on cue, Martha stood up.

"Ladies, we have good news and bad news," she stated in a strong confident voice they hadn't heard before. "The good news is I'm a millionaire!" she said smiling. "But there's a hitch, I need to prove that I am related to Jim's daughter, Mae Bell. This luncheon is to brainstorm how we can do that."

Letting that sink in she sat down as the room erupted in their typical manner of responding to unbelievable news.

This time Marie didn't whistle. The sounds of the ladies laughing and talking was so joyous to her. She couldn't help thinking of her own life, how she was brought here. These women had become such a big part of her life, they were her family. Now they were adding another family member,

Martha! She knew these strong loving women would find a way to prove her kinship.

"Martha, did your mother ever tell you any stories before she left," Maggie asked.

"I don't remember much of her, she never married my father and left before I was two. My Grandmother, Mae, raised me. I believe my Grandmother was carrying on the female family name. I'm the first I think that didn't have Mae in their name. My mother's name was Sadie Mae, we all know now who she was named for."

The ladies spent the next two hours eating, drinking, there was some wine involved in the meal and brainstorming. The first idea of course was courthouse records. Birth certificates, death certificates and deeds to land that James and Sadie had owned. Another was of course the internet sites that prove ancestry. With renewed excitement they finished their lunch and planned to start their search in the morning.

Leona felt a nap coming on, too much wine she thought. Martha grabbed the bus home, she didn't want anyone driving after indulging. As she rode, she looked out the window. How strange she thought, I left home one person, now I'm returning another, or am I? Her surroundings looked the same, although the sun looked a tad brighter.

She hurried up the steps to her apartment, opened the door and dropped her coat on the chair, then stopped. Looking around she suddenly realized how stark her apartment was, she kept it that way for a reason. But now she had every reason to make a home, a real home, with roots. Martha felt the silent tears roll down her cheeks all the while praying they would find the connection to great grandmother Mae Bell.

Fixing herself a bowl of mac and cheese, Martha sat at the table thinking of her plan for tomorrow. Out of the corner of her eye she spotted the box of Mae's belongings from the assisted living facility. She felt a tinge of regret. She should have spent more time with her, listened and learned from her life stories. Why didn't she share them with her, why did she want her to make her own way? More questions with no answers once again.

Pulling back the flap to the box, the first thing she saw was her picture, as a child in a frame. Taking it out and running her fingers over the picture she tried to remember being that young.

The rest of the box yielded clothing and personal things such as hair brushes and ribbons. In the bottom of the carton was a small mahogany box. She carefully removed it and opened the top, inside were letters. All she could do was stare at them, stunned and afraid of what they might or might not say.

Martha went to the closet and pulled out a bottle of Carolina Sweet Wine, opened it carefully and poured herself a glass. So what if she already had some at lunch, she needed some liquid courage to open those letters. Taking a deep breath she took the first letter from the top, yellowed with age it felt like it could crumble.

"Sadie, my love,

I'm sorry, there is nothing else I can say. I am innocent of the charges as Martin has informed you. You must take Mae Bell and go north, he will make all the arrangements. If you stay here Mae Bell will hear the rumors and will ask questions.

For both your sakes please listen to Martin. There is a bank account set up for you both and enough money for you to live comfortably. Martin and Deardre are family, trust them, I have.

May my heart follow you wherever you are my darling, Jim

She returned the letter to the envelope, letting the words sink in. I wonder what it was like for poor Sadie, having to up and move to a strange city, she thought. She opened the next letter.

"Mae Bell, my darling child,

Your old pappy loves you, I know you're probably confused and scared but you can depend on your Uncle Martin and your Momma. Things will work out, it will be ok. I have left you some deeds to land on the peninsula to build a home once you get married. That is if you wish to move back. Uncle Martin has them in a safe place. If you ever need anything go to him, he'll help you.

I love you baby girl, your Pappy"

Well another letter talking about the deeds, that might help her cause. Continuing on she grabbed the next letter.

"Sadie Mae,

Congratulations on the birth of your child, Mae. We were so pleased to hear the news. Thank you for naming her for your grandmother. She would have been so pleased. I wish we were closer so I could visit but I still don't feel comfortable in Charleston. I am pleased you have found your way home. Remember all the wonderful stories we were told before the great tragedy, please pass them on to your daughter, he must not be forgotten.

Love from your loving mother, Mae Bell"

The great tragedy they called it, the accusations against Jim! Sadie Mae moved back to Charleston, that's how Mae ended up here. There were only two letters left in the box, she was almost afraid to open them. One if the letters looked new, it wasn't yellowed like the others. When she opened it, it was her name on the top,

"My sweet baby girl, Martha,

If you are reading this it means I have gone to live with my ancestors. What I couldn't or wouldn't tell you while I was alive, I can tell you now. Your ancestors help build this city. James Harris was a partner with Martin Harrington in a construction company. The letters in this box can explain better than I. There was a great tragedy that separated us physically but never in our hearts. The Harrington family watched over our family for generations. You have many family members yet to be discovered. I pray the spirits lead you to our extended family wherever they may be.

Thank you for allowing me to be your mamma, I love you,

Mamma (Mae Harris)"

Martha was sobbing as the cell phone rang, wiping her eyes with the back of her hands she answered, "Hello"

"Martha, it Leona, I had to call you, are you ok?"

Martha assured her she was ok, still sobbing and now laughing at the same time. The ladies spent the next thirty minutes talking, Martha told Leona about the letters she found and Leona told Martha about her dream of Mae smiling. They had the proof!

CHAPTER THIRTY SEVEN

One Mystery Solved, Now Another

The Charleston Grill had never seen such a celebration! They were all there, her family, without them this party would never be happening. Never in a million years would she have thought she was related to the Harrington's! But she was, her cousin Herbert was a direct descendant of Martin. The same Martin that was half brother to Jim, her kin. Martha stood and raised her glass,

"To my new family, without y'all none of this would have happened! I am so blessed to know each and everyone of you. I will never be alone again, cheers." A huge hurray was heard throughout the room with clinking of glasses.

"I wish my Herbert were here to see this, but I know he probably had a hand in it from above," Leona laughed as she hugged Martha, "I know what you mean about being alone. After Herbert died I had no one, but always felt a piece of me missing, until Marie and now you," she said and they both laughed.

As everyone ate and visited the room was alive with joyous noise, noise that Martha loved. It seemed that her lifestyle had certainly changed inward as well as outward. She gazed from one to the other, silently thanking them for being there and caring for her; Leona, Maggie, Geraldine, Florence, Marie, Dora, Allison, Boyd and Allison's parents, Brook and Blair. She had invited Donald McKenna, who had ended being a friend but he declined due to a meeting at the courthouse.

Thinking back to the third meeting she had with Donald made her smile, he had been so gracious. It was just the two of them, signing papers, lots of papers, when he looked at her and said with sadness in his eyes,

"Martha, I have something to tell you, something that will probably make you hate me. It's about our families," he paused and couldn't look at her.

"Donald, you have become a dear friend to me, what happened decades ago matters not today. We, you and me have made our choices to be friends. That's all that matters to me," she took his hand and smiled.

"You knew? And still came to me?"

"I think the spirits knew our families needed to heal. Thank you for taking care of me," she stood and hugged him, both had tears in their eyes.

As her friends got ready to leave the celebration they made plans to meet over the weekend. After all Martha would need her friends to help her decide where her forever home would be. Leona thought how bright Martha's future looked, she was so happy for her. There was still something gnawing at her, Martin's letter, the last part, about Jonathan's family coming together with Martins. But for now she would just be happy for Martha and her new big extended family.

CHAPTER THIRTY EIGHT

Memories

Geraldine and Granny had gone back to New Orleans, having spent a month away. They were happy to be home. The weather had just started getting humid yet again, but Granny loved it. It reminded her of days gone by, it seemed she was remembering these days more and more lately. Maybe it had to do with that feeling of something missing, that feeling she's had all her life. Why now, why was it getting stronger.

Geraldine decided to go back to the tourist trap part time, she loved the people and it kept her up on the latest goings on in town. She was so proud of the woman Maggie had become, they had the fates against them when she was born, but they made their way, both of them with Grannys help. Geraldine sat by the window looking out over the square, her life story flashing before her.

Mamma and I have been through some tough times, but always found our way. The spirits have always been there to correct any wrong paths we have chosen. We have free will that sometimes gets in our way, when our ego rules, we almost always make the wrong decisions. Take for example my pappa, who I never knew. Mamma let her ego get the best of her. He said the things she wanted to hear, and here I am, the result of that. But spirit corrected that timeline, brought us together from another lifetime to make things right this time around. Some people don't believe what we do, that's ok, it's an individual journey we're all on. Looking back, it's been one hell of a ride.

I think I fell in love with him the very first moment I set eyes on him. He felt the same, knowing of sorts, like we had done this before. I was working at a little tourist trap shop, the kind that sold trinkets, like strands of multicolored beads, foil covered chocolates that looked like money and voodoo dolls. We made most of our yearly income during Mardi Gras season, the tourists needed something to bring home to prove they were here, we were happy to oblige.

He walked into the shop and just moseyed around, not really looking at anything in particular. Once in a while he'd pick up an item, look at it, then put it down. I watched him for a few minutes, thinking, "look at me." I longed to see his face. It was the strangest thought, almost an obsession. Before I could approach him another man asked me directions to Jackson Square, I looked away to answer him and when I turned back the mysterious man was gone. When I got home that night I told Mamma about what happened.

"Oh Geraldine, his spirit was reaching out to you. He didn't know it consciously, but his subconscious did. He'll be back, spirit doesn't give up," she laughed as she hugged me.

It took about a week, I was stocking shelves of beads when one of the boxes I was reaching for fell over while I was on the step ladder.

"Here let me help you," he said picking up the box, looking up as he handed it to me.

I felt like a wave of pure joy shot through me, it was him, his face was known to me.

"Oh, thank you," I stammered, hardly able to breath.

The ladder wobbled and I lost my footing, as we both toppled over he caught me, I will never forget the heat of his touch. The look on his face told me that he felt it also, although it confused him.

"I'm so sorry, thank you again, I can't imagine why that ladder moved, I feel like a fool," I said barely whispering, as if others were listening, but there was no one else around.

"It's no problem, really. In fact, I really don't know what brought me here today. I guess it was to save you. I'm sorry, my name is Greg," as he laughed it was music to my ears.

They talked for a while, mostly about him, he was in the military, stationed in Biloxi Mississippi. At Keesler Air Base, but grew up in Iowa. He loved coming into New Orleans, he said the city had a living spirit within it. Geraldine laughed to herself at that one, more like the dead she thought. He was in training for the next six months then would be sent to who knows where. He wanted to see the world. He had enough of farming and cold winters that's why he joined the military.

Before leaving the shop he asked Geraldine,"I come to town whenever I can grab a ride from one of my buddies, so I never know too far in advance which day. Would you have dinner with me next time I come?"

"Yes, that would be fine, sounds like fun. Here's my number, just give me a call when you know and I can meet you," she said, handing him a slip of paper.

Geraldine was on pins and needles every time the phone rang.

"Will you calm down child, he'll call, just give the spirits time," Momma said

She was right, he called two days later and they planned to meet at an outdoor cafe near Jackson Square.

Geraldine arrived early to get a good table with a view of the river. The sun was setting and it reflected off the river like shimmering diamonds. There was a gentle breeze, just enough to make the humidity bearable. She had on her multicolored floor length skirt with a matching scarf wrapped around her head. Her jet black hair, inherited from Momma, was loose down her back. The bracelets she wore made a clicking sound every time she moved her arms, which she did nervously now.

He came up behind her, after watching her from across the street for a few minutes. She looked like a gypsy woman, maybe that's the hold she had on him, a spell of sorts he thought smiling.

"Good evening, you look lovely," he said, leaning over to kiss her cheek, as if it was perfectly normal for them.

"Thank you, as do you," she giggled

"Great spot for dinner, the view is unbelievable," he said gazing out over the river.

They settled into reading the menus and small talk. This time he asked her about her life. She told him of her and Mammas many moves and journeys over the past 23 years. Theirs was a different kind of family, their roots were in the spirit world, they had a sight. If that didn't scare him off nothing would she thought. But he was intrigued, wanted to know more, he had a hunger.

The next month they grew closer. He borrowed cars from friends to get him into town more often. They spent every moment they could together. She taught him of their craft and he learned so quickly that Momma thought he'd done this in a previous life. He loved his visits with Momma, especially her Jambalaya nights! She embraced him, knowing that I loved him, but she also knew something I didn't. Our relationship would not last this lifetime.

Greg's six month schooling at Keesler was complete. His new duty station was overseas. Unfortunately it was in a battle zone in Afghanistan, at a war office for a general. He would have to leave in two weeks.

"Marry me, Gerry. Marry me now. You can join me when my deployment is up, wherever they send me," he pleaded.

"Greg, you know I love you and would follow you anywhere but marry you, it's not me. I can't be tied, it's my nature," she said sadly, "I will be here when you return, I will always be here for you, just not on paper. We are spiritually bound already."

He left with the understanding that she would join him after his deployment, they wrote letters everyday, he even got to call once or twice.

It had barely been two months since he was gone when Geraldine realized she was pregnant. After the panic lifted she was excited.

"Momma, I have news."

"I am to be a Grandmere," she said smiling at her daughter. "You forget my sight, child. I knew before you even realized it."

"Oh Momma, Greg will be so happy. He will insist I marry him now."

"Let the spirits lead, child, they know the way. Whatever is right will happen," she said, but Geraldine thought she said it with a sad voice.

Geraldine was right, as soon as Greg heard he insisted they make it legal, for their child's sake. They planned a courthouse wedding when he returned in six weeks.

Those next five weeks flew by. I was busy with baby stuff. Going into my second trimester I was feeling much better, not as tired. Momma helped me find items we needed at the local flea markets and thrift shops. We made a game of it. Asking the spirits ahead of time where to find our items. They helped guide us in the right direction, sometimes finding things we weren't even looking for. We had just finished our tea when Momma got real solemn,

"What is it Momma? Are you not feeling well?"

"I feel darkness," she said looking directly at Geraldine.

There was a knock on at the door. They both looked at each other, neither one moved. There was another knock. Geraldine knew she had to answer it, it was her darkness at the door.

It had now been two weeks since Greg's friend from Keesler knocked on the door, it still seems like yesterday. There had been a missle attack at the base Greg was stationed at. Four troops were killed. When he told her Greg was one, she fainted.

Momma had stayed by her side for the next few days, worried for her daughter and baby. Somehow she managed to pull herself together. She went about the last few days still in a fog, half expecting a letter to come from him. What did come was a letter from the military explaining that Greg had left his life insurance policy assigned to their baby. She was to notify them once the child was born and she would receive a check plus whatever survivors benefits were available.

Five months later, on November 11, 2000, during a full moon, Magdalene was born. She was beautiful, inheriting the jet black hair of her feminine lineage. Geraldine and Florence, now Grandmere, fell instantly in love. Maggie was now the center of their lives. She started to show the sight at an early age, especially with healing. She'd find injured birds or mice and bring them home to cure. Thanks to Greg's insurance policy the three of them lived comfortably. Florence still worked part time in the cafe and Geraldine worked full time at the tourist trap. They arraigned their schedules so that Maggie never had to be without one of them.

It was August 29, 2005 that their lives changed yet again. Hurricane Katrina destroyed their home. They had evacuated a week before taking with them all they could carry. They boarded a bus for the unknown along with everyone else in New Orleans. When it was over they found their way back riding with another family in their car. The old rooming house had a room for them temporarily until the insurance could pay them off. Thankfully a friend of a friend knew a family who was moving out permanently. They had enough of the storms. They owned a two bedroom condo in the Quarter. After meeting Flo and Geraldine they agreed to rent to them.

Once again they were on the mend, Flo set up her altar and crystals, consulted the spirits and made a cauldron of Jambalaya to celebrate! Maggie seemed happier in the Quarter, she fit in better. She discovered that she wanted to be a healer, nursing school was in her future.

And the future was now, she had become a caring compassionate nurse who loved her patients. The cell phone ring snapped her out of daydreaming. It was Maggie checking on them, funny how she always knew when I was thinking of her.

The past month has been a whirlwind of emotions. Martha had settled into a condo on East Bay Street. Maggie and Allison helped her with decorating. The eclectic look was actually very inviting, a touch of old and new. That had become Martha's new motto. Going from her stark surroundings to the new homey look made her smile.

A huge overstuffed sofa with a leather recliner bought from B&B Antiques faced a floor to ceiling window overlooking the bay. The coffee table was actually a huge piece of driftwood that they bought from the vendor at the Old Slaves Market. A pole lamp that looked like an octopus with eight tentacles stood in the corner, complete with different colored light bulbs. The girls were going shopping for Martha's bedroom next week.

As Martha sat in her leather chair gazing out the window over the bay her mind drifted, how she missed her Grandma Mae. She had a brand new family but somehow they couldn't take the place of Grandma. Sometime during her daydreaming she fell asleep. Her dreams took her back to the hospital where Grandma died. She was lying in the bed smiling, smiling at Jim who was standing at the bedside. They both turned their faces toward Martha. Jim smiled and Grandma winked. The sound of a boat horn woke her. Realizing the gift she had just been given she laughed, stood up, walked to the window and placed her fingers on her lips. Kissing them gently she blew the kiss at the window. Somehow she knew her kin had just crossed over and she would never see them again, except in her heart.

Marie was back at school doing very well. In fact a local architectural group had their eye on her since the showing at school. Only a few more months till graduation and she had three interviews lined up already! There also seemed to be a man in her life After three dates she brought Tim home to meet their blended family. Tim was from up north, a yankee, but they didn't hold that against him. They met at school and he already had a position at a prestigious firm after graduation.

Leona and Dora resumed their regular luncheons once a week, just not at the Charleston Grill, that was for special occasions. While Dora decided to visit her daughter in Atlanta, Leona decided it was time for spring cleaning. She would start with the library. There were so many old books and knick-knacks to go through, it would take days. Maggie had volunteered to help in between her days off and helping Martha. Allison brought over boxes from the store to pack things for donation and things to store away.

The books started piling up on the floor everywhere. How would she decide what to keep and what to donate. The local librarian had given her a list of books they could use and Leona decided to start with that, which led to the piles. It was easier to pack away the knick-knacks she called dust collectors than the books. After working for hours she made herself a cup of tea and sat in her comfy chair to drink it. She started thinking of everything that had happened in the past few months, lives changed forever. Just as she was starting to doze off there was a loud noise behind her. Startled, she jumped up spilling her tea on her lap. What the heck, she thought, looking around she saw two books had fallen off the shelf.

Wondering what would have caused it, she walked over to the shelf. She looked up thinking, maybe the other books she removed were keeping them in place. Actually, there were no other books on that shelf. Herbert's desk used to sit in front of this bookshelf before he died. She had Ronald rearrange the room after his death to make it more like a library than an office. She picked up the books and looked at them, strange. She didn't think he went in for this kind of reading. But after making their recent discovery it made sense. The Lineage of New Orleans Founders and Spirits of Our Ancestors. Why hadn't Herbert ever told her, but then she remembered how their relationship started on lies, now more lies.

As she placed the books on the coffee table, one slipped out of her hands and as it fell to the floor a note paper fell out. She picked up the paper and read it. Once again it had her grandparents names on it, just like the bank statements. Only this time there was something very different, a lineage, a lineage of different names. Getting her bearings she knew what she had to do.

CHAPTER THIRTY NINE

Granny's Story

After seeing what the spirits revealed in the past month Florence had hopes. Hopes that maybe her questions would be answered. For some reason these women together attracted the spirits that needed to cross over. Maybe just maybe her parents were waiting for her to find them. She thought back on her life as she gazed out the window at the river. The water had a flow that reminded her of a heartbeat, swish, swish, swish, almost hypnotic.

As far back as she could remember she had "the sight." At the Lafayette Foundling Home they punished her for foretelling things to come, called her evil and even possessed. If she slipped up and appeared to be using her sight, she was beaten. She learned to bury it, not speak of it, until she literally ran away and ended up living with gypsies.

She had just turned 12, but looked all of 16, tall with jet black hair and green eyes that appeared dead. They had just beaten her for the last time. Never again she vowed, never again will I be hurt. She left with the clothes on her back, she had no possessions. By the time they found her living under an overpass outside New Orleans she was half starved and had lost her fighting spirit.

"Child, who are you? Where are your kin?" one of the old gypsies asked her, shocked at what they saw.

"There's no one," she whimpered, "I'm alone."

Not wanting to scare the girl, two women sat down next to her and offered her some bread. She grabbed it hungrily and ate as if she hadn't eaten in days.

"What's your name, child?"

"They just call me, girl," she replied shyly

The old women looked at each other and decided right then she would be one of them. She told them of being brought up in a horrible foundling home. They never named her because no one would adopt a possessed child. There had been a name, but she couldn't remember it, something like Beament or Buemont. She only heard it a few times when the headmistress was talking with potential parents. The clan took her in, fed her and clothed her. She became Florence. They soon realized that she too, had the sight.They traveled from town to town in southern Louisiana, usually with carnivals. For the first time in her life she had people who cared for her.

Florence soon flourished into a beautiful young woman. Although she loved the gypsies, she didn't love moving from town to town.

"It's time Grandmere, I need to settle in one place, make a life for myself, find my people if possible."

"Yes, my Flo, you were not meant to wander. Find your place, your spirits will guild you, as they did when they brought you to us," she said sadly, knowing it was time.

The clan made sure she was settled into a rooming house in town before moving on.

She had found a job as a waitress in a small cafe on Bourbon Street. The tourist loved saying they ate there, just for the cafe name, The Cafe de Bourbon Spirit. It had a funky voodoo vibe to it, the walls were painted a deep purple and green with day glow paint that sparkled under the black lights. There were beads of all kinds from past parades hanging from the ceiling and lights. Incense burned from opening to closing, blending in with the smells of hot Cajun food that made your eyes water at times, but the people loved it. They had a big local following, especially on tuesdays. The special was Jambalaya and crusty French bread and once it was gone, that was it. Some days there were lines for lunch outside the door.

Florence settled in nicely, she loved her job. On her off nights she went down the street to a club called Bayou Blues where she'd listen to the soulful sounds of the horn instruments. They called to her, at times their voices very distinct. The club was on the corner of St Louis St and Dauphine Street. It usually was only frequented by locals who would play for free just to showcase their talent.

It was one such night, as she was walking in the door she heard, "He's the one with the answers," Not one to question the spirits she sat down and ordered a drink. As the evening went by she realized that she wasn't sure who "He" was. She listened to two sets of soulful music, falling under the spell of the horn that she had learned to love. Then they introduced a newcomer, it was his first time playing there. Her ears perked up, waiting. Then he played the most sad music she ever heard. It brought tears to her eyes. The horn moaned as if alive, she felt every note he played. By the time he was done she realized she was crying. The crowd went crazy and rushed the small one step up platform to congratulate him. She couldn't bear the sorrow and had to leave. Whatever that man's soul was carrying, it was painful to her.

She didn't go back to Bayou Blues for a few months, fearful that she would see that man and absorb his pain. Instead, she found a new little dive, closer to home. There she met Roberto, he was swave and good looking. He knew all the right things to say to make her feel wanted. Their relationship got serious just after three weeks. She was sure she was in love. Somehow they always ended up at her place, his excuse was too many roommates at his. Eventually he just moved in. They worked different shifts so she wasn't sure what he did during the day, other than sleep. His caliber of friends should have warned her but she was too much in love.

"Baby, I might have to go out of town for a while, it's business, probably a week or so," he told her one morning as she made breakfast.

"What? why? I thought you worked at the hotel?" she said questionly

"It's just a thing, you know. I told you about that guy, my friend, gotta help him," he said unconvincingly.

He was gone a month later, he took all her savings she had hidden in her freezer and left her pregnant. As it turned out, he never worked at the hotel. It was all a lie. She vowed never to trust a man again.

She was devastated, her world fell apart. Why had her spirits failed her, why didn't they warn her. Then she realized, they did tell me! "He's the one with the answers."

She knew she had to go back to Bayou Blues. It took another month before returning. With trepidation she walked in holding her breath. Please, spirits, help me to know what to say to him. Please let him be here, she thought. No longer drinking alcohol she ordered a sweet tea and sat in the corner, waiting. The horns didn't fail her, they took her to a place of peace. She closed her eyes and floated into their notes, feeling relief for the first time in weeks.

"Excuse me, may I sit?" It was him, the "He"

She looked up to see him. Although he looked vaguely familiar she did not know him. It was strange, the harder she focused on his face the more the sunlight coming in the window behind him blocked her view of him.

"Yes, of course, sure," she stammered.

He sat down across from her, the sun forming a ring of light around his head. She shifted her gaze to his chest so not to stare. They sat listening to the music for a few minutes. She waited, knowing her spirits were at work.

"You're searching," he said, not looking directly at her.

"I am," she barely whispered.

Once again they sat for a few more minutes in silence, absorbing the music, closing her eyes, letting it relax her. She barely heard his next comment through the music, something about a last name, but she distinctly heard Geraldine!

"Your last name is Beaumont, but your blood is another name. I can only answer that one question for you now. But in time your blood name will be revealed. Name your child Geraldine for her grandmere."

Her eyes snapped open and she was alone. She searched around her, stood and walked to the door, looking. But he was nowhere! Had she imagined it, dreamt it. No, she knew the spirits sent him. He came with the music, lived on the notes, and was gone just as the song ended. She had a clue. Beaumont, did she hear right. it sounded like that,it made sense, the name she thought she heard as a child sounded just like that. What a wonderful name, but there were many of them. It was a popular last name in Louisiana, where did she start.

As the months rolled by she prepared for her baby. She knew it was a girl, she trusted the spirit that told her. A retired nurse, Sarah, lived just below her in the rooming house. She was the happiest person Flo had ever met. Her eyes sparkled when she smiled. She actually reminded Flo of what a grandma would look like,short and plump with a crown of short gray hair. Sarah watched over Flo's pregnancy making sure she got her vitamins and ate properly. She also volunteered to babysit after the child was born so Flo could continue working. Florence was not one to just take. She made sure that she brought food home from the cafe for Sarah after each shift. Their friendship grew as Flos' belly did.

Florence found many Beaumont families but none of them seemed to have a missing child. Strange thought Flo, someone must know something. How did she end up in that home without a trace. She thought about going back and questioning them. But it had closed a few years back after the state received numerous complaints of child abuse. She sent a letter to the state inquiring about the files from Lafayette but hadn't heard back at all.

The baby came into the world just as silently as she was conceived. Flo hardly had time to call Sarah and she was born. The spirits had given her a good child. She named her Geraldine Beaumont, for her grandmother that neither knew. When the baby looked at Flo her eyes sparkled green as if she already knew her mother in another lifetime. Sarah noticed it first. Your child is special, she would say every time she saw her, Florence agreed.

They grew up together, Flo liked to think, never having a childhood. She experienced all the fun things with Geraldine and never squashed her personality. There was so much to discover. They became sisters in spirit. Sarah had helped raise Geraldine and became a surrogate mother when Flo, who had no knowledge to fall back on raising a child, needed her. The three of them were happy, until one evening when Geraldine was ten, Sarah died of a heart attack. Once again Florence's life was turned upside down.

The two of them buried Sarah. They mourned their loss, but celebrated that they were able to share in her life. Two weeks after the funeral a letter arrived from an attorney. Flo and Geraldine sat at the table scared to open it, thinking it was information about the foundling home.

Geraldine handed the letter to her Mamma saying, "It's ok Mamma, it's good news, Sarah has sent us a message."

Flo looked at her daughter, she had the sight. Oh praise the Goddesses, she thought. They opened it together. It was in fact a message from Sarah. She had left them both her life saving since she had no family. It was enough to buy the house in the Ninth Ward.

Florence and Geraldine bought the house on St Claude Avenue three months later and moved in. The first thing she did was make an altar to the spirits in the living room, thanking them for all the blessings they had sent. From that moment on Florence consulted her spirits for everything. She tried to teach Geraldine, but she was too interested in having fun. It was then that Florence became known to the neighborhood as Granny, the one with the evil eye.

Now that they were settled yet again, Flo started her search for her Beaumont roots. She always felt something more was missing, a part of her.The closest she came to finding kin was a couple who had died in 1952 in a horrible train wreck. She knew that she was born in 1950. They were named Jonathan and Geraldine Beaulieus. She had gotten so excited, finally, her mother! The names weren't the same but close enough. But sadly there was no record of them having children. How could this be, her name was Geraldine. There had to be a connection, she would find it, someday.

Maybe that someday was getting closer. She still felt there was a connection in Charleston. There was a special feeling there, like home..

CHAPTER FORTY

A Day Off

Maggie sat at the table in the break room. She noticed all the gray metal lockers that lined the walls. Some had pictures taped to the front of their kids, others had stickers of all kinds. She wondered what she'd find if she opened each one. The personality of each nurse was inside with their prized possessions needed for work. Each locker represented that person. Were we like a locker? Hiding away our most prized possessions?

"Hello? Earth to Maggie…."

"Gosh, I'm sorry, I didn't hear you come in, I guess I was daydreaming again."

"Not getting enough sleep lately?" Ally asked with her usual one eyebrow cocked up.

"I guess the extra shifts are catching up to me. By three o'clock I feel like I hit the wall, I could use a day of doing nothing!" she smiled.

Ally sat down next to her and sipped her coffee, she too had worked extra lately.

As both girls zoned out for a minute the door opened and a nurse's aid burst through.She was all excited, the man in room 1106 had just woken up! He was actually talking. The girls looked at each other and jumped up.

"Blessed be, I hope he doesn't have any memory of what happened," Maggie muttered to herself. He had been mugged in a small town miles from Charleston and air lifted here for care. They really knew nothing about him, in fact he was admitted as a John Doe, unconscious with no identification.

The hallway around room 1106 was busy with people going in and out, doctors of all sorts barking out orders, nurses making sure those orders were followed. Neither Ally or Maggie had been assigned him as a patient today so they stayed to the side. In the past few weeks that he had been in their unit they had taken care of him a few times. It was sad to see such a handsome man lying there bandages with tubes everywhere to keep him alive. Thankfully he was not on a ventilator, but the feeding tubes, IV tubes and urinary tubes were still a sight. As they watched an orderly whisked a gurney into the room, off to CT unit one nurse said walking out of the room.

"What happened?" Ally asked her as she walked by.

"It was the weirdest thing. I was straightening the room, getting ready to change his dressings. I always hum while I work on a patient that I can't talk to. Anyway, I was humming this really sad jazz number I heard, it just stuck in my head for some reason."

"Yes, yes, what happened?" Maggie interrupted impatiently.

The nurse looked at Maggie with a hard stare then continued,

"The sun shone right through the window on his face as I turned to remove the bandage and he opened his eyes. Oh, they are so blue, like deep pools of water I could fall into!" once again going off the rails with the story thought Maggie who held her tongue this time.

"Anyway, he just said 'Hi,' I said 'Hi,' then I realized he spoke! I'm afraid my bedside manner got a little excited. I hit the call bell for help and everyone came running."

"Did he answer any questions when the doctors got there," Ally asked

The nurse went on to explain in between her gushing about his blue eyes that he indeed did answer questions. He didn't remember what happened. Maggie gave a silent prayer of thanks, although now they couldn't catch the people that did this. But the other strange thing was he didn't remember his name, complete amnesia!

The girls all returned to their other patients, happy for the handsome blue eyed man. Only time would tell on his recovery. Maggie stopped into Shamus's room and sat with him for a moment, she told him of the man in 1106 waking up,

"I know you're in there, you can do it, too. It's just taking time, don't worry we're here for you. When you're ready the spirits will help you come back to us."

She went on to tell him about Martha and her windfall, how exciting it was to finally solve that mystery. Maybe one day he could write a story about her, if he ever woke up. The remainder of the shift was thankfully quiet, oops, never ever ever use that word if you're a nurse, it attracts all hell to break loose.

With their twelve hour shift over, Maggie and Ally decided to walk home together. The evening was beautiful and the air felt good, even if there was a hint of humidity. They talked about their next outing which they both needed.

"How about exploring the other side of the Ashley River, didn't Herbert's family own a plantation there once?" Ally asked.

"He did, but by now it's probably fifteen different housing developments. But we can drive that way, it will give us something different to do."

When they got to the corner deli they parted ways. Ally went towards King Street as Maggie continued down Rutledge. There was something gnawing at Maggie about the handsome blue eyed man, she couldn't put her finger on it. She wondered why he responded to the sad jazz song, it reminded her of Grannys story.

Maggie woke the following morning stretching, not wanting to leave her warm comfortable bed. She thought of today's adventure with Allison. West Ashley was a part of town she hadn't been to, visiting old Plantation homes should be fun, as long as no spirits hitchhiked back home with them, she thought smiling. She showered, dressed and made her way down to the kitchen. The smell of fresh coffee had a way of drawing her in. Marie was already sitting at the table, she had an interview today with an architecture company. Dressed in a sleeveless pale blue dress, she looked cool as a cucumber. But Maggie could see she was nervous,

"Good morning, don't you look pretty, big day, ya."

"Oh Maggie, I'm so nervous, I really want this job."

"I'm sure you'll nail it, your work is awesome. Try to imagine the people with no clothes on," she laughed.

"My luck I'll get a big old fat man and laugh at him," she said giggling

Marie finished her coffee, hugged Maggie for luck and headed out the door.

There was a car horn beep outside the alley back door. Maggie grabbed her sweater and ran out. Dressed in jeans and a tee shirt was fine for the sun, but walking on the plantation grounds in the shade of the trees could get chilly. As Ally maneuvered through traffic Maggie asked where there first stop was,

"I thought we would head to Magnolia Plantation, it's one of the oldest and largest I think," Ally said while checking her mirror to switch lanes.

"Sounds good to me. Any word from work on that John Doe?" Maggie asked

"I haven't heard anything more. They will be keeping him until he's more stabilized I guess, he still has a ways to go."

They rode in silence the rest of the way, which was only another thirty minutes or so.

As they approached the entrance Ally slowed. It was stunning. The landscaping and out buildings made you feel like you were back in time. They parked the car and got their first glimpse of the house. How magnificent it stood with its many white columns and wrap around porches spanning the second floor. They joined a tour group and followed a period dressed woman explaining the history of Dayton Hall. When the inside tour was finished the woman encouraged the group to do a self tour of the grounds, but watch out for our resident spirits she chuckled as she walked away. Maggie and Ally looked at each other,

"I was afraid of that," Ally said.

"Me too!" Maggie said laughing.

Their morning quickly went by with sightseeing on the grounds and thankfully no spirits approached them. Heading north on Ashley River Road they came to their next stop,

Middleton Place. This plantation was different then the first. The original house had been destroyed during the war of northern aggression. What was left standing was a modest brick home later used by the family after their return. The grounds and gardens, which were over two hundred years old, were lovingly preserved by the family over the centuries. They were again encouraged to wander the gardens, which they did. Maggie saw him first, an old black groundskeeper. He was kneeling in a bed of yellow rose bushes weeding.

"Excuse me, sir, may I ask you a question."

Looking up, the old man's wrinkled face smiled, "Why yes you may. What can I help you with, Missy, my name is Leroy?"

"I was wondering if you ever heard of the Harrington Plantation?" she said, crossing her fingers behind her back.

The old man grabbed his rake and pulled himself up. Standing in front of her he was taller then she would have thought.

"Now that's a name I haven't heard in a good long time," he looked at Maggie and Ally with a questionable stare. "Are you kin?"

Maggie didn't want to go into the whole story about the family so she just explained that a family friend had said they might find another plantation to tour that day. He seemed satisfied with that answer and went on with his story,

"Round about the eighteen fifties, there was a family who were named Harrington that owned land out here. But the war destroyed the family home and from what I learned from my grandpappy it just about destroyed the family also. Anyways, the land was divided up and sold between the neighboring owners, the Middletons and Magnolia in 1875. Some of what used to be Harrington's land is right here," he pointed all around him.

"Your grandad knew these people?" Maggie asked.

"He didn't, but his daddy did. His stories would go on for hours," he chuckled.

The girls thanked him for his story of the Harrington's, shook his hand and decided to wander down near the old rice fields.

"Y'all be careful down there. There's some old slave spirits that come out in the early evening, y'all hear them singing them old spiritual songs," he laughed and walked away.

"What's with all these warnings of spirits, do we look like we need warning?" Ally said.

With that they both looked at each other and burst out laughing,

"It takes one to know one I guess," Maggie said as they walked down the path.

They finished their self guided tour just as the evening spirits would have come out. Laughing, they walked back towards the car. A parking attendant had just parked one of the plantation vehicles when the girls approached,

"Did you ladies enjoy our gardens today, it sure was a good day to visit," he asked.

"Yes, it's so beautiful, so much care. We especially enjoyed talking with your groundskeeper Mr. Leroy."

The attendant got a startled look on his face, "You talked to who?"

"Leroy, nice old black man, infectious smile," Maggie said.

"Ladies, I'm afraid we have no one on staff named Leroy at this time. But…."

"Oh no, don't tell me, he's a spirit!" Ally moaned.

Joe, that was the attendants name, told them about Leroy, "He did work here, but has been dead for over what they think is a hundred years now. While doing some reconstruction work out in the lower garden they found a grave marker that simply read 'Leroy, who loved this garden, may he Rest In Peace'. We believe he must have lived and worked here as a servant back then. Funny he only appears every now and then, usually to people that have a connection to the old Harrington family. Do you ladies happen to know any Harrington's?"

Maggie and Ally fell into such a fit of laughter that he probably thought them crazy. They told him the only Harrington they knew of was the Doctor from the Medical University. Then quickly thanked him and left.

Since it was close to dinner time they decided to stop and eat. A few of their coworkers had raved about a barbecue place right on Route 17, called Bessingers. They thought they'd give it a try. Pulling into the parking lot they noted that there were a lot of people who seemed to like this place, it was packed. Standing in line the smell of BBQ was making their mouth water,

"I didn't realize how hungry I was," Maggie said.

"Me either, gosh it smells like hog heaven," they both laughed at the pun.

The food didn't disappoint, it was so good they got a sandwich to go for a snack later.

"We'll have to come another day for lunch and bring the gang." Ally laughed.

CHAPTER FORTY ONE

Preparations

Leona knew what she had to do. But it would take a slew of private detectives digging to find the answers and she didn't have time for that. The only way to get her answers was to bring the dead back to life! A spirit seance, that would be the fastest way to get s answers. But would the others agree. They all had the sight, Maggie's family especially. She would need them all here. Flo and Geraldine had just gone back home a few weeks ago, would they come back for her wild goose chase? There was only one way to find out. Ask them, ask them all!

Maggie and Allison came home first, laughing as they walked through the door.

"Well, girls you look like you've had a good day off. By the way, Ally, you have some sauce on your chin," Leona giggled.

The girls told her everything of their day, the spirit Leroy and the best part about locating the old Harrington land. They thought Leonia would be happy with that news but she seemed preoccupied with her thoughts.

"Is everything all right, Leona? You seem a little distracted?" Maggie asked concerned

"Oh, yes, fine, just fine. But I need to have a meeting with everyone. I have found some information I need to share. Can you help me get everyone together for maybe this weekend? I will need your mom and grandma here also, Maggie."

"Geez, Leona, are you going to make us wait till then? I mean it will drive us nuts. It's only tuesday. What am I supposed to tell my family to get them to come back?" Maggie said, sounding upset.

"Tell them I need to bring the dead back to life, a seance!"

With that she walked away leaving Maggie and Ally standing in the hallway with their mouths wide open.

Accepting the fact that Leona wasn't going to say another word about this weekend was no easy task. Every time she saw her, Maggie wanted to give her the third degree. Explaining this to her family was a bit different. Just the statement of bringing back the dead had Granny on board. It only took the word seance to convince Geraldine. They agreed to fly in on Friday afternoon. Maggie was working so Leona said she would pick them up.

Thank goodness Marie had news that distracted them. Her interview had gone well and she was keeping her fingers crossed that the job was hers. It only took two days when she heard.

"I got it, oh my goodness, I got it," Marie said yelling, hanging up her cell phone.

Leona and Maggie had been sitting in the kitchen when she came in with the news.

After hugging them both she sat down,

"Can you believe it, my first professional job!"

"I am so proud of you, your father would have been also," Leona said with tears in her eyes.

They decided to celebrate, dinner out, just the three of them. In fact, Leona was so proud that she phoned up the Charleston Grill and made reservations,

"There's nothing too good for my granddaughter!" She smiled as they all went to get dressed.

CHAPTER FORTY TWO

The Handsome, Blue Eyed Man

As Granny and Geraldine prepared to fly to Charleston, Maggie was busy at work, thankfully, keeping her mind off what was coming this weekend. The day had started off the same as any other work day, meeting Allison at the deli, coffee, cinnamon bun and onto The Tower. The girls discussed the upcoming seance and what they expected Leona might be revealing.

"I still can't believe this is all happening, it must be something bad, bringing your family back so soon and all," Ally said.

"I know, it worries me, Leona has been so solemn about the whole thing."

They made their way to the step down unit where they worked, they finished their coffee in the break room as they put away their purses in their lockers.

Maggie's assignment today included the man in room 1106, John Doe. She was anxious to see what progress he had made in the last week. She entered the room introducing herself.

"Good morning, my name is Maggie. I'll be your nurse today, how was your night?"

The man just looked at her, a strange glaze came over his eyes.

"Are you ok, sir?" she said, as she was assessing his mental responses, finding him to be in no distress she allowed him time to respond

"Magdalene?" he said slowly and deliberately.

Maggie had to find a chair before her legs gave out. What the heck, she thought.

"Why, yes, but people here call me Maggie," she said, trying to sound in control of her whits.

There seemed to be a stalemate. He didn't speak and neither did Maggie. Both waiting for the other to respond. Maggie went about straightening the room and the bed linens.

When she got to his pillow he looked her directly in the eyes and said, "You're a Beaulieus, your great grandmother was Geraldine. This message is for you. Let the others know tomorrow," with that his eyes fluttered and he passed out."

Maggie hit the code button on the wall. Within seconds doctors, residents and other ancillary departments were at the bedside with her. After twenty minutes the doctor called it, time of death 11:11. Maggie was stunned. He seemed fine, had just spoken to her, she informed the doctor who was questioning her about the patient. Could she be mistaken? he asked.

"Mistaken, how could I mistake someone talking to me?" she answered rather indignantly.

"Maggie, please sit," the doctor said pointing to the chair. "This man has been in a coma since they brought him here. The severe beating he took to his head probably killed him."

"But he woke up, the other day. I was here," she questioned.

"He did, but that was only for those few minutes. It was his last ditch effort to stay alive I believe."

Maggie never repeated her conversation with John Doe with any of the people at the hospital. They looked at her with sadness, imagining her thinking she had spoken to him. Ally, who was working another hallway rushed to Maggie's side.

"Mags, are you ok? I heard John Doe just passed."

"We need to talk, but not here, lunch, outside, in the courtyard," she said and walked down the hallway, leaving Ally standing there totally bewildered.

Lunch couldn't come soon enough for both Maggie and Allison. They met up in the elevator and rode down to the first floor. Exiting, Ally headed toward the cafeteria as Maggie grabbed her arm.

"No time for food now, we have to talk," she said, pulling her towards the door to the courtyard.

"Geeze, Mags, I've never seen you this agitated, spill."

They sat down on a cold concrete wall, far from any other people. Maggie looked around as if she was checking to see if someone was listening. When she was satisfied she told Ally the details of her morning.

Finishing she asked, "Am I crazy, I can't be, I've heard those names before, or at least similar ones."

"First off, you're not crazy. That message came to you the day before this big shindig Leona is planning. It must be related somehow. You need to write down exactly what you heard," Ally said.

Maggie explained that she did just that the minute the doctor stopped questioning her and she could be alone. She showed Ally the paper,

"Maggie are you sure you got this right?" she asked.

"Yes, every detail, I could never forget those eyes."

"But your name is Beaumont not Beaulieus," Ally stated, looking at Maggie questionably.

Maggie knew she got the name right. She knew because he spelled it out in unspoken words, just as other spirits had done, with mental telepathy. Sitting on the concrete wall for another twenty minutes helped sort some things out, but then stirred more questions. The girls still had six hours of work left before they could continue their conversation. Agreeing to meet at the time clock after work they headed back to their unit.

Maggie and Allison couldn't walk fast enough to the house on Rutledge! Maggie had suggested that Allison come home with her to help explain what happened today. When they walked in the alley back door they found everyone around the kitchen table, Leona, Granny, Geraldine and Marie laughing. The mood wasn't as somber as it had been for the past few days. Leonia loved spending time with Granny, it lightened her mood. The girls made themselves a sandwich, got a beer and sat down with their friends. Ally explained that they missed lunch and were famished, while looking at Maggie for some clue what to say next.

"One of these days you guys are going to have to teach me this secret eye language you all have, Maggie. You and Allison are doing it again," Marie stated

They all looked at Marie and started laughing, "Oh, Marie, it will come naturally to you I promise, the older and wiser you become," Leona said, still smiling but looking at Maggie. "Ok, what's up? I could see it in your eyes the minute you came through that door."

Maggie took a deep breath and retold her story of John Doe, the handsome blue eyed man. She took a curled up paper from her uniform pocket and laid it on the table.

Looking directly at Granny she asked, "What is our last name?"

After hearing Maggie's story she was starting to wonder herself. She explained to them all, "I had no name when the gypsies found me. I was just called "girl" at the home. They were frightened of my sight, so I squashed it, but they still hated me. When a spirit appeared to me many years later, it was in a jazz club, very sad music was playing, he told me my name, I might have misunderstood, I don't know."

"In a jazz club?" Maggie blurted out "Ally, remember when John Doe woke up the first time? The nurse said she was humming an old sad jazz tune! I knew there was something that bugged me about that," She continued, "Granny, you told me that story many times, maybe this was the same spirit, trying to get it right this time."

Granny jumped up from her chair, so excited she couldn't speak, just repeating oh my god, oh my god, over and over. Leona and Geraldine tried to calm her down,

"Mamma, what is it, tell us."

"When I was researching years ago I came across Jonathan and Geraldine Beaulieus! They died in 1952 in a train wreck, but there is no link to any children. This has to be them, my parents. My spirit told me to name you Geraldine and now Maggie's spirit said her great grandmother was Geraldine. This can't be a coincidence," she said looking from one to another.

After a great amount of discussion they all agreed that Leona's seance tomorrow would hopefully answer their questions. They decided to each write down a question or two for the seance, just to make sure they covered all their bases.

Maggie started off reading her question. It was simple and direct, what's my real last name? Granny asked who her parents were? Leona wanted to know why she felt something or someone was missing all her life. And why did her grandparents never tell her of her parents? Geraldine wanted to know if Greg was ok, did he think about us? Marie's was did my parents really love each other? And finally, Allison wanted to know who the heck Mr Calhoun was? She laughingly asked, not really having a spirit led question.

CHAPTER FORTY THREE

Seance

Saturday morning couldn't come fast enough. Maggie and Leona were up by six a.m. drinking coffee in the kitchen. Granny wandered in wearing her fluffy slippers and robe thirty minutes later looking for coffee. She poured herself a cup and sat down.

Looking at the others she said, "Anxious ladies?"

Maggie just shook her head, yes. Leona mumbled something like, it can't come soon enough. Marie stumbled in. Seeing the coffee pot was almost empty she made a fresh pot and sat down.

"What time is this happening?" Marie asked

"Romona will be here about ten. Who wants to shower first?"

The ladies discussed who would shower first as they finished their coffee.There were two bathrooms but the water pressure in this old house left a lot to be desired. Marie cleaned up the kitchen as the others went on their way. Leona asked Geraldine to help her set up the dining room table as Granny showered.

"I have a pretty lace table cloth in the buffet, second drawer down," Leona said

They spread out the white table cloth and Leona brought over a few candlesticks from the buffet top. Geraldine brought some chairs in from the kitchen to make sure they had enough, counting on her fingers as she called out their names. Stepping back they looked at the table. Everything was in place, now they just had to wait.

The doorbell rang at 10:45 and Maggie opened the door to see a smiling Allison, "Good morning, are you ready for this Mags?"

"Yup, should be interesting, that's for sure," she said, closing the door behind her.

The ladies were all sitting in the drawing room when the doorbell rang next. Nearly jumping out of her skin Leona got up.

"It's go time ladies" she said as she walked into the foyer.

Romona walked into the house, or Maggie thought, floated into the house. Her movements were so fluid you couldn't tell she was walking, just moving. Her hair was a bright red falling on her shoulders in ringlets. Her kimono type dress made up of swirls of different shades of green was accentuated by her hair color. When she introduced herself to Leona her voice had a sing-song sound, almost like she could break out in a musical tune at any time.

Smiling, she faced the others, "Good morning ladies, are you ready for some fun?"

They all moved into the drawing room and found a seat. Romona instructed them to make sure their cell phones were turned off and out of the room. She didn't want any outside interference or influences. They settled in and waited for her to unpack her toys, as she called them. She lit the sage and walked around the room, corner to corner waving the smoke in all directions. Placing a grid on the table she laid out her crystals carefully then took out her Oracle cards. Looking up she took a deep breath.

"Angels of the light, we ask your protection. Cover us with light, do not allow the darkness in. We are your children in search of answers, Grace us with your presence if it is your will, Blessed Be," she closed her eyes and rested her hands on the table. "I will take your written questions now if you like."

No one moved, Romona looked at Maggie as she handed her the paper. No one breathed. Romona read it to the spirits, closed her eyes and waited.

"I can tell you it is not what you think" Romona said, "but it's not the other either."

Maggie was even more confused, "That makes no sense, which one is it?"

Romona explained, that was the answer the spirits gave, she knew no more.

Looking now at Granny, she reached for her paper, read it to the spirits, closed her eyes and waited.

"Your spiritual parents were the gypsies. They saved you, loved you as their daughter. The man and woman who made you were only here a short while. They are coming to reveal themselves, but not today."

Granny nodded, accepting the inevitable, she had waited this long.

Turning now to Marie, "Your parents were deeply in love, you are a result of that love. They found each other out of loneliness and were separated out of hate. They are eternally bonded together now and are standing besides you always."

Marie had been holding her paper out for Romona, "You never read my paper, how did you know?"

Romona explained that her parents' love for their daughter was so strong that they came through with the mention of her name. "You are very blessed, child."

Marie and Leona had tears running down their cheeks as they looked at each other, Marie thinking of her parents and Leona thinking of her son.

Geraldine held out her paper before being asked, she could wait no longer.

Romona read it to the spirits, closed her eyes and waited. "Your Greg is standing behind you, his hand is on your shoulder. His only regret is not marrying you and seeing his daughter grow up. He says he knew you before and will find you again."

Geraldine touched her shoulder as if she could feel him, and smiled at Maggie.

Romona looked at Leona, "Please, your paper."

Leona passed her paper to her holding her breath. Romona read it to the spirits, closed her eyes and waited.

"Your answers are coming in a package yet to be revealed. There is a letter, that is the answer to what you're missing."

Before anyone could say anything else, Romona turned to Allison, "Your Mr Calhoun thanks you for remembering him, he is delighted. Please tell your parents that he watches over their shop, it was once his."

She explained that his spirit came through without being asked because he had helped them recently with another problem.

Romona bowed her head and thanked the spirits for their help, asking them to watch over this house and all who sat at this table. As she rose to leave the candles that had been burning on the table blew out with a gentle breeze that filled the room.

It was as if they couldn't wait for Romona to leave, they had so much to discuss.

Thanking her for her spiritual insights they all gave her a hug and she floated out just as she had floated in.

Maggie was the first to have a say in her answer, "I'm more confused now, how can neither name be right?" Looking at Granny she asked, "How many names can we have, first you have none, now we have three?"

Granny and Leona both voiced their opinions, all will be revealed was really what Romona had said on their questions.

"We must be patient, I feel it's closer now," Granny said.

Marie and Geraldine both got the answers they had longed for. They were loved and missed. Both knew they weren't alone in this world, their loved ones would always be with them. Allison laughed when she thought of Mr Calhoun and couldn't wait to tell her parents.

The ladies decided tea and biscuits were in order. Marie and Allison set out to the kitchen to put the kettle on and gather some biscuits and cookies. Geraldine and Maggie headed towards the drawing room with their heads together laughing. Leona asked Granny to stay with her in the dining room for a moment.

"I have a letter, Romona was right, I need you to tell me if I should share it."

Granny looked at her strangely, "Is this letter why we are all here?"

"Yes" she said meekly, "I needed you all, I thought a seance would answer all our questions. But yet again, it left us with more questions," she sighed.

Granny smiled and hugged her, letting her know that whenever she needed them they would be there.

"We might not be blood but we have become family! Let's go join the others and you can tell us all about the letter."

The ladies headed into the drawing room where the others had just poured their tea.

Leona begged their pardon, she had something to tell them. Yes another puzzle piece that maybe with all of their heads together they could figure out where it fit. She told them about donating some of the books to the local library. And that While she was going through the books that had piled up on the floor, some books fell off the shelf. As she showed them the genealogy titles a few eyebrows raised.

"Have those books been there this whole time? Why would they just fall off?" asked Marie.

Leona went on to explain about Herbert's desk being right under that book shelf before she had Ronald rearrange the room.

"It seems our marriage that started off with secrets, had many more lurking in the background" she continued her story. "When I went to pick up the books this letter fell out." Holding up the letter she said, "This is why you're all here, I thought a seance would end all our questions."

"Well, are you going to read?" asked Geraldine.

Leona opened the envelope and removed the yellowed paper, "Dear Doctor Harrington," she looked around to see their surprised faces, not expecting the letter to be addressed to him. Continuing on she read, "Our investigation has had many twists and turns. It seems your wife's family has buried much information quite well. What we can tell you at this juncture is that your wife, Leona, had a twin sister Lucinda." There were gasps from them all. She didn't dare look at them for fear of not being able to finish the letter. "This information comes to us by word of mouth. A kindly old woman who lived near Leona's grandparents volunteered this information. We need to verify it so we can move on to find her parents for you. We have a few leads that I will be forwarding to you in the weeks to come. I pray this gift you are giving to your wife will end in joy not sorrow. Adam Barstow, Lead Investigator, Barstow Detective Agency"

Leona looked up holding her breath. Tt had only taken seconds and they were all around her, hugging and crying! There were a multitude of questions from each one of them, all wondering who and where the heck Lucinda was!

Granny whispered in her ear, "you're halfway there, now you know what you were missing, it was a who, Lucinda!"

"Leona, when was that letter sent?" asked Maggie.

"Two weeks before Herbert's death. I believe he was trying to surprise me. I had told him so many times of how I wished I knew my parents. My grandparents never spoke of them. All I ever got when I asked was, terrible tragedy, you don't need to live in the past. I never knew any other relatives so I assumed I was an only child."

"Well you're not! And we're going to find Lucinda!" Granny said sternly, "after all we have the internet now. I bet we can even do one of those DNA tests!"

"That's a great idea, Mom, there are all sorts of links to those," Geraldine chimed in.

It was decided right then and there, their mission was to find Lucinda. Maggie was going online to order a DNA test kit. Allison volunteered to visit Martha at the courthouse to see if there was anything under her name there. Geraldine and Granny were flying home the following day but promised to search on the internet once they got home. Marie had started her new job so she could only help once the others had some clues to follow. Leona just sat back and listened to her family and friends, thinking how blessed she was.

CHAPTER FORTY FOUR

New Orleans

It had been a long weekend. Getting back from Charleston late they decided to pick up take out food for dinner. The corner BBQ joint was the closest, its awning of red and white checkered material had matched the table cloths inside. It was an old building but clean and smelled of delicious food. The owner made a point to come speak with them. He had known them since they moved in after Katrina.

"I was wondering, my wife, she is suffering from bad headaches, the doctor says it's stress, the business and all. You have told us of herbs before that helped her legs, maybe you know one for headache?" Nickoli said with a Cajun accent.

"Of course, I will be happy to bring you a herbal tea mixture that should help. Will tomorrow afternoon be alright?" asked Granny.

They agreed on meeting at three o'clock after the lunch rush was over. Saying their goodbyes, they took their order and headed home.They loved visiting Maggie and the others but it was always good to be home. After dinner Granny and Geraldine went on with their nightly rituals before turning in. While Granny was gathering her herbs for the morning she thought, I wonder if there is a connection with our families.

Dared she dream that she was Lucinda. That would be too easy, they had never found any paper trail in that direction. I guess all southern names tend to sound the same.

Monday brought a rainy dreary morning. Looking out over the street, it was empty. Tourists tend to stay inside on days like this. The riverboat horn sounded its boarding call for all passengers willing to brave the rain. Geraldine daydreamed about Greg again, since the seance he had been on her mind. I wonder what life would have looked like if he lived, the places they would have traveled to in the military. She missed him more than ever now, even though it was way over twenty years ago. She could almost feel his presence. Closing her eyes she heard in a faint whisper, *"no time exists with love"*. She knew it was him. Thanking him silently, she said I love you in a whisper and turned from the window. She had decided to stop by the Tourist Trap where she worked. They didn't know exactly when she'd be home so she wasn't scheduled to work until Wednesday. Dressing in her raincoat and favorite yellow galoshes she checked with Granny before going out the door,

"Mom, I'm running over to the shop. Do you need anything?"

Granny came out of her room also dressed to go out. She pointed at Geraldine and they both laughed, "I guess great minds think alike. I'm running over to the herb shop. I ran out of camomile and lavender that I need for Nickoli's wife," she said as they walked out together.

"I have had a craving for a muffuletta sandwich, if I pick one up for lunch will you eat half?" Geraldine asked.

"Absolutely, sounds good, see ya then," she said over her shoulder as she went the opposite way of Geraldine.

Granny walked along Dubois Street as a slight drizzle of rain continued. The stores were just opening, owners were sweeping away standing puddles in front of their doors. The cobblestone streets tended to hold water rather than drain it. Every now and then she could smell the fresh brewed chicory coffee from the nearby cafes.

The Oily Herb Lady's owner, Eleanor had just put her "Open" sign out.

"Good morning Miss Florence, it's good to see you on this day. Mother Earth is getting her nourishment today, may She feed us well." she said as she held the door open.

"Yes, Eleanor, may She feed us well."

"It's been awhile. How may I and the spirits assist you?" she said, smiling.

Flo explained what she was looking for now. In addition she decided to replenish her herb cabinet. After taking a sweet grass basket to hold her herbs, they wandered up and down the small shops aisles together. They discussed the herbs and essential oils that had new blends. Eleanor suggested a cup of herbal tea after Flo made her purchase. They sat down at a white wrought iron table for two, tea cups painted with beautiful flowers held the tea.

"You've heard from the spirits, I see it in your aura," Eleanor said, more of a statement than a question.

"Yes, Charleston, but as usual they present me with more questions than answers."

"Ya, that is their way. They want you to find your answers, it is within you to see."

Elleanor had reminded her of the old gypsies, her advice always brought back memories of growing up. They finished their tea and conversation, but there was one more thing that needed to be done. Before leaving her shop, Elleanor would gaze at your palm. Flo held out her hand, Eleanor took it and turned the palm up. Gently tracing the palm with her index finger she looked up at Flo.

"A letter, your answer is in a letter," she winked, turned and walked away.

Florence walked out of the shop thinking, letter? Did that mean Leonias letter? Could that be the answer? Or, was there another letter? Geez, more questions. She daydreamed as she walked. Not paying attention she nearly bumped into Boyd.

"Miss Flo! I'm so sorry, I seem to bump into your family a lot," he laughed.

"Oh, Boyd, it was my fault, not paying attention. What are you doing in New Orleans?"

"Hopefully on my final business trip. I've accepted a new position with my company that will keep me in Charleston full time," he said smiling.

They chatted for a few minutes since he was between meetings. Florence invited him to dinner.

"We're having a cauldron of jambalaya tonight if you would like to come by, dinner at six?"

"I've heard so much about your famous jambalaya, I wouldn't miss it! If you give me your address I'll find it with my GPS."

Florence was laughing, "You don't need GPS, it's just across the street, there, second floor up." she pointed.

Laughing, they made plans to meet later. He even volunteered to bring the French crusty bread and wine.

Geraldine arrived home about an hour after Florence, holding a bag that smelled so good it reminded Flo she was hungry. They set out the plates and cut the huge round sandwich in half. Geraldine picked at the olives that fell out as she cut. As they ate Florence told her about bumping into Boyd and him coming to dinner,

"Oh Momma, that's great. How fun to see someone here in New Orleans from Charleston. Maggie tells me that Allison and Boyd are getting pretty serious. I wonder if that's why he's taking the new position."

They finished lunch and Florence went into her room to finish up the herbs she was preparing for Nickoli. Pieces of camomile, lavender and lemon were placed in refillable tea balls. Then another bag was filled with the same ingredients for use at a later time. She prepared a small vial of peppermint essential oil to be placed under the nose and on the forehead. She placed it all in a gift bag she had specially made for her friends.

Geraldine came into the kitchen to see how she could help with dinner. She watched her Mom for a minute, thinking how blessed she was. What a strong woman she was, raising her alone, then helping her raise her child alone. It was just the three of them most of the time. Now they had a bigger family. Their spiritual family had grown since Maggie moved to Charleston. She watched her stirring her cauldron, to the right, always the right,

"What can I do, Momma?"

"I guess, set the table. Boyd's bring the bread and wine," she laughed, "That sounded too religious for me."

Geraldine laughed along with her as she set the dishes out on the table. The bowls had been a gift from Flo's gypsy grandmothers. The swirls of beautiful colors covered them inside and out. Flo often said you could read them but she didn't know how.

The doorbell rang at five thirty, it was Boyd bearing gifts.

"Oh Boyd, it's so good to see you. Isn't this a surprise, come in, come in."

"Good evening Miss Geraldine, yes, this was a pleasant surprise. To be honest I was getting a little homesick," he said, walking into the living room, "Something smells really good." He handed the bottle of wine and crusty bread to Geraldine. Flo called out from the kitchen for the two of them to make themselves comfortable. She was just finishing up. As Geraldine opened the bottle of wine, Boyd walked over to the window and commented on the view. He didn't realize you could see the river from here. The night lights across the river made it look magical.

He seemed to be deep in thought as Flo came into the living room wiping her hands on her apron, she sat down.

Looking at Geraldine, Flo rolled her head towards Boyd, "Are you okay Boyd?"

"Oh, yes ma'am, I'm sorry, it just….."

"It's a wonderful idea," Florence whispered, smiling

"You know? How did you know? I just made up my mind," Boyd stammered.

Florence walked over and hugged him, explaining, her spirits suspected this afternoon but weren't sure till he saw the twinkling lights on the river. He told them that he loved Allison, and loved her since that night in the carriage ride. It was true, he took the job to stay close to her.

"I saw those river lights and knew this was where I wanted to propose to her," he said smiling shyly.

They were all hugging and crying with happiness. Geraldine had to convince him how strong the spirits were in their new family, secrets were hard to keep. Dinner that evening turned into a celebration!

Geraldine was having her morning coffee when her cell phone rang. She almost didn't answer it, not recognizing the number. It was her friend at the post office, Laura. It seemed that while they were doing some renovations to the mail room, they found a few letters that had fallen behind a countertop years before. She wanted to know if her mother was still in New Orleans. She had a letter for her mother that was addressed to their old house in the ninth ward. Geraldine made arrangements to pick up the letter that afternoon. Thinking it was no big deal she neglected to tell Florence until she handed it to her hours later, the return address read, "Lafayette Foundling Home"

CHAPTER FORTY FIVE

At The Same Time!

Leona, Maggie and Marie were going shopping, then out to dinner. Their afternoon was planned this morning at breakfast. It would be fun, something they hadn't done in awhile. Maggie and Marie filled in the morning with chores around the house while Leonia worked in the garden. Lunch was light since they knew dinner would be early. They finished up the dishes and headed upstairs to freshen up and change clothes before going out.

The afternoon of shopping turned out to be an afternoon of looking. No one bought a single thing. Strange but nothing called out to them, in fact the exact opposite. It was as if this was not where they should be. They decided to stop home before going out for dinner since it was still early.

Before they could get halfway up the steps a UPS van pulled up, Maggie, being closest to the street turned around and met the delivery man at the curb.

"Sign here lady," he said, holding out the package.

Maggie signed his hand held computer and took the package. It was wrapped in brown paper, strange, she hadn't seen that in a long time. Leona and Marie had joined her in the foyer, both looking at the package.

"Who's it addressed to?" Marie asked.

Maggie looked down to read the label, with a startled look she turned her head to Leona.

"It's addressed to Mr Herbert Harrington! And it's from The Barstow Detective Agency! Leona this package was mailed years ago, how could this be?"

The ladies made their way into the drawing room in a strange silence. Maggie set the package down on the coffee table, looking at Leona to make some sort of decision.

Marie sat in the overstuffed chair near the window and watched the two other women. There was an unspoken conversation going on and she watched in awe.

Leona stood at the coffee table, reached out to touch the package and quickly drew her hand back, looking at Maggie with sad eyes. Maggie put her hand on Leona's shoulder and led her to the sofa.

"Well, I guess we should open it," Maggie said breaking the spell.

"No, not yet," Leona whispered, "We need to wait for the others."

Maggie joined Leona on the sofa, they sat holding hands and agreed to wait.

Not totally understanding who the others were, Maggie and Marie looked at each other. Maggie shrugged her shoulders as if to say, "oh well, here we go again."

"I'm not sure I want to go out right now," Leona said looking at them both.

Maggie and Marie agreed, this package put a damper on their plans.

"Let's raid the fridge, I'm sure we could come up with a fun dinner. I think there's left over cheesecake, for dessert or for dinner," Marie laughed as the others agreed and stood to follow her into the kitchen. Maggie looked back for a second to look at the package on the coffee table, just another thing I have to wait for, she thought impatiently. The cell phone in her pocket rang as she entered the kitchen. Looking down it said MUSC, work, she thought, they must be short staffed.

"Hello."

"Maggie, is that you, I've exciting news," Carol exclaimed.

"I'm here, what's up?"

"Shamus McGinnis woke up!! He's asking for you!"

CHAPTER FORTY SIX

New Orleans

Geraldine handed Florence the letter. As Florence touched the yellowed envelope she knew it had answers.

Looking questionably at Geraldine, "Where did you get this, how?" she barely got the words out.

Geraldine had to assist her Momma to a chair. She was pale and she had never seen her so shaken. She explained about the phone call, thinking it was just an old piece of mail she forgot to tell her. It was then that Florence told her of Eleanor's palm prediction. They looked at each other, were they scared or excited, their emotions were all over the place. Was this the letter Florence hoped for years ago, would it answer her questions. She looked down at her hands that held the letter. Geraldine moved closer and put her arm around her mother. Florence gently lifted the flap of the envelope and pulled out the folded paper. Unfolding it she saw the insignia.

Lafayette Foundling Home
Lafayette, Louisiana

She read the letter aloud, which was barely a whisper.

"Dear Ms Beaumont,

Since it has been over twenty years, we are able to release information.

We have reviewed your request for information on a child that resided here during the time period that you requested. There were no Beaumont's listed.

Could you have been mistaken with the last name? I understand your need to find your family,maybe these two names might help, they are similar to Beaumont. The first is Anna Lee Boidenesse and the second is Lucinda Beaulieus.

I hope this helps you.

Sincerely, Thelma Portman"

CHAPTER FORTY SEVEN

Charleston, The next Day

Leona knew she was coming, she felt it. We can't keep secrets anymore sister.

Florence and Geraldine boarded the flight with barely time to spare. Grabbing the first flight out turned into a nightmare with traffic. As they settled into their seats she thought, I'm coming sister!! It was only nine thirty in the morning but Geraldine needed a glass of wine, she rang for the stewardess and ordered two glasses of white wine.

"Geraldine, it's too early."

But when the stewardess came with the glasses it was Flo that drank her's down first.

Once again Maggie stared at the brown paper package on the coffee table as she drank her morning tea. What did Leona mean, wait for the others? Marie wandered into the drawing room, also holding a cup.

"It seems to be pulling us in here, doesn't it?" she said, pointing at the package.

As Maggie was about to agree, Leona came in.

"Good morning ladies" she said, sounding unusually chipper for this hour of the morning.

Leona asked Maggie to call Allison and Martha,

"Can you see if they're free for an early dinner, say around four, here. I need my family here when we open the package."

Maggie and Marie looked at Leona, then at each other. Not wanting to question Leona's reason, she agreed. It was a Saturday so she knew Martha was off. Allison wasn't working either but Boyd was in town and she might have plans. After contacting them both, they readily agreed to come. Martha volunteered to bring a few bottles of her favorite Carolina Sweet Wine.

It was noon before Geraldine and Granny were standing at the house on Rutledge's front door. The bell rang and Leona let Maggie answer it. She knew it was them but wanted Maggie to be surprised.

"Oh my goodness!!! What are you guys doing here....oh the package!" she laughed hugging them both as she winked at Leona.

They made their way into the drawing room where the infamous package sat on the coffee table, all of them looking at it like it was a ticking time bomb.

"Maybe a light lunch is in order after you gals freshen up. We can't stand here and stare at the darned thing all day," Leona said.

After agreeing,Geraldine and Granny made their way upstairs to the guest room. Maggie, Marie and Leona went into the kitchen to prepare a luncheon. There was so much excitement now, anticipating the package being opened was like Christmas morning! The ladies spent the next few hours after lunch sitting on the veranda trying to relax before Allison and Martha joined them. It was no easy task, the anxiety was like humidity, you could cut it with a knife. Granny and Geraldine hadn't told anyone about her letter yet. They were waiting for later, when the package was opened. Neither Leona or Granny let each other know they felt it, their relationship. It was more, they were sisters, they just needed proof!

Allison called Martha earlier to see if she could pick her up later that day. Martha was happy to ride with Allison since she'd be carrying a few bottles of wine. They arrived early, at three fifteen.The anticipation was too much for them also, and what the heck, none of them were doing anything but sitting around. As the ladies said their hellos and hugged, not surprised to see Geraldine and Granny again so soon, they headed into the drawing room. Before they could sit the doorbell rang again, this time Leona answered it.

"Yes, yes, this way, in the kitchen will be fine. Can you please set up the dining room also, we will eat there. Thank you, I'll be in the drawing room if you need me." they all heard her say.

Leona told them she had dinner catered, those were the staff from the Charleston Grill. The ladies were astonished, "what?" could be heard from all of them. Leona assured them that this was going to be a special occasion, even not knowing what was in this package. It was still going to give them some answers. She was sure of it.

They each found a seat. Looking at Leona to take the lead they were surprised when Granny spoke,

"Before you start, Leona, there is something I need to show you and the others."

She took out the yellowed envelope from her pocket and handed it to Leona. With trembling hands she opened the flap and took out the letter. As she read tears flowed down her cheeks, handing the letter to Maggie she looked at Flo,

"Oh, my God, I knew it. I felt the connection from the very first meeting," she said now hugging each other and crying.

Maggie read the letter out loud to the others, they were all astonished! How wonderful this was, two sisters reunited. But now there were more questions, how? why?

Granny was sitting in the overstuffed chair crying still, "Am I truly Lucinda?" she asked Leona, "We have no proof, all my life I have been searching for my real name."

"Yes, dear sister, you are Lucinda, we will prove it!" she said looking at the package. "It's time ladies, let's see what the spirits have delivered us!"

Leona moved her chair closer to the coffee table as the others watched. She gently pulled apart the wrapping. It was so old and crinkled, inside was a manilla envelope.

She heard a collective breath as she opened the end and pulled our various certificates and a letter. Putting the certificates aside Leona read the letter aloud.

"Dear Mr Harrington,

I hope this information finds you well, I believe you will be pleased with these results.

The certificates I have enclosed are proof of what I am about to tell you. I must say this has been the most interesting and strange case I've ever worked on. To begin, we must go back many generations of family history. There were two brothers, Jonathan and Martin. Due to the civil war Jonathan moved to New Orleans and for some reason changed his name to Beaulieus. So now you have two family lines with different names. Martin's family, yours, is the Harrington line in Charleston.

Your concern is with Jonathan V born 1910 who married Berth in 1929, she was also born in1920. These are the grandparents that raised your wife. Before you freak out, you are by now very distant cousins, your marriage is fine. Jonathan and Bertha had a son also known as Jonathan VI born 1930 he married Geraldine in 1950. They had twin girls named Leonia and Lucinda born 1951. Unfortunately Jonathan and Geraldine were killed in a train wreck in 1952. The children were separated apparently because the grandparents could only care for one child. Your wife has a sister who was placed in the Lafayette Foundling Home.

As I stated before, the certificates will be proof enough for you. They include birth, marriage and death certificates of all those above. I'm not sure why this was kept a family secret but us southerners have our pride, maybe the grandparents were ashamed of how they had separated the girls, no telling. My bill will be forthcoming under separate cover.

Sincerely, Adam Barstow."

There was such an uprising in the drawing room that the staff from the kitchen came running.They found the ladies crying, laughing and hugging each other all at the same time! Granny, now known as Lucinda, was looking at their birth certificates. She was born first, then came Leonia. Geraldine was blown away by the information. Leona was actually her aunt and Maggie's great aunt. Marie was their cousin!!! It was all too much to take in. Martha had slipped into the kitchen, grabbed the bottles of Carolina Sweet Wine and had one of the staff bring a tray of glasses to the drawing room. For a moment she watched as they all came to the realization that they were truly family, in spirit and blood. She was also bonded to them through their great great grandfathers, what a story! Looking over at Marie she smiled, winked and held up the bottle. Finally Marie was understanding this non verbal conversation women had, she put her fingers to her lips and blew. They all turned and looked at her.

"I think Martha would like to make a toast."

They all took a glass as Martha filled them. They raised their glasses as she said,

"To Martin, Jonathan and Jim, may they finally Rest In Peace knowing we have all found each other! To family"

The others said in unison "to family!"

CHAPTER FORTY EIGHT

Waking

Nora, the unit's Charge Nurse, dressed in white scrubs with her graying hair tucked neatly in a bun, made her way down the corridor. Morning rounds were her opportunity to assess the census on the unit and give each patient a rating. One to five, five being the patient that needed the most care. It was imperative for assignments that nurses carried the same load. Entering each room with a friendly "Good morning" she had enough years under her belt to make an assessment of a patient in minutes. She held a clipboard and check sheet armed with her favorite pen. Nurses always had favorite pens, and if you laid one down near a nurse, it would find its way into her pocket. The previous night shift charge nurse had given her the clipboard which she now carried when she heard the alarm go off. Hurrying down the hall she was joined by Cindy, who had been assigned Mr Christian Belle that morning. Cindy was also a seasoned nurse with fifteen years on the unit, she was considered a back up charge nurse. Unfortunately, Cindy was as round as she was tall, which led to her moving a tad slower in emergencies. However, her assessment skills and knowledge were just as sharp as a doctor. At first glance entering the room

Mr Belle looked to be in no distress, Nora went over to the ventilator and turned off the ringing alarm checking the setting as she went about assessing the machine.

Cindy hurried to his bedside and gasped,"Oh Lord, his eyes are open."

Nora immediately called the resident and the respiratory therapist on call for the unit. All kinds of commotion ensued for the next hour. Although Mr Belles eyes were open, the sedatives he was given were still keeping him down. Waking up on a ventilator can be very scary. Feeling a large tube in your throat could panic a person into pulling it out too soon, hence the restraints on his wrists.

He looked at them questioningly, Cindy calmly told him where he was while holding his hand and crying.With Mr Belle awake they could start the weaning process off the ventilator. Although he was awake they weren't sure how much he was understanding. He had been in a coma for some time. They wouldn't be able to assess his mental capacity until he could actually answer questions. And that would entail the tube being removed from his throat.

Slowly the process began, until they were confident he could breath on his own and then the tube finally came out. Cindy encouraged him not to try and talk, just nod yes or no to their questions for now. Did he remember the accident, he nodded no. Cindy explained what happened. His eyes got wide and he pointed to his wrist. Not quite understanding at first, she figured out he wanted to know how much time had gone by. A month she told him. A tiny tear rolled out the corner of his eye. Next he held up his left hand slightly motioning to his ring finger. Yes, your wife knows.

As the hours progressed the doctor ordered some thickened juice, making sure his swallow reflexes worked well enough to start fluids by mouth. By now the charge nurse had reassigned Cindy's patients to other nurses so she could stay with Mr..Belle.

The next few days would be hard on Mr Belle. Physical therapy would have to evaluate his strength after lying in bed for so long. Respiratory therapy would do constant readings to make sure his breathing was adequate and, of course, occupational therapy evaluations to assist in small motor movements. It was really a dance to get a patient up and moving after a month on a ventilator.

It was the second day, Cindy had just brought him a liquid lunch and the nurse's aide was helping him sit up when he said in a whisper,"Is Maggie working today? I always looked forward to her sitting with me," he remembered all the times she sat and talked to him, kept him sane, her funny family and all their escapades.

"Maggie? I don't think we have a nurse named Maggie working in this unit."

"What about Allison?" he whispered.

"No definitely no Allison, why do you ask?"

Shaking his head, he looked at Cindy, not understanding. Maybe he was wrong,

Could it have been a dream, then again maybe it was the spirits. Then he remembered something she said, "Maybe someday you'll write a book about us." She had laughed when she said that.

CHAPTER FORTY NINE

Christian Belle

Maggie did exist. So did Leonia, Geraldine, Allison and all the rest. It hadn't been a dream. She did in fact work in The Tower, but on a completely different floor. Her story was all true. How he knew it all was the question, but he did know it and wanted to know more. He never really spoke about it after that first day, thinking maybe he was crazy. Or maybe some kind of ventilator psychos had set in.

His recovery took months in a rehabilitation unit. His once long lean powerful legs were more like jello after months in a coma. The hands that used to write were atrophied inward as if holding a ball, which he had been doing to keep them from completely cutting into his palms. He had graduated from a wheelchair to walker in just one week. He hadn't lost his determination to live. With the help of occupational therapy, his hand and finger exercises helped regain enough strength to hold a pen. It was the headaches that plagued him. When they came he needed total darkness, the light would make them worse. The neurologist explained that they would eventually go away. But for now, his brain was still recovering.

The rooms here were more comfortable than his hospital room. They had a recliner and sofa made of soft leather. The dresser and mirror matched the masculine feel of the furniture. His days were filled with all kinds of therapy, after dressing in street clothes and taking meals in a patient dining hall. But the evenings were his loneliest. He had very little visitors now that his wife was long gone, too self centered to care for him. She had divorced him right after the accident,while he was still in a coma. She only visited out of pity. Her life as a social butterfly lended no time for a debilitated husband. Once every couple of weeks a member of the Charleston Literary Guild would stop in to check on him. But these were mere acquaintances. They probably only did it out of respect, after all he was the pride of Charleston's historical mystery writer. It was then that he realized that having no family meant that he was completely alone.

The rehabilitation unit was within the Medical University so it was easy for him to start his first quest, find Maggie Beaumont! You would think it would be easy. But with all the new HIPPA rules for patients the same rights applied to staff. It took a few weeks before one of his physical therapist recognized her name,

"I think I know her, a nice girl, works on a step down unit on the seventh floor. She's sent a few patients my way in the past."

Christian felt like a military strategist. Having found her now he just had to think of a way of approaching her. After all he couldn't just blurt out her whole life story.

As the weeks went on and he was able to, he began writing again. He knew exactly what his story would be. In fact it was already written in his head, 'The Charleston Harringtons.' His one problem still remained. Without actually getting her permission he would have to change the names and he didn't want to do that.Her story was all true. How he knew it all was the question. But he did know it and wanted to know more.

CHAPTER FIFTY

Strategy

It just so happened that a certain Dora Fowler was a member of the Charleston Literary Guild. How Christian came about this knowledge was quite easy. He had a copy of their latest issue which had a list of members in good standing on the inside cover. Funny how people loved to see their names in print, especially those in the Charleston social circle. Knowing that Dora was a friend of Leona Harrington, he had to find a way to get Dora to meet with him. This was really going in the back door, so to speak, to get to Maggie, he didn't want to scare her off with direct contact.

It would take patience, after all he had all the time in the world. He phoned up the president of the Guild and asked if Dora Fowler could visit him next time they sent someone over to check on him. He was more than happy to ask her. In fact they were having lunch the following day so he assured him he would discuss it with her. His plan worked. The next week Dora Fowler dressed in an emerald green suit with modest low heeled shoes to match appeared at his door. What drew his attention was the pale green feathered hat she wore almost like a crown,

"Mr Belle, I'm Dora Fowler. I understand you wanted to see me?" she said, walking into his room.

"Yes, it's a pleasure to meet you. Please come in, can I get you anything?"

"No, thank you. How have you been? Terrible accident, I hear."

They had a few more minutes of small talk before Christian brought up Maggie.

"Miss Dora, I might have brought you here on false pretenses."

Her eyebrows raised as she cocked her head to one side and said, "And just what would that be, young man?"

He told her his story, of Maggie sitting by his bedside, telling him of all the questions and answers they delved through. He told her that according to the nurses that cared for him Maggie never came to his room physically. But he knew all the heartwarming family stories and Allison's love story, oh he couldn't forget her little Charleston Grill set up for Marie that Dora arranged. He did get a chuckle out of her with that one.

"This is quite a story you have here. How on earth do you know all this? You've been in a coma that whole time. Leona really must meet you, do you mind if I bring her here?" she said quite excitedly.

"I'd be delighted. I must confess, I really want to meet Maggie. I need to know why she came to me in my coma. But I don't know how to address her without scaring her off," he said hopefully

"Oh, don't you worry son, between myself and Leona we'll find a way," she smiled.

"Now let's get down to business!"

Leona had just finished her second cup of coffee after having a light lunch. She was sitting on the second floor veranda thinking of everything that had happened over the past few months. Lucinda had stayed with her for a month after that evening of discovery! They had gotten to know each other, not as friends but as sisters. The spirits had brought them all together she thought. They were truly a family.

When she heard Dora's voice, "Leona, my dear, down here!"

Looking down into the courtyard she saw Dora, decked out in her feathered green hat.

"Dora, what are you doing down there? Come in please."

"I would my dear, but the door is locked and no one answered the door when I knocked." replied Dora.

Leona quickly made her way through the kitchen to the back door, unlocked the door and met Dora coming up the stairs.

"What on earth, Dora! Why didn't you call?" Leona said exasperated.

"We need to talk, this is phenomenal, something I couldn't tell you on the phone, we really must find a way, it's just ...."

"Stop!, slow down, you're not making any sense, one thing at a time." Leona tried to get Dora to organize her thoughts.

Leona went to the refrigerator and took out a bottle of Sweet Carolina Wine, grabbed two glasses and sat down at the table. Looking at Dora, raising her eyebrow, Dora nodded. She poured two glasses and handed one to Dora who gulped down the whole glass. Handing her the glass back, Leona refilled it.

Dora, having calmed down after two glasses of wine told Leona Mr Christian Belles story. By the time she finished, Leona had finished her second glass. They both agreed that the spirits had somehow picked up Maggie's intuition and transferred them to Christian. But why? Oh,here we go again, more questions with no answers.The two old ladies had to figure out a way of getting Maggie to meet Christian. They wanted to see if there was a trigger when they saw each other.

When Marie and Maggie came home from work that evening they found the two older ladies a bit tipsy. Their first clue was Dora's green feathered hat hanging dangerously to the left ready to fall off. The second was two empty bottles of Martha's favorite Sweet Carolina Wine.

"I hope you ladies saved some of that for us. I could use a glass after I clean up," Maggie said peeking into the kitchen.

"Ladies, are we celebrating something?" Marie asked as she sat down at the table while Maggie headed upstairs to shower.

As soon as they knew Maggie was safely upstairs they gave Marie a run down of what had happened earlier that afternoon.

"How is this possible?" Marie said, looking at them both questionably.

"We're not sure, but we do know the spirits are involved somehow. I guess we need to follow their lead. Any ideas on how we can get Maggie to meet Mr Belle?"

The ladies opened another bottle of wine and put their heads together. One thought maybe she could get assigned to work that unit, but that wouldn't work. How could they explain that to Maggie's supervisor. Another thought maybe they could wheel Mr Belle to the courtyard and accidentally on purpose run into her. No, that would also take too much coordination.

Sitting for a moment in silence Dora suddenly said, "I've got it! Leona, you and I will invite Maggie to lunch. Then, when we are on our way I will say that I need to stop by the hospital to deliver a paper to one of the Guild members. Leona, you will say, why don't we all go up, stretch our legs or something."

"I think that might work!" Leona said excitedly.

"I agree." said Marie.

CHAPTER FIFTY ONE

A Lunch Date

Dora had just pulled into the rear alleyway to pick up Maggie and Leona for lunch when her cell phone rang. It was Christian, were they coming? Was everything working out the way we planned? He rambled on so that Dora had to assure him that they would be there shortly and abruptly hung up as Maggie got in the back seat.

"Is everything all right Dora?"

Seeing a perfect opportunity to start her little fib she replied, "Yes, my dear, I hope you don't mind, that was one of our Literary Guild writers that asked me to stop by so he could give me his latest article. He's at the rehab unit at the Medical University just down the street. We'll just run by on our way to lunch," Dora said eyeing Leona, who sat in the front seat next to her smirking.

They pulled into the parking garage. Dora always seemed to talk her way into a perfect parking space with the garage attendant. Of course, the ten dollar tip each time helped.

"Why don't we come with you, I'd love to meet one of your writers," Leona said, getting out of the parked car, "Come on, Maggie, you can point us to the rehab unit he's in."

"Sure, just where I want to be on my day off," she said smiling.

They made their way past the lobby and up the elevators to the second floor. Maggie looked at Dora and pointed her in the direction of the nurses station. The group made their way down the hallway between patients in walkers and wheelchairs. Dora knew right where she was going which seemed a little strange to Maggie, but she just followed along.

"I believe this is his room, let me just peek in first," Dora said.

Opening the door she saw Christian sitting in the leather recliner with a pad and pen in his lap. His eyes opened wide when he saw her and attempted to get out of the chair.

"Please, Mr Belle, don't get up on our account. I am just here to pick up your article," Dora said, winking at him.

Leona and Maggie followed her into the room, introductions were made. As Maggie held out her hand to shake Christians hand a strange tingling feeling came over her. It was as if she was watching this unfold out of her body. As he took her hand and smiled, looking into her eyes she fainted.

"Oh my goodness, Leona, do something!" Dora screamed as Christian caught Maggie and gently placed her on the bed.

"Me! What the Sam Hill am I going to do? Anyway it looks like Christian has it handled."

Dora went to get some water while Leona gently patted her hand, "wake up Maggie."

Christian found a nurse in the hallway who bought orange juice and extra sugar, nurses always treated low blood sugar with a quick dose of OJ.

Maggie slowly opened her eyes and realized where she was, lying on the bed, embarrassed she said, "Oh lord, I'm so sorry, I don't know what came over me," as she attempted to get up.

Everyone insisted she rest for a few minutes and drink the sugared orange juice. The nurse said probably a blood sugar problem, mumbling on how she sees it all the time.

Sitting up she assured them she felt fine, looking from Leona to Dora she knew there was more to this then they let on.

"Ok, ladies, what's going on? You both look guilty, I'm the one who screwed up not you."

Christian helped Maggie to the sofa and sat down beside her. Again her body tingled, but this time she didn't faint. She looked directly into his eyes.

"Oh, my God, I know you. I mean I knew you, from before, way before," she stammered and looked at them all. "We have a history," she whispered with tears suddenly rolling down her cheeks.

Before she could stop herself she threw herself into Christians arms. He held her and she was home, how could she tell them.

Leona and Dora had slowly backed out of the room, the scene had become too personal for them.

"I can't wait to hear this one," Leona said with an astonished look on her face.

"I never in a thousand years thought she would react like that, what do you think she meant?"

"Dora, my dear, they were lovers in another life, of course," she said matter of factly.

As Maggie held Christian on the sofa she suddenly realized that he may have no idea what she was talking about. He probably thought she was deranged. Embarrassed once again she extradited herself from his arms.

"I'm so sorry, you must think I'm crazy."

"Actually, no, no I don't. I have a confession to make Maggie. You were brought here under false pretenses, I need to explain," he said.

Christian explained everything from start to her illustrious finish. Then he sat in silence as he waited for it to sink in. The one thing he didn't tell her was that he had seen her many many times in his travels around town, not realizing until just this morning who she was.

CHAPTER FIFTY TWO

Explanations

Leona and Dora sat nervously in the waiting area. A TV was on the weather channel repeatedly giving out the same information over and over. It was as if you just turned it on and hadn't heard it ten times already.

"Good Lord, can someone turn that TV off, it's getting on my last nerve!" Dora said exasperated.

"Calm down, dear, you're just on edge about Maggie. I'm sure she's finding her way," Leona said, patting Dora's hand.

The two old ladies sat for a few moments longer when Maggie appeared at the doorway signaling them to follow her back into Christian's room. Getting up slowly, as most old ladies do, they looked at each other. Both anxious about what would happen next.

Christian was still sitting on the sofa as the ladies came in, he stood.

"Please, ladies, my apologies if this caused any trouble. Have a seat and I'll try and explain."

As they found a chair to sit in, Leona and Dora assured him no apology was needed, just some answers.

Maggie looked at the woman she had grown to love and admire, "You both have taught me so much over the past few years, I love you. I think the spirits have been working overtime and maybe both of you can help connect the dots for us."

There was nothing these old ladies loved more than a good spirit led mystery!

"Let me ask you something, Maggie, have you ever crossed paths with Christian?

Bumped into him in a cafe? Anything?" Leona asked

"No, up until today I never set eyes on him," she answered.

"That's not entirely true, Maggie," Christian said sheepishly.

"Really?" Maggie questioned.

"Do you remember waving to a certain bicycle rider?"

"Was that you! All those times?"

"Yes, in fact, once I saw you a few times I became infatuated. Don't get me wrong, not the stalker kind. I just felt like I knew you," Christian confessed.

Leona and Dora agreed, they did know each other in another lifetime. They went on to explain that we all have a Twin Flame, a great love, one that was destined to be repeated over many lifetimes. That was why Christian was drawn to her when she smiled and waved to him and why when Maggie touched his hand her heart knew.

"The love you have for one another is very powerful, it overcomes all obstacles.The spirits saw to that," Leona said smiling.

"The one thing I don't understand is, how did Christian know all these stories?" Maggie asked.

"That might be something only the spirits can answer I'm not sure, maybe in time," Leona replied.

It was as if a light bulb suddenly went off in Maggie's brain, she stood up and smiled.

Maybe, she thought, just maybe she could connect the last dot. Dashing out of the room she yelled back,

"Don't anyone move! I will be right back, hopefully."

Maggie walked as fast as was allowed in the hallway and headed for the elevator. Tapping her foot impatiently for the doors to open she prayed this was the answer. Riding down to the second floor took forever. Finally weaving her way to his room, she took a deep breath and pushed the door open.

"Good morning, Shamus!" she said, noticing he was sitting in a wheelchair.

"Ah, lass, I've been expecting you," he said with a sly smile. "Shall we go?"

Not another word was spoken, not on the elevator, nor the long hallway back to Christians room. It was as if neither wanted to break the spell.

Shamus McGinnis was an old soul, not just in years, but in eons. He had many lifetimes and remembered then all. Some happy and then some very sad. He was a special kind of spirit, one who helps join others to find their twin flame when they are lost. Maggie opened the door and pushed the wheelchair through, a spark went off in Christians eyes as he took a long look at Shamus.

"Do I know you?" Christian asked before Maggie could do the introductions.

"Yes, in a manner of speaking, yes you do," he winked at Maggie.

Leona and Dora sat with their mouths open, they felt it, his presence was overwhelming. Dora whispered under her breath to Leona, "A true spirit in the flesh."

Leona nodded, still awestruck. Maggie went on to explain what she thought helped them connect the dots.

"I took care of Shamus when he was unconscious. I would tell him all the experiences I had had during the weeks and months. He was the only one besides you all," pointing to Leona and Dora "that I told these stories to. Even Ally doesn't know some of them. Somehow Shamus transferred my stories to Christian while he was unconscious. Am I right Shamus?"

Shamus nodded yes, then with a smile that lit up the room proceeded to tell them of his other lifetime. One, over a century ago, Christian was his son, they shared a bond that will last many lifetimes.

"The people we are drawn to in this lifetime are no mistakes. We gravitate towards ones that we have known before, good and bad. Our souls know each other and if you're lucky you find each other without help. In this situation," he looked at Maggie and Christian, "you needed a wee bit of help."

CHAPTER FIFTY THREE

The Weddings

It had been six months since what Maggie liked to call the big Reveal! So much had changed. The spirits never failed to point them in the direction they needed to go, even if it was off the beaten path. Boyd had proposed to Ally in New Orleans, just as he planned. She never suspected.

And Christians proposal really wasn't a proposal at all, more like an understanding.

"Maggie, it seems our lives have been entwined many times before. Let's not stop here," he said to her one evening as they walked along the battery.

And so it was decided a week later that the girls would have a double wedding!

After a date was chosen, October first, agreeable to all, the preparations started. The couples wanted to keep the occasion small and intimate. Dora's wedding gift to them all was reserving The Charleston Grill for a small and intimate reception, which ended up not so small and not so intimate!

The summer humidity seemed to hang on longer this year. Usually by September it started to break. The girls were doing their best to stay in shape, jogging along the battery and Colonial Lake. The wedding dresses had been fitted and they didn't want to have to alter them by gaining any weight.

"I can't wait to eat the biggest piece of wedding cake I can get," grumbled Ally while eating an apple.

"I totally understand, I can't believe how that seamstress lectured us about not gaining weight. I mean I usually stay pretty much the same weight anyway. Now I'm paranoid," replied Maggie laughing.

Leonia had taken care of ordering the flowers. Ally's parents and Geraldine paid for everything else. The wedding was set for October 1st at 3:00 pm, outside in Battery Park at the gazebo.

"I love the idea of getting married in the gazebo," Ally said, "It will look so beautiful draped in purple and pink carnations."

"Just know there will be a lot of people mulling around the park watching us that aren't invited," Maggie replied.

"Very true. But we'll be the stars that shine!" Ally said as she looped her arm through Maggie's laughing.

Two weeks before the wedding, things started to go awry. A strong weather system was headed for the caribbean and it hadn't been determined yet which direction it was going. Granny tried to channel her inner spirit for some kind of forecast, but got nothing. As the final arrangements were made they watched The Weather Channel anxiously.

"Oh, my goodness, I can't believe this! I wouldn't mind a little rain but a hurricane, no way!" Maggie complained to Leona.

"I'm sure it will be ok. The fates haven't brought us this far to mess it up now," she said, trying to reassure Maggie.

Thinking they should have a back up plan a meeting was arranged, dinner at Leona's that evening. As the group gathered together later that day, the anxiety in the room was palpable. Everyone was talking at one time. Marie, who is known for handling these kinds of situations, put her finger to her lips and gave out a loud whistle. Everyone stopped and looked at her,

"One person needs to take control here or we're not going to get anything done," she said as she sat down with an exasperated look on her face.

"You're absolutely right Marie, thank you. I think Maggie and I will now hear reasonable ideas," Ally said looking in Maggie's direction.

"Why don't we call The Charleston Grill and see if you can hold the actual wedding there? I mean, just in case the storm comes this way," Dora suggested.

"I think that's the best way to go also but....." Ally's mother, Blair, started to say and was cut off by Granny,

"If that storm ends up coming this way the restaurant will be closed, we will have nowhere to go."

"As I was trying to say," Blair continued, "in a worse case scenario, our warehouse is big enough to do it all, but that would mean a lot of work in the next week and we're not even sure it's coming here." Everyone was looking at Blair, she usually sat very meekly and didn't say much. This great idea surprised them all.

"Oh, Mom, that's a good idea. Can we just wait a few more days, see the predictions, then make a decision," Ally said, really not wanting to get married in a warehouse.

"I agree," Maggie said, almost reading her mind, "Let's give it two days, then make our final decision," she said looking at Christian and Boyd, who both nodded.

Good news came the following day. It looked like the storm was going north of them, the Outer Banks of North Carolina! They would probably get rain but nothing like was originally predicted. Dora phoned The Charleston Grill and made final arrangements for the wedding ceremony to be held there with the girls permission.They all continued to watch The Weather Channel. These storms were known to make a turn at the last minute and they didn't want any surprises.

The morning of October 1st was overcast with a few showers. The weather report showed the storm heading towards North Carolina skirting the South Carolina coast.

Leonia was having tea in the drawing room with Granny when it happened, the picture of the sea captain fell over!

"Oh no, not now Granddaddy!" Leona moaned.

"What do you mean?" Granny asked.

"Remember the hurricane last year. This picture predicted it, I can't let Maggie know this, it will spoil her day worrying about something that might never happen."

"We'll keep this between the two of us for now," Granny replied.

Keeping one eye on the weather the ladies prepared for the day.

By the time the limousines were scheduled to pick up each girl at 2:30 the bands of rain from the storm were getting stronger. Thank goodness for the large overhang in the alley entrance, it helped keep Maggie as dry as possible. Lifting her long skirt she ducked into the car, followed by Granny, Leona, Geraldine and Marie.

Laughing they all managed to get in without getting wet, "Mom, the rain seems worse, has anyone checked the weather report?"

"Yes, it's coming pretty close but we'll be inside soon and no worries there," Geraldine tried to sound confident.

At the same time Allison and her family were being picked up by their limousine. They had been glued to the tv and knew it didn't look good.

By the time they had all arrived at the Charleston Grill the storm had changed course. It was heading right to Georgetown, sixty miles north of Charleston, not the Outer Banks! There was no time now to change any plans. Everyone who was coming to the wedding was already there. It was decided to go ahead with the wedding ceremony. The restaurant already had staff and food prepared. It would be unsafe to send anyone out in the storm now. The manager of the Grill made preparations for the staff and party goers to stay at the Charleston Hotel, attached to the Grill until the storm was over.

The wind howled as the rain belted the windows sideways. The rain bands were getting closer. The group gathered at a room in the center of the building, chairs and tables were moved to keep them safe from the huge windows that could shatter from any flying debris.

"Let us gather together. Come closer as we join these couples in their love," said Dora as she motioned to the crowd.

The shuffling of feet was barely notable above the sound of the wind and rain.The young woman officiating the service was a friend of Marie's who had just become an ordained minister. This, in fact, was her first wedding. Anita placed both couples in front of her as she faced them. Looking out into the group she said before beginning the ceremony, "Let the rain and wind be a good omen, wind to blow away your troubles and rain to cleanse your heart," smiling she continued with the ceremony.

As the couples said their 'I do's' and everyone clapped in joy, a group of very wet and scared people burst through the door.

There was so much commotion that once again Marie's whistle seemed to quiet the group. Evidently the streets had started to flood. People in low lying areas were asked to find higher ground. This particular group of people had been hunkered down in a building two blocks away when the flood waters started coming in. They made their way to the hotel in the attempt to get away from the water which now had made its way into the first floor of all the homes on the peninsula!

"We are so sorry," a young woman started to explain…

"There is no need to apologize, we are happy to have you join us," Leonia said, as she found some towels for them.

"You are too kind, we've ruined your celebration."

Maggie and Ally made their way over, embraced the young woman and assured her that it was all fine. In fact the more the merrier. We can't help what Mother Nature sends our way, we just embrace it and they all laughed. Knowing how bad the situation had become, and knowing they were all stuck here for the next eight hours they newlyweds made an announcement,

"We've asked the servers and cooks to join us, and any other employees that were unable to leave," Boyd said.

"We will make the best of things so everyone feels at ease. So let's help the cooks bring out the food and enjoy this time together, as true Charlestonians do!" said Christian.

As they all gathered together the party atmosphere gradually became lighter. Laughter could be heard as new friends were made. The staff of the Grill and Hotel were so grateful that they offered the two newlywed couples a free weekend stay, when the weather was better of course.

Maggie noticed a young woman staring at Allison,

"Ally, do you know her? She's been staring at you."

"Who?" Ally said, as Maggie pointed to the young girl.

"No, I don't."

Allison decided to introduce herself to the young girl, as she walked over she got this strange feeling that she did know her.

"Hi, I'm Allison, have we met?"

"No, we haven't, my name is Victoria. It's really strange, I know you. Do you know Mr Calhoun?" she asked.

Allison went pale, so pale Maggie noticed and walked over to the girls.

"Ally, are you ok?"

Allison looked at Maggie and burst out in laughter. She was laughing so hard it attracted her parents, who walked over to them.

"Maggie, we have another guest, Mr Calhoun!" Ally said, now giggling.

"Not today Ally, not today…..today is for the living! Mr Calhoun, you'll have to wait."

Made in the USA
Columbia, SC
05 July 2021

41422691R00183